If you haven't read a Colin Bateman novel before, this is what you're missing

'As sharp as a pint of snakebite' *The Sunday Times*

'A joy from start to finish . . . witty, fast-paced and throbbing with menace' *Time Out*

'There is more to Bateman than a racy plot. His prose is intelligent as well as aesthetically satisfying, his dialogue toughly funny and tone-perfect' *Mail on Sunday*

'Bateman has barged fearlessly into the previously unsuspected middle ground between Carl Hiaasen and Irvine Welsh and claimed it for his own' *GQ*

'Terrific mordant wit and a fine sense of the ridiculous . . . the writing is great' *Evening Standard*

'If Roddy Doyle was as good as people say, he would probably write novels like this' *Arena*

If you have read Colin before, you're already an addict

Also by Colin Bateman

Divorcing Jack
Cycle of Violence
Of Wee Sweetie Mice and Men
Empire State
Maid of the Mist
Turbulent Priests
Shooting Sean
Wild About Harry
Mohammed Maguire
The Horse With My Name

MURPHY'S LAW

Colin Bateman

headline

First published in 2002 by
HEADLINE BOOK PUBLISHING
A HEADLINE paperback

10 9 8 7 6 5 4 3 2 1

ISBN 0 7553 0243 5

Typeset by Palimpsest Book Production Limited,
Polmont, Stirlingshire
Printed and bound in Great Britain by
Clays Ltd, St Ives plc

HEADLINE BOOK PUBLISHING
A division of Hodder Headline
338 Euston Road
London NW1 3BH

www.headline.co.uk
www.hodderheadline.com

To Andrea and Matthew

PROLOGUE

Murphy hates this place.

Scotland Yard. Nobody says New Scotland Yard, like it says on the tin; they say, Scotland Yard. Scotland Yard. Like it's something out of a 1950s *Wizard* or a B movie. Worse, a British B movie. Like it's something special, not just a big building with paperwork. They like to think of it as the nerve centre. He likes to think of it as a Christopher Reeves kind of nerve centre, everything's there, but it doesn't quite work, but one day, one day there might be a revolutionary breakthrough, and then watch out, you, you dastardly criminals.

He comes here as little as possible, and more recently, never at all. He slumps in the back of the lift as they rise to the eighth floor, uniforms all around him. He's wearing his own uniform, of course, it's just a different one: black jeans, one knee gone to white, black T-shirt, bomber jacket, zips on the arms for the little pockets where you can hide things like squares of chocolate or surface-to-air missiles. He ran a comb through his hair this morning, big sense of occasion and all, but all it really did was drag the mess to one side, making him look ever so slightly foppish. He soon fixed that.

He really hates this place.

Maybe he should have shaved, actually cut his hair, put on a nice suit. It's not like he's been working and has to stay shabby. Make the effort, Marty, make the effort. But no. He was up half the night writing a song; and as usual, when he came to look at the lyrics in the morning, his head thumping with Carlsberg, probably the worst hangover in the world, and a tiny, tiny amount of dope, right enough, they were shit, primary school lyrics. So he's feeling rough and sad and annoyed that he has to be here.

He sits there, Rebel Without An Ashtray.

Dr Coates arrives after a few minutes, full of apologies and the flu. She's quite cute but self-important. She has a pile of folders, and Murphy knows from past experience that his is the thickest, and growing. Fair enough.

She begins to fill in a form, then looks up at the sound of his lighter. She glances around theatrically at the sign behind her, then back to Murphy, who nods and removes the cigarette. She returns her eyes to the file, only to hear the lighter again and she looks up angrily to find Murphy now has two cigarettes in his mouth.

'Go on,' he says, 'give us a smile.'

There's no smile. Murphy removes the cigarettes.

'You've missed three out of your last five appointments, Martin,' she says. He nods. 'This is important. We're trying to help.'

'I'm feeling better,' Murphy says.

She nods, but is not convinced. 'Martin, the death of a child—'

'It's none of your business.'

They lock eyes. She doesn't blink. How does she do that? Perhaps Scotland Yard has developed an android. Perhaps there are so many crash and burns victims the regular psychobabblers all imploded. Or exploded. Covering the walls in gore and meaningful notes. Perhaps . . . Murphy blinks first.

'Yes it is,' she says, stern, but still trying to be family. 'Let's be frank here. If it wasn't for your history, you would have been retired on medical grounds months ago, but the fact is certain people don't want to lose you. That doesn't mean we can just ignore . . .'

He's laughing inside, really. Your history, your medical grounds. Like he's Mel Gibson in *Lethal Weapon* or Clint Eastwood in . . . anything when he had big hair. Clichés aren't clichés for nothing, Missus. Maybe he should act all manic like Mel. Maybe they'll assign him a partner to help see him through this difficult time, and by the by solve the big case. A buddy. They'll be total opposites of course, they'll fight from beginning to just before the end, but they'll learn to love one another along the way, and then one of them will die. And it won't be Murphy, because he never dies.

He sits forward. 'I'm OK. I just need to go back to work.

Look at me, you're trained, you can read me like a book, you can see I'm ready.'

'It's not as easy as that, Martin.'

'Yes it is. Just read me.'

'Martin, psychiatry—'

'I can read you.'

'What?'

'I'll do you a deal. If I can get you off like . . .' and he clicks his fingers, 'then you put me back on active. What do you say?'

'This isn't a game, Martin. I really don't think—'

'You're in the process of splitting up with your husband.'

'What?'

'You're in the process of splitting up with your husband.' He isn't even looking at her. He lights his cigarette and takes a drag. She ignores it. 'You've been on holiday with him to try and patch things up, but it didn't work out. You're at that can't live with him, can't live without him stage. You tried to talk things through with him last night, but you had too much to drink and you slept together.' He takes another drag. 'How am I doing?'

Dr Coates looks pale and annoyed. 'You can stop this right now.'

He doesn't, of course. In for the kill. 'You're like most freckled women who go away to the sun. You sit on the beach for two weeks but you don't quite get a tan, you just look a little bit dirty. That said, I can see by that band of pale skin that you wore your wedding ring while you were away, but no longer. You've had stale drink on your breath since you walked in—'

'I said stop it.'

'Now look at your nails – they're not false, are they?'

'No, I . . . Martin, this is getting—'

'Then consider your forehead.'

'I—'

'There's the remains of quite a hefty spot there. You've covered most of it with make-up, but I can tell by the skin around it that it didn't die of its own accord, it's been squeezed to death.' Her hand begins to move towards her forehead, but she manages to stop herself. 'But you see, Dr Coates, a spot requiring that much violence, there'd be nail marks, and there's none. So someone with short nails. It's not the romantic sort of thing you'd ask or allow a boyfriend to do, but a husband could do it without a second thought.' Marty takes a final drag on his cigarette, then stubs it out, half smoked, on the floor. He looks up at her after a moment. 'Right or wrong?' he says. With the Belfast brogue and the light in his eyes, it somehow comes across as vaguely charming.

Still, she's a professional, and there are standards to maintain. 'You're very good, Martin, nobody doubts that.'

'So put me back where I belong.'

'Yes,' says Coates, 'I do believe I will.'

Life, when you boil it down, comes to this: sitting in a canteen full of policemen trying to find a word that rhymes with orange, but mainly thinking about the difference between success and failure: how, on a different day, Bob Dylan would have been thrown out of his first record company for daring to sing with a voice like that. How, on a different day, if something hadn't sparked his imagination, if he hadn't suddenly hooked onto the zeitgeist, he might have turned 'Blowin' In The Wind' into a comedy song about flatulence and scored a minor but forgettable hit. Chance, and the decisions that seem small at the time but are sometimes huge and significant and historic.

Someone he used to work with comes across and says, 'Murphy, how're you doin'?'

'OK,' he says. 'Do you happen to know a word that rhymes with orange?'

And the someone laughs and walks off like he's not serious.

All these hundreds of people around him, the camaraderie, the confidence, all with one purpose in life: to do good, to help people, to save the world. Well, at least, that's how it's supposed to be, but Murphy knows different. They really want to be Travis Bickle in *Taxi Driver*, they want to go out there and cleanse the world of all the filth and degradation. But they won't, because it's against the rules, somebody might file a report, they'll sit in this canteen and talk about sport and mortgages and forget for a while the evil that's out there, and when they are forced to go out they'll do their weary best but it won't get them down because they realise they're fighting a losing battle, so why exert yourself? Do the bare minimum, get by, get by. De Niro fiddles while Rome burns.

1

He sees dead people.

Every day of the week. Six times a day. Fat, thin, mostly thin. Young, old, mostly old. Heart, cancer, road accident, broken heart, oh she died of a broken heart, never got over the loss of her Tom, he sees them every day, and there's not a flicker of emotion. There can't be, really, it would kill you.

Mitchell stands at the back of the chapel in his black suit and white shirt and black tie and his austere haircut, nodding glumly as the mourners file in. He has the look of a man who would pass the interview for the position of guard at a small to medium sized concentration camp, but might stumble on the written test.

Today, today is different, and while death is all around him, this is the day he lives for. They don't come along that often, but the adrenaline is already pumping around him with a vigour that is entirely absent from the corpse in the box at the front of the church; his fingers are tingling with the anticipation, an anticipation completely opposite to that of the small band of pallbearers who will shortly lift the coffin and carry it through the chapel and outside to the hearse; theirs is an anticipation of fear, of being a shoulder's width and a few lousy millimetres of polished wood from death. You never get closer to a corpse than that, unless you are one, or unless you're Mitchell, five-year veteran of the Fond Farewells funeral home – funerals, embalming, cremations, all at a price you can afford.

Mitchell checks his watch. It's nearly time.

Come on, get a move on. Let's get out there and stick her in the ground.

His pulse is racing.

Oh, it's good to be alive.

At Fond Farewells, Terry Hatcher is escorting an elderly couple around the showroom. The coffins on display are polished up and look sleek and new and heavy like they'll keep you safe and sound, underground, but they also look like they'll cost you a fortune, and you can't afford that, not on your pension. But don't worry about it. Hatcher believes in looking after folk, in not charging them extortionate rates; this is, after all, life's final journey, what sort of a man would he be to make money at a time like that. Oh, he's good, Terry Hatcher. He'll sell them.

'It's entirely a matter of personal taste, of course – from this simple pine box, this is the Abraham model, to this more flashy, solid bronze, velvet lined Dartmouth model, which is the BMW of the casket business, but listen, you're in luck, I'll tell you, this line is being discontinued, we need the space for our new stock, I'm sure we can work something out . . .'

And he'll cut them a deal even though it means there's virtually no mark-up for him on it at all; he may not tell them that they're shelling out for wood but after the mourners have gone they'll end up in a plastic casket that costs practically nothing, just like the rest of the stiffs. Why would he tell them? Mister, when you're dead, you're dead, doesn't matter what you're lying in.

Hatcher checks his watch. It's nearly time.

This is London, north London; outside, the traffic thunders by, drowning out the soft weeping from the newly bereaved in the waiting room, and the sounds of Johnny upstairs, getting their guns ready. Johnny likes his guns. He's a big guy, like Hagrid with attitude, hair tied back in a ponytail. He can take the weight of a coffin, including contents, over his massive shoulders. Then hurl it across a room.

Not the same demand for this as, say, tossing the caber, but you never know when it might come in handy.

Not far away, not more than a mile as the crow flies but thirty minutes in traffic at this time of the morning, Jimmy Warbeck's getting ready for work. He's had a nice time in bed with Mary – three months married, how long will this sex every morning last for? They hadn't lived together and they'd only made love once before they got married. Jimmy thinks this is some sort of record, and he's probably right – and now she's downstairs with a bowl of Special K and watching *Good Morning*. He's on flexi-time, so he's a couple of hours later than usual going into work. He shaves. Normally he uses an electric shaver, but they had a late honeymoon in Florida and he accidentally left the shaver behind. Now he curses as he cuts himself with a Bic. He presses toilet roll against it. At the weekend, he would just leave it, but this is work, and blood against a white shirt collar doesn't look good. There now. Not too bad. He puts on his shirt, but doesn't button the top button just yet. He pulls on his uniform. Smart, he looks smart. He carries his hat downstairs. He kisses Mary on the top of the head then comes round in front of her for inspection. She puts down her bowl and carefully peels off the little scrap of toilet roll from his neck. My, he's looking good. She buttons the top button then gives him a big kiss. He pats her stomach. She's nearly two months gone. A late honeymoon baby. They're in love.

He drives to work, though it would be quicker to walk. He's not sure what it is – he's not embarrassed by the uniform, or the job, loves them both, but there's something about walking the public streets in this uniform that makes him feel vaguely silly. Like, if you're into all that shit, why didn't you become a policeman, instead of a jumped-up little Hitler of a security guard? They don't know he used to be a cop, they don't know he had to leave because he broke his leg, knocked down by a joyrider, and couldn't face a desk job. Still, he's not going to hand out leaflets about it. So he drives to work.

Security. Head of security. Lots of responsibility. Always millions in diamonds on the premises. And he doesn't have ten thousand tonnes of paperwork and dog's abuse from the public to deal with. Oh, he's happy; good job, reasonable pay, beautiful wife, baby on the way.

James Warbeck, on his final day.

Security here at International Diamond Exchange is state-of-the-art.

Unfortunately human beings are rarely state-of-the-art.

Or perhaps they are: they respond to crisis in a pre-programmed manner, and each according to what their particular programme is: cool and calm, panicked, disastrously, unexpectedly; it's in the genes, it's in the DNA, it's in the eyes and the heart; none of it you can predict, not James Warbeck, in the control room, watching the video monitors, his colleagues beside him, not Hatcher or Mitchell or Johnny, sitting just a couple of streets away, their guns ready, just in case, but really, they're not going to need them. It's down to James Warbeck now, how he responds. If he goes for it, then they'll get the diamonds; if he doesn't, then they'll drive on, no harm done, and pick another target.

But he'll go for it.

Hatcher's done his research. He knows people. The quick and the dead.

He lifts the mobile and dials.

'Security,' is the response.

'James Warbeck please,' says Hatcher.

'This is Warbeck.'

'Ah, first time lucky.'

'What can I—'

'James. Tell me one thing. Have you ever heard the sound of a woman dying?'

His blood freezes. Everything goes into slow motion for James, just like the movies, except there's no music but drums, and the drum is his amplified heart. He sees everything in absolutely microscopic detail: dust mites in the air caught in the sun through the window; Mason, his pal, chewing gum by the monitor; the subtle vibration of the coffee percolator. There's a rush of blood in his ears like sea in a shell.

'What . . . who is this?'

'Listen, James, to little pregnant Mary.'

He hears a panting sound, distorted, distant, and then a scream of pain . . . His legs almost give way, he is transfixed by terror. 'Mary . . .' he whispers.

'Now here's what you're going to do, James. No hesitation, no questions, any deviation from my instructions and she's dead. Now, you have access to a gun, do you not?'

There's no point nodding on the phone, you actually have to make a sound. James manages a strangled grunt. This isn't happening. It can't be. Not to us. Not to us. Oh Mary, please, no.

2

By the time he appears outside International Diamond Exchange, James Warbeck has shot one person dead, wounded two others, and is carrying a bag of diamonds. He is without hat or jacket, and there is blood splattered over the front of his white shirt. He stands, breathing hard for a moment, his head spinning, looking, crying, heaving, waiting for salvation, waiting to wake up, knowing it's a nightmare, and knowing it's not. He feels drunk and hungover at the same time, his body isn't his, it has been usurped, there is an alien inside eating away at him, determined to burst out.

Then the people carrier with the blacked-out windows screeches to a halt, a door slides open, and he's hauled in.

Three men. None of them disguised. And in that moment he is certain he's going to die.

If he was to live they'd be disguised.

Death.

He's flat on the floor, one foot on his back, the other on his head. They don't even bother to take the diamonds off him, not yet. They're in traffic. Not speeding. Patient. He hears the indicators. They're so calm. Since when did robbers bother with indicators? Turning left. Turning left again. Turning right. Traffic lighter. Road bumpier. What's that? The sound of a boat. The river. He smells the river.

'Please tell me about—' but before he can finish, his face is pressed hard into the floor. He smells shoe polish. New leather. Wintergreen.

Brakes, then he's hauled up. He sees that he is indeed close to the river. There's an old factory, or warehouse, or something industrial behind him. But long gone. There are holes in the roof and the windows are smashed. There's a great black crow watching him.

He's pulled out of the vehicle and tossed onto the rubble-glass-concrete. He gashes his knee but so what? One of the men takes the bag off him; he doesn't look at their faces, a million to one shot that they'll let him go if he doesn't look at their faces again; he doesn't look but he's had glimpses and he'll remember those faces until the day he dies.

Today.

'My wife, please tell me . . .'

Johnny laughs down at him. 'You tell us. We haven't had the pleasure.'

'Sucker,' Mitchell says. 'Gets 'em every time.'

Then Hatcher pushes Johnny to one side and glares

down at James Warbeck. 'Where's the fucking rest of them?'

'I don't—'

Hatcher grabs him by the shirt and pulls him to his knees. 'Where are they?'

'I brought everything I—'

'You fucked us!'

'I swear to—'

Hatcher hurls Warbeck backwards, then turns angrily away. He has over a million in diamonds, but it's not enough.

Mitchell is sloshing petrol over the interior of the people carrier. There's another vehicle, same make, different colour, sitting behind it. They'll be out of here soon. Mitchell is buzzing. Tonight will be good. Party time. Noreen, she'll be up for it too, she loves it when they get a result. He looks at Hatcher, red with anger, but they're still doing OK. Diamonds are worth their weight in gold. Mitchell laughs. He thinks he's a smart cookie, though he would probably spell cookie wrong. He throws the empty petrol can into the back of the getaway car.

'Tuesday's not a good day . . .' Warbeck is whining.

'You can say that again,' says Johnny.

'I brought everything . . . I shot people . . . I did everything you asked . . . please . . .'

Hatcher stands over Warbeck; he reaches into his jacket and James prepares for the worst.

Holy Father.

My beautiful wife.

My beautiful baby to be.

I love you.

Except the man going for the gun, maybe he's changed his mind; he removes keys instead. He tosses them into the puddle behind.

'You've ten seconds to get out of here,' Hatcher hisses.

Disbelief. 'What?'

Johnny smiles. 'Ten,' he says.

Mitchell is beside him. 'Nine,' he says.

James scrambles round. The puddle is shallow, but it's murky-dark; he's in there with both hands, his fingers urgently searching out his passport to life.

'Eight,' says Johnny.

Please Jesus!

'Seven,' says Mitchell.

He has them. He jumps to his feet. He doesn't look at their faces. He races to the vehicle. He tries to put the key in the ignition, but his hands are shaking so much that he drops them to the floor. He reaches down.

'I'm going, I'm going . . . thank you . . . thank you . . . I swear to God I won't say a—'

'Six,' says Johnny, taking out a cigarette.

'Five,' says Mitchell, lighting it for him.

James has the keys, he fumbles to get the right one into the ignition.

'Four,' says Johnny, lighting the cigarette.

'Three,' says Mitchell.

The engine starts.

Thank Christ!

Mitchell takes the cigarette from Johnny's mouth and tosses it into the back of the people carrier.

James Warbeck doesn't even see it.

He races the vehicle forward. He has ten metres and four seconds of hope and freedom, of living again, of seeing his wife and holding his baby, before the whole lot explodes in a ball of flame.

He screams and he screams and he screams.

Johnny and Mitchell stand impassively. They see dead people every day.

'We agreed on ten,' says Johnny.

'I know,' says Mitchell, 'I cheated.'

Up above, the crow caws then takes off. Hatcher watches it go, follows its trajectory through the smashed glass and exposed rafters of the warehouse roof. He wonders if it's symbolic of something, the security guard ascending to heaven, the Devil watching them work. Mitchell is watching it too, and is thinking of his favourite song, 'You Are The Wind Beneath My Wings', which is about as deep as Mitchell gets.

3

It's late autumn cold, it's barely past lunchtime and it's already getting dark.

He's on his way to a gig, stopping off for a couple of pints, quelling the pre-minstrel tension. The temptation, as ever, is just to stay here, put it off to another day, but he forces himself up and out. Buddy Holly didn't get anywhere by sitting in a bar all day. Michael Stipe was on the road with REM for eleven years before he met with any real success. You put the work in, you get the results. Murphy finishes his third pint, then lifts his guitar and heads for the road. Now it's just a matter of deciding where the gig should be. Indoors, he thinks.

He wears the kind of pre-baseball tweedy cap that Bob Dylan used to wear, a heavy jacket with buttons rather than zips, and sometimes he has a mouth organ, but not today.

Murphy busks for a while at Charing Cross tube station.

His repertoire is wide and varied, he can give you 'Needles & Pins', 'The Kids Are Alright', 'Is She Really Going Out With Him', 'No Woman No Cry', a country version of 'White Riot', and he might even give you his *a cappella* 'Strange Fruit', but his voice is likely to give out halfway through that one and then he'll have to rent a slug of Special Brew off the emaciated Scot lying on the tartan rug at the foot of the other moving escalator.

It's all about making eye contact. Most of them keep their heads down and keep walking, but if he manages to make eye contact they invariably feel embarrassed enough to give him a few pennies. The Japanese are the best, they're usually worth a few pounds. Maybe he should go tour there: Marty Murphy, Live at Boudakan. He will embrace Japanese culture – the World Cup, Hiroshima, *Farewell My Concubine*, Sumo, kimonos, Sparks album, *Kimono My House* is still a favourite and of course his video of *The Bridge On The River Kwai*.

Americans are pretty good too. They think it's quaint. When he spots Americans he chooses American songs, because they really don't like foreign things at all; big old historical buildings sure, they're cute, but what they really want is a little bit of home. He'll give them 'American Girl', 'Do You Know The Way To San Jose' and Marty Robbins' 'Ballad Of The Alamo'. And when they've put money in his paper cup he'll say, Have a nice day. And they'll say, You have a nice day too. And sometimes he'll say, But I hope you have a better one, and really it could go on for ever.

When the cop comes to move Murphy on, he goes

without a fuss, pausing only to collect his coins. The cop leaves the Scot alone. Murphy knows the Scot is not actually a down-and-out but an avant-garde performance artist impersonating a tin of Edinburgh shortbread past its sell-by date, his comment on commercialism, cultural colonialism and political independence, but he says nothing. Murphy might try another pitch, but just as likely he'll adjourn to a pub to spend his change. He'll stash his acoustic behind the bar. He probably won't remember to take it with him when he leaves, but that doesn't matter, he'll get it again, or a similar one, on some future visit. He has them stashed in bars all over this part of London, like food dumps on the way to the Pole – or was it on the way back?

He loves the music. But it can make him think too much.

He loves the drink. And it dulls everything.

He has been with four women in the past year, all of them when he was drunk, and they were too. Not drunks, just drunk. He does not know what he would do with a sober woman. Make her a sandwich and ask her for a word that rhymes with orange.

One pub, two, three, he does a tour because he's pissed off. He had resolved to switch his brain off for twenty minutes, just long enough for Dr Coates to see that he'd wised up and was OK to return to duty, but he couldn't even manage that. She winds him up the wrong way. Time before last she asked him if he kept a diary, and when he said no she suggested that he should start and that then they would look at his thoughts together, perhaps it would be a cathartic experience for him.

So he brought his diary in the next time and she flicked through it with increasing annoyance.

It read like this:

Tuesday 23rd: Dentist. Sore.

Wednesday 24th: Launderette. Found extra sock.

Thursday 25th: Wild sex with Kim Basinger. Woke up.

'This wasn't what I had in mind at all,' she said.

'I know.'

'Everything's locked up inside you, Martin, it needs release.'

'Ah, right. Like that Dutch farm girl.'

'What?'

'The Dairy of Anne Frank.'

'Martin, this isn't funny.'

'I know. It's really annoying.'

He smiled, she glared, session over.

The Laughing Policeman. No one remembers that record now. A novelty song, but also the stuff of his childhood nightmares.

He finds himself climbing out of a taxi off the Fulham Palace Road. He can't really see the money he gives the driver, so he holds out his hands, full of drinking change, and lets him pick out as much as he wants.

'What about a tip?' the driver says, chancing his arm with the drunk.

'Don't sleep in the subway,' Murphy says.

The taxi roars off, and Murphy has a pee up against a wall.

Then he's putting his key in the door, except it won't fit, no matter which way he twists it. He looks blearily at the key. Somebody else's? Did some fair damsel slip her key into his pocket and say later? Well, there has to be a first time for everything. He leans against the door for support, then rings the bell, rings it again and again and again. When it seems like he might finally wear out the battery, a window shoots up high above him and Lianne's head appears.

'Wassa big idea, lockin' the bloody—'

'Martin,' she hisses, 'will you go away.'

'That's lovely, that is!' Murphy shouts.

'Martin, please!'

'Just open the frickin' door!'

She glares at him for a moment, then slams the window shut. He leans against the door. He hears hurried footsteps on the stairs, the bolts being drawn back. He pushes himself off the door and readies his charming yet triumphant smile. Except when the door opens there's a mountain man in a dressing gown standing there and before Murphy can say anything, a fist shoots out and catches him on the side of the nose. The force and the shock of it propel him backwards. There's a blinding light and a sudden stench of well dogged pavement, and then darkness.

Norman has been living with Lianne for three months;

she tells Murphy this in the bathroom where she's doing her best to fix his face. Norman paces outside the closed door, worrying because his lady is in there with her ex-husband and she's hardly wearing nothing at all, and Murphy's thinking exactly the same, that she's hardly wearing nothing at all. Her right breast is peeking out at him, almost waving, but sobriety has arrived quickly – concussion and blood on the footpath can do that – and he resists the temptation to cup that breast in his hand, just for old time's sake. He looks at her, squinting up while she dabs at the back of his head – ouch, jagged cut, hairs stuck in it – and she looks just as pretty and just as angry as he remembers.

'Are you OK in there?' Norman asks.

'Yes. Go to bed, I'll be fine.'

She knows he won't go, and it makes her happy. He'll protect her. He'll look after her. Her Norman. She shakes her head down at Murphy. 'Oh, Marty, what am I going to do with you?'

'Anything you want,' he says, and smiles, then drops it when she doesn't return her own wonderful smile. 'I'm sorry. I forgot. I was . . .'

'I know. Martin, you're putting me in danger.'

'No I'm not. That's all finished.'

'No it's not. You know it's not. You're putting yourself in danger, and you're putting Norman in danger.'

'Well, forgive me if I don't lose sleep over—'

She drags his face round with her hand. It hurts a little, but he goes with it. Listen to mother. 'Listen to me! I'm serious! You promised! You swore!'

Hold it, hold it, hold it . . . ah, too late . . .

'Yeah, well, you promised to love, honour and—'

'We lost our son! That wasn't me!'

'Oh yeah, right, fucking dead on!'

She begins to cry.

There's a knock on the door. 'Lianne?'

'Go to bed!' she shouts.

But he won't.

She wipes at her eyes. 'Just go, Marty, please.'

Murphy stands, patting gingerly at the back of his head.

'And don't come back.'

He looks at her sadly, they've made love ten thousand times and now she can't bear to be in the same room as him. But they'll always be joined.

'I watched the tape again last night,' he says.

'Don't, Marty.'

'You never asked for a copy.'

She sighs.

He opens the bathroom door and steps into the hall. He closes the door. He takes a deep breath. He sighs. There is a slight movement to his right and he turns to see Norman standing there, arms folded, brow furrowed, eyes intense. He's a big man, and quite heavily muscled, but he's been letting it go, he's at the stage now where it could very easily turn to flab. At this point Murphy should offer his hand, respect, men of the world, look after my woman. Instead he raises his eyebrows and says, 'She's still a great kisser,' then takes off down the stairs at the speed of sound, with big Norman in his dressing gown in hot pursuit.

4

He's up all night again, working on a song. It's called 'Carla's Last Stand' and it's a beautiful ballad, although this child of punk is slightly embarrassed by it. Then he thinks of the Beatles and 'Hey Jude' and 'Let It Be' and decides it's all right to come over all ballady once in a while.

He falls asleep around six, a glass of red wine spilled unnoticed over the quilt so that when the phone rings four hours later he jumps up like he's been shot, then looks at the quilt and thinks he really has been shot, and it's several long moments before the panic subsides, moments he uses to feel under the bed for the gun that's strapped there. He has it out in his hand and pointing at shadows while the answer machine clicks in and his voice on the tape cracks in with: 'WHAT? WHAT DO YOU WANT? GO AWAY! Alternatively, leave a message after the . . .' and it beeps and then there's a young woman's voice drained of emotion saying: 'DC Murphy, please report to James Warbeck at Chelsea Royal Infirmary at . . .'

He lies back in bed, breathing hard from the panic, slowly relaxing, then trying to think about the message and what it means. Dr Coates has changed her mind? Or they've managed to get me voluntary work as a hospital porter.

He gets out of bed, stows the gun, then looks at his lyrics. If he likes them, he'll go and see what they want; if they're shit, he'll stay where he is and work at them.

He amazes himself. They're good. The tune is good.

He goes to the shower, humming his own song. He'll be singing it on *Top Of The Pops* by the end of the year. Or *Opportunity Knocks.* No, wait, they cancelled that twenty-five years ago.

He sighs.

If the water is hot, it's a sign, and he'll go; if it runs cold then the Gods don't want him out of the building and he'll crawl back into bed.

The water's burning hot; so hot it makes the cold feel warm. Under the shower he thinks about Lianne and what they had and what they lost and he knows he can never have it back; he knows he doesn't want it back; that it's gone for good; too much said, too much hurt, too much blame. When he gets drunk he goes home, or to what was his home before they split, the way other people put on their favourite records. He will have to change his ways. She's right. It's too dangerous for him just to turn up like that. They could be watching. Even now, after it's all supposed to be over.

Two hours later he's striding down the hospital corridor, a big black orderly a couple of steps ahead of him. He has written James Warbeck on a piece of paper, which the orderly is now carrying.

He hates the smell of these places. Reminds him of . . .

'This way,' says the orderly and pushes through the swing doors, examining the piece of paper as he goes. 'James Warbeck,' he says to himself.

Three more sets, then they're in the morgue.

Murphy doesn't want to be here.

If he'd known he was coming to the morgue he would have stayed in bed.

The morgue has a smell all its own, separate from the tinny antiseptic of the hospital. He can't quite pin it down. It's morgue-smell, and it defies description. The orderly looks up at a bank of drawers, counts along and down, glances at the paper again, then pulls out the drawer, not much more than a thin metal shelf. He turns back to Murphy and says, 'James Warbeck, be back in ten,' nods, then exits.

This is James Warbeck: drained and brained by the autopsy, but before the undertakers have had a chance to get at him, to pretty him up, fill him out, apply the make-up, pump in the embalming fluid; he's a mass of teeth and scorched flesh; he's purple and black and yellow and oozing and—

'Fuck!' Murphy jumps as a hand is brought down on his shoulder.

He spins, ready for unarmed combat, or at least to plead for his life, only to find Murdoch standing there, and behind him a young man with a wispy moustache he does not recognise.

'Jesus,' says Murphy, 'don't do that to me.'

'Martin,' says Murdoch, 'you look like you've seen a ghost.' He gives it a big belly laugh, while his mate smiles thinly.

Murdoch's pushing fifty, one realistic eye on retirement, the other fantastically set on late-life promotion to the dizzy heights. It has the effect of making him cross-eyed, at least metaphorically. Unfocused. He has been Murphy's boss since Murphy dragged his sorry arse across the Irish Sea, bruised, battered, destroyed, determined to start again, but needing careful handling. Actually, Murdoch's a good guy. What you would call old school, but not in the club tie and pipe sense; more the doesn't mind going for a pint but stopping off on the way to give a suspect a surreptitious slap down a dark alley. He's a little paunchy now, not like the other cop, standing there in his nice suit, a folder under his arm, bright blue eyes, ready smile. Alan Carter. Call me Alan, he says. Shit, Murphy doesn't even know Murdoch's first name.

'So what's the story, morning glory?' he asks.

Before Murdoch can reply, Carter, Alan, steps forward, opens his file, looks up at Murphy, down at the corpse, and then returns his attention to the file, like he's giving the reading in church. 'James Warbeck, thirty-two, married, wife expecting, head of security at International Diamond Exchange, suddenly pulls a gun, shoots his best friend dead, wounds two others, then makes off with a million in diamonds.'

Murphy ignores Carter for the moment, addresses his question to Murdoch. 'So how'd he come by the suntan? Guilty conscience?'

'Yeah,' laughs Murdoch. 'When was the last time you came across one of those?' He lets the laugh settle for a moment, then looks gravely down at the horror on the table. 'Told his colleagues that his wife was being held hostage, that they were going to kill her.'

'Meanwhile,' says Carter, 'the wife was in Sainsburys.'

Murdoch sighs, then nods at Carter. Carter turns to the back of his folder and removes a series of black and white photographs. Fumbling slightly, he passes them to Murdoch. He takes a look at the top one and passes it to Murphy. Murphy sees three white guys in black funeral suits.

'Ah,' says Murphy, 'suspects.'

'Guy in the middle, Terry Hatcher. He's known locally as the Undertaker.'

Murphy rolls his eyes. 'Everyone must have a nickname. It's the rule.'

'He runs a string of LCD funeral homes,' says Murdoch. 'Also has interests in a number of pubs and clubs across the city. Goes without saying he's into protection. He does some small-scale dealing, mostly E, and now, it seems, he's into diamonds.'

'He mixes E and D,' Carter says, and neither of them rewards him with a smile. Carter clears his throat and continues. 'Until now he's been strictly second division, been called in a few times, hasn't done any time, but you know how it is with these guys, once they get a taste of it they want to play in the Premier League all the time.'

Murphy nods thoughtfully at Carter for several moments, then turns abruptly to his boss. 'I didn't know you were running a youth training scheme,' he says.

Carter's eyes nearly pop. He spits out: 'Yeah, it's to replace all the burn-outs.'

Murdoch guffaws – yes, a genuine guffaw – and steps between them. He pats Carter on the shoulder. 'Easy there, Alan. Murph's only kiddin', aren't you, Murph?'

'Of course I am, Alan,' Murph says, then adds a needless: 'Ho, ho, ho.'

Murdoch tells Carter he wants to have a quiet word with Murphy, and there's a brief moment when a hint of childish hurt and self-pity flits across Carter's eyes – why will nobody play with me? Why can't I do anything right? – before he nods and leaves, though when he goes he leaves the door a fraction open.

Murdoch closes it, leans against it, smiles at Murphy. 'He's OK, Marty.'

'I don't doubt it. Anything else?'

Murdoch shows him a second photo, of Hatcher entering a pub called the Crook and Staff, with a blonde woman.

'Her name's Annie Guthrie.'

'And after nicknames, there's always a blonde.'

Then there's a third photo, grainy, long-distance, through a window, looking down. Hatcher naked on a bed, a blonde woman on top of him, also naked.

'Wham, embalm, thank you, mam.' Marty smiles to himself. He likes that line. He can use it in a song. 'Photographer's got the plum job, hasn't he? Think he could run me up some private copies, purely for research?'

Murdoch ignores him. 'We believe this is the third diamond snatch they've done in the past month. But the first time someone's been killed. If they've stepped up to murder, then there's no telling which direction they'll go next. The boss wants this stopped.'

'You have a boss? I thought you were the highest of the high.'

'Very funny, Martin.'

Murphy takes a deep breath. He smells death, burns, antiseptic, a hint of aftershave. 'So,' he says, 'this is where I come in.' Murdoch nods. Murphy looks at the top photo again. 'And apart from the cast of *Reservoir Dogs,* you've nothing to go on.'

'Marty, you failed your assessment. This three strikes and you're out thing doesn't just apply to crime. You've failed your third evaluation. You shouldn't be here at all.'

Murphy shrugs. 'You called me.'

'I fought to get you onto this. It really is your last chance this time.'

'Yeah, me and Mel.' He nods sagely for several moments. He should leave it. Just say thank you, boss, I won't let you down. Instead: 'Another way to look at it would be, everyone else turned this down. Nobody else was stupid enough to volunteer. Even the boy wonder.'

'You're very cynical.'

'Cynical and alive, as opposed to dead and gullible.'

'For your information, they were all fighting to do this. Even Carter.'

'Carter? You'd send him undercover? As what, Greyfriar's Bobby?'

Murdoch nods, without smiling. They stand silently for several moments. There are a thousand things Murdoch wants to say to him; he knows all the details, and Murphy knows he knows all the details. Murphy knows Murdoch is a good, warm man who would be his friend.

'So how're you doing, Marty?'

'OK.'

'Dr Coates wasn't overly impressed.'

'Got me on a bad day.'

'I get the impression most days are bad days.'

Murphy shrugs. 'I'm fine. I have a problem with psychiatrists.'

'It's the way it's going.'

'Don't I know it.'

'So what do you say?'

'Would I be right in thinking there's a promotion in this?' Murdoch nods. 'For you rather than me?'

'I'm too old for this shit, Marty. I need a desk job. I need a desk. So are you on or not?'

Murphy takes a long, lingering look at James Warbeck, and thinks that no wife should be allowed to see her husband like this.

He has been down this street before, and it's a dead end.

He pushes the drawer back into the bank. A corpse behind each door. He shudders and turns back to Murdoch.

Outside, in the car, Murdoch finds Carter flicking through his tapes, and is a little flustered to have been caught doing it. Murdoch's a little flustered as well. In some of his more ludicrous moments Murdoch imagines himself to be Inspector Morse. Cultured. And able to solve a crime in one hundred and twenty minutes with ad breaks. Ah, if life was just like that. But it isn't, and the truth is he hates this Dvořák shit he's been trying to love, but he will persevere with it until Carter is out of earshot.

As they drive away from the hospital, they pass Murphy walking along the street, shoulders hunched, eyes cast down. Carter shakes his head.

'Not impressed?' Murdoch asks. Carter shrugs. Murdoch smiles paternally. 'Most of them burn out after a couple of years,' he says. 'Murphy, he was burned out before we got him.'

'So why keep him?'

'Because his worst is better than most people's best.' Carter keeps his eyes steady on the road, but Murdoch can tell he's not convinced. He's cocky, Carter, but he'll learn. 'Murphy's a natural,' he explains. 'Most of them think it's about acting. It's not. All actors forget their lines at some point. You do that in this business and you're dead meat. You have to live it one hundred per cent.'

'If you live it one hundred per cent,' Carter says dryly, 'wouldn't you be on the other side?'

'Let's not go there, please,' Murdoch says, and eyes the Mantovani tape on the dash.

He has to go into the Big Building again to sort out his background and cover, but there's really not that much to do. He's not a friggin' master of disguise; he plays himself, a feckless Irishman on the loose in London. Ex-army, so couldn't settle in Belfast, no particular trouble, but a few minor convictions they can check out and approve if they have the right connections, and most of them do. Nothing anyone's going to trip him up over. Doing odd jobs, building, driving; shit, anyone could have seen him out busking anyway.

It's about getting inside, but not making it obvious.

Joining the gang by chance and contrived circumstance, not by trying to ingratiate himself. To make them want him, rather than the other way round.

He will become, to all intents and purposes, the Singing Detective, although with better skin.

He tries to tap petty cash for a new guitar, but they laugh and roll their eyes like he's not serious.

'I am serious,' he says. 'It's part of my character.'

'Yeah, right, Murphy.'

'It is. For Jesus' sake, ask Murdoch. I need a guitar. It doesn't have to be expensive. I'll supply my own picks.'

'Yeah, yeah, Murphy, very funny.'

'Come on. It doesn't have to be top of the range, just something I can bang a tune out on.'

'Tell you what, Murphy, you buy the guitar, and bring us the receipt, then we'll see what we can do.'

Murphy nods warily at them. 'What about a mouth organ?'

5

The manager, John Duffy, is in a bit of a panic because Hatcher's in tonight and he doesn't want to look like a disaster, yet they've been advertising 'The Man in Black', the sounds of Johnny Cash, all week, and now the bastard has phoned to say he's been pulled over by the cops. What's Duffy supposed to do? The place is filling up. There's no cover charge, but what's to stop them drinking up and moving on when they realise Johnny Cash ain't coming to town? What the hell is Johnny Cash doing riding round in a stolen van for anyhow? Is he, like, a Method-impersonator, really wants to go to prison so he can pretend he's at San Quentin or something?

Then the funny little Irish guy who's been drinking in the Crook and Staff all week comes up and says, I hear you're having a Cash-flow problem, and Duffy snaps back something smart and then the Irish guy says, I'm a singer, I'll sing for you. Duffy says something about it not being amateur night and the Irish guy says please yourself and walks off. Duffy calls him back and says are you any good? Irish guy says yeah, I'm brilliant, that's why I'm getting pissed in the Crook and Staff, do you want me to get up or not?

He has balls. Duffy likes that. He puts his hand out. 'Duffy,' he says.

'Murphy,' says Murphy. 'What do you pay?'

'Sod all,' says Duffy, 'but you can have free drink at the bar, and if you're not beaten to death by the punters, you can play again another night, and then I'll pay you.'

Murphy thinks about that for a moment. 'Fair enough.'

'What sort of shit do you play?' Duffy asks.

'All kinds of every shit,' says Murphy.

'OK,' says Duffy, 'but if you can do Johnny Cash I'll pay extra.'

'You're not paying me at all.'

'You can have crisps as well.' He winks and moves on, out into the bar to check that everything's OK with Hatcher.

Fucking Hatcher. He hates that bastard, but then everyone hates their boss, don't they? Or is there something different about Hatcher? Sure there is. His handshake is, what, clammy? Duffy knows why that is. Because he fucks around with dead people all day. Touches them. Touches them up for all he knows. Removes things. Or inserts them. Ugh.

Hatcher's in with his full crew tonight: Johnny's there, half pissed already, Mitchell, Noreen, that new girl they have working down there, Annie, good-looker, but knows it. The old man's there too. Hatcher Snr. Now there's an old gent, sitting there coughing and spluttering in his wheelchair. Well, at least one thing's for sure, he'll get a good deal on a coffin. Duffy has heard that Hatcher Snr was a bit of a hard nut in his time as well, but looking at him now it's hard to believe it. Legs like sparrows'. Snap them in your hand. That sucked-in look the terminal always have. Likes a drink though. And, Duffy seems to remember, a Johnny Cash fan.

Duffy goes across. 'All right for drinks, gents?' he says. He sees now that they're on champagne. 'What's the big occasion, Mr Hatcher? A result on the gee-gees?'

'That's right, Duffy,' says Hatcher, 'our horse came in.'

'Or should that be hearse,' roars Mitchell, and they all erupt.

Duffy laughs along with them, but inside he's stony-faced. 'That's great, Mr Hatcher. Another bottle of bubbly?'

He organises the champagne and then heads into the kitchen. The chef – hah! – has clocked off, but before he goes he always leaves out something in cling-film for Duffy, and tonight there's a nice breast of chicken in sauce and some mash. Duffy stands eating it, cutting the chicken with his fork, mixing it all up like a casserole. He hears the Irish guy coming on and waits for the booing to start, but, dammit, if he doesn't knock them down with three Johnny Cash's in a row. 'I Forgot To Remember To Forget', 'Ghost Riders In The Sky' and 'A Boy Named Sue'. By the second song Duffy is eating his dinner in the kitchen doorway. The reaction is good, the applause loud. Maybe too good; he glances at the bar and sees that nobody's up buying drink, they're all too busy watching. He checks to see if Hatcher has noticed, but no, he's enjoying the music too much.

Hatcher leans forward. 'Get you another drink, Dad?'

'I'm OK, son.' The old man runs a spiderish hand down his chest, gives a pained expression. 'I think one's plenty, with the way I am.' He brightens a bit as he looks up to the stage. 'Good lad, this,' he says.

Hatcher nods in agreement. He's feeling good now, he's over his anger. So they didn't get as much as he'd hoped. Nobody's fault. They'll just have to do another one. There's time yet. D-day isn't until . . . everyone around him begins applauding as a song finishes. He joins in. Yeah, enjoy tonight. Noreen is looking at him. He smiles. He takes a drink. She turns as Mitchell whispers something in her ear and then giggles. Annie sits drinking her champagne tentatively, still a little nervous in their company. He thinks she thinks this is all a little downmarket for her, but she's trying to hide it. She is very pretty, but you can hire pretty every day of the week. There's something else about her, something cool and mysterious, like she knows she could have every man in the room but it'll be entirely up to her which one she has; she won't be seduced, she'll do the seducing. He likes that, likes it a lot. But he won't be panting around after her, that's not his style. He'll be cool, like his customers. He smiles at the thought of two cold fronts meeting; what would the weather man say to that?

Up on stage Murphy is tuning the acoustic, and nodding at the applause. 'Thank you, thank you . . . oops, there we go . . . sorry, first night nerves 'n' all. I ah . . . was wondering, how do you know when the Lone Ranger's going to the toilet?'

There are a few heckles from the audience which he doesn't quite pick up. He laughs anyway, then leans into the microphone. 'To-the-dump, to-the-dump, to-the-dump, dump, dump . . .' he sings and there are groans aplenty in response. 'Sorry,' he says again. 'OK, I'll stick to the singing. Now, I'm gonna need a volunteer for this one. Is there anyone called Annie out there tonight? Any Annies? I'll accept Anne. But not Diane.'

Mitchell sticks up his hand and points at Annie, who immediately blushes and tries to lose herself down the back of the booth.

'OK, we have an Annie!' says Murphy.

The crowd begins to applaud, Hatcher, his dad, the whole gang too.

'I'm not—'

'Go on!'

'Come on, chicken!'

Annie relents; she takes a long drink of her champagne, nearly chokes herself, then splutters and coughs her way to the stage – hah! – where Murphy has already pulled up a bar stool for her to sit on. He pats the seat for her to get up, and she does so rather self-consciously.

Murphy moves the mike a little to the side so he can cover her as well. He smiles. 'Annie, is it?'

'Yes.'

'Nice name. What's that short for?'

She thinks for a moment, then realises he's raking her. 'What?'

The audience laughs. He pulls the microphone back round. 'Only testing. OK, Annie, all I need you to do is sit there and look beautiful.'

She gives a little embarrassed laugh, then looks down like she's Lady Di. It's a nice touch; he wonders for a moment if she's up to her arse in diamonds as well or is she just Hatcher's arm candy? He strums.

Marty sings 'Annie's Song', his voice honed by months of busking on and battling against the acoustic violence of the tube. He sings strong and pure and clear. He's singing John Denver, and people are suckers for John Denver. He might be pushing up seaweed, but he can silence an audience inside a verse. Not quite rock 'n' roll, but needs must. Annie's face changes as he sings: from embarrassed get me out of here to grudging appreciation to a kind of dreamy this is really nice but where am I?

When he finishes, the applause is thunderous. He sees Hatcher's whole table – save the old guy in the wheelchair – up on their feet cheering. Annie just sits there with a benign look on her face.

'That's it,' Marty says softly, and it yanks her back to the real world.

She looks embarrassed again. 'Oh,' she says simply, laughs at herself, then hops down off the stool.

6

Forty minutes later he's drained, sweated out. He's given them everything he has. Not just going through the motions like some two-bit cabaret crooner, but really pouring his heart into it. In his head he's playing the great arenas. It's not just Marty Murphy and his guitar – it's Marty Murphy Unplugged. He has recorded the gig and will listen to it later, searching for mistakes, intent on perfection. He realises that on Bruce Springsteen Unplugged you probably can't hear the sound of cash registers from the bar, or the toilets flushing, or the bouncers throwing out a Rasta guy selling drugs; on Nirvana Unplugged there's no one gagging for breath after choking on a pork scratching, or the slimy bar manager calling out charity bingo numbers between songs. But at least he's up there, performing, in his element, living a little bit of his dream. That and he gets to catch bad guys as well.

He's a superhero really – by day, mild-mannered musician, by night the Scarlet Pimpernel.

He's in his dressing room – hah! – getting changed when the door opens and Annie's standing there, smiling a little nervously. He's wearing boxers, socks and a fresh T-shirt; he raises his folded jeans protectively over his groin and says, 'The ladies is down—'

'I . . . I know, I just wanted to say, nice song. Not sure I enjoyed being up there, but I enjoyed the song.'

She ventures just a little forward into what is otherwise known as the men's toilets. Two urinals, a cubicle – lock broken, no paper – and a stench.

'Yeah,' he says, 'if you can forget about the James Galway version, and John Denver's teeth, it's actually a lovely wee number.' He turns away slightly so that he can pull his trousers on.

She averts her eyes for a moment. 'First time here?' she asks while he zips and buttons.

'Aye. I got fed up playing the big arenas. They're so impersonal, don't you think?' She smiles. 'So I said to my agent, I wanna get back in touch with my people.' He stops with a comic double take. 'Wait a minute, I don't have an agent. Ah now, I know your game. You're an agent. Your car broke down, you took shelter in this dive and now you think you've discovered the next Chris de Burgh, but cooler – Ice de Burgh . . .' This time Murphy laughs. 'You can stop me any time you want, there's two batteries just in the back of my . . .' He trails off. 'Sorry. I'm a bit juiced after . . . adrenaline . . .'

'Sorry,' Annie says, 'I'm not an agent. I'm with friends. They want you to join us for a drink.'

'And you?'

'And you what?'

'And do you want me to join you, and your friends, for a drink?'

She kind of shrugs and looks away. 'Nice dressing room,' she says.

'You should see the support act's,' and he nods at the half-closed door of the cubicle. 'Listen, the drink, sorry, I'm knackered, another time. You'll explain to your friends?'

She nods, and looks a little relieved. 'See you around,' she says.

Some of Hatcher's resolve has evaporated by the end of the evening. He's looking at Annie as they laugh and joke and thinking how wonderful she is, so when she goes to the ladies he arranges with Johnny to run the old man back to the nursing home, saying he's got some business to attend to. Mitchell gets the hint and comes over all horny with Noreen, though she's clearly not the slightest bit interested. Still, Mitchell calls the shots, so by the time Annie comes back from the loo, Noreen's up and pulling on her coat, muttering away to herself the whole time. After they go, Annie says she'd better be getting on too. Hatcher says he'll give her a lift. After what you've drunk? I'll walk you to a taxi. She seems happy enough with that.

They're still laughing and joking when they come out of the Crook and Staff. He says how about going into the

Chinese next door, but she says again she wants to go home, but thank you.

They're about a hundred yards along, close to where he knows he'll pick up a taxi, when there's the sound of glass smashing and then sudden movement from a doorway to their left and this street dweller, all ripped parka and stench of urine, comes hurtling towards them. He has a jagged broken beer bottle in his hand, flecks of foam spit and foam in his mouth as he says, 'Give me it, give me it, give me it, you fuckers . . .'

Annie lets out a little scream and instinctively moves behind Hatcher, who holds out his hands, fingers spread, palms down. 'Just take it easy,' he says.

'Gimme your fucking money, you fucking poofy fucker.' He jabs the bottle at Hatcher, who takes a step back. But he's not ruffled. He really isn't.

'You don't want to do this,' Hatcher says.

'Just give it to him!' Annie shouts.

A thin smile appears on Hatcher's face. 'OK,' he says quietly, 'if that's what the man wants.'

He's unbuttoning his jacket. He will slip out his gun and he'll put it in the tramp's face and sees if he's still so keen on taking his money.

His fingers are just curling round the gun when there's movement, to his right this time, and he thinks for a moment that he's been blindsided, shit, I should have expected it, it's the fucking champagne. But it's not what he thinks or could have imagined – it's the fucking singer!

Murphy wields the acoustic guitar like a pickaxe, up

over his shoulder and crashing down on the tramp's head. There's an explosion of bum notes and splinters and the tramp lets out a howl and hits the deck. Even when he's on the ground, curling up, half crying, Murphy goes after him, hitting him twice more with the neck of the guitar.

Hatcher stands back, happily surprised. He removes his hand from the gun in his jacket. 'Hey, hey,' he says, 'music man to the rescue!' He feels Annie up beside him, grasping his arm for protection. He steps forward and kicks hard at the tramp, once, twice, three times, four. He could probably kick him for ever and the bastard wouldn't feel a thing, he's that drunk.

Annie produces a mobile phone from her bag. 'I'll call the police,' she says.

Hatcher and Marty turn as if choreographed and say, 'No!' at the same time. Then they look at each other and laugh. Hatcher says, 'No harm done, Annie, just some pond life looking for the next drink.'

She hesitates, looks to Murphy.

'No problem with me,' he says.

She turns back to her boss. 'But Terry—'

'Leave it. Occupational hazard round here, love. Place has gone to the dogs.'

Hatcher looks at Murphy, standing there awkwardly now, his passion spent. He looks mildly embarrassed by what he has done. He picks up the bits of his broken guitar and even the tramp's broken bottle and places them in a bin. He comes back to them and says, 'Well, if you're OK, I'll just . . . mosey along . . .'

Hatcher takes out his wallet and begins counting some notes. 'Fair's fair,' he says.

'No, honestly, it's OK.'

'You'll need a new guitar,' says Annie as Hatcher proffers the money.

'No, seriously. Obviously you haven't heard my "Bohemian Rhapsody" on a tambourine.'

Hatcher stuffs the money into the top pocket of Murphy's jacket anyway, and then they're all distracted by the tramp making a sudden and remarkably lithe break for freedom. Murphy swings round as if to go after him, but Hatcher grabs his arm. For a brief moment he feels tense muscle.

'Relax, son,' he says, 'he's not worth it.'

Murphy takes a couple of steps after the tramp, then stops and nods. 'Suppose you're right,' he says. 'I just hate . . .' He trails off.

'Well, thanks,' Hatcher says, 'thanks a lot.'

Murphy nods, first at Hatcher, at Annie, then gives a little wave and says he'll see them around.

Ten yards down the street, Hatcher calls after him. 'Hey!' Murphy turns. 'I might have a job for you!'

'What sort of a job?'

'Do you do birthday parties?'

It's a question Dylan doesn't get too often, but Murphy's not thinking about pride right now. He shrugs, he appears nonchalant, he procrastinates until Hatcher jacks up the fee. But he agrees in the end. Of course he does. He's one step closer to the gang and if it's not exactly Live At the Albert Hall, it's another gig, and you never know who might be in the audience. Gangsters and showbiz, they go hand in hand. The Krays and all that. He might arrest a killer and score a record deal on the same night.

Hey rock 'n' roll.

When he's sure Hatcher and Annie are gone, Murphy returns to his van. His equipment is packed away already – every singer worth his salt has his own PA, you can't depend on a pub having anything decent. As he opens the driver's door he's suddenly thrust hard up against it and pinned there. Something digs into the side of his throat.

The stench of the tramp is almost overwhelming. 'Money or your life,' he hisses, 'and this time there's no fucking cavalry.'

Murphy sighs. 'I have no money, and I have no life.'

Abruptly the tramp drops two blunt fingers from Murphy's throat. 'Well, could you at least give me a lift home?' he asks.

He reaches up and pulls down the hood of his stinking parka. It's Murdoch. He also peels off a matted beard and stuffs it into his coat pocket; he unzips the coat to reveal the padding within. He rubs at his head. 'Did you have to hit me so bloody hard? And you were supposed to stick to the body.'

'Gee, I guess I'm just careless,' Murphy says in American. 'Now will you get in the fucking van?'

7

Through to dawn Murphy writes three, count 'em, songs, he's on a high over his show, and with getting in with Hatcher so easily. A master in so many fields. He drinks red wine and wonders what he should do with his songs, he nearly has enough for an album. He hasn't yet had the nerve to play them in public. He thinks people are slow to welcome new songs in a live context. Even when you go to see huge bands, people get impatient when the singer announces, 'This is a song from our new album, it's out next March'; they're not interested, give us the fucking hits. You need people to be familiar with your work for them to appreciate it live; so what he thinks about doing is maybe going into a studio and making a demo. Then he can hawk it around some of the record companies. He knows he's too old to be a pop star. And too young to be Perry Como. But somewhere in the middle maybe. A song-writing craftsman, like Elvis Costello or Van Morrison. Yeah.

He leaves his apartment at ten, not having slept at all. He has a fry-up in a cafe, then heads out to Kensington by tube. There he gets lost a couple of times before he finally locates the Mount Merrion Kindergarten. He wasn't quite sure how he was going to approach her while she was teaching, so he's relieved to see her standing with her back against the playground's razor-wire topped fence, watching the toddlers tumble and cavort. He goes up behind her. He knows she's dying for a fag, but it would be a sacking offence in front of the kids. Her body is probably peppered with nicotine patches. She might even have emergency cigarettes Sellotaped to her chest.

He says, 'Lianne,' and she jumps. There's an oh, you scared me look, a hint of warmth, then she remembers, and the thunder mask descends.

'How did you know I was working here?' she snaps.

'I'm a policeman. I know everything.'

'I thought you were sacked.'

'Reports of my sacking were premature. It's seems I'm indispensable. At least to the police.'

She makes a bit of a face, but can't resist a smile as well. Then she looks up and down the street. 'You come to my home, you come to my work. You might as well just give out flyers.'

'Peace has broken out back home, Lianne, nothing's going to happen.'

'Oh good. Let's just move home again, we've nothing to worry about.'

He sighs. 'OK. I just came to apologise.'

'What, by doing exactly the same thing again, except sober? This is even worse.'

'I can't win, can I?'

She sighs, this time. 'OK. Just . . .'

'I know.'

He puts his hand on the fence, traces the outline of the diamond patterns. Diamonds. Hatcher. Work.

'So how's stormin' Norman?' he asks.

'Not happy with you. Happy with me.'

'Good. I'm pleased.'

'Are you?'

'No.'

She smiles wanly. 'So,' she says, 'any women in your life?'

'Kate and Naomi. The usual. Won't leave me alone.'

'Marty.'

'I'm serious. I'm telling you, once they get the war paint off, they're not that special. Especially that Kate, you could break her like a twig and use her for kindling, she's that skinny. Taller than you'd think, though.'

She's looking at him, and she shakes her head. 'You always did talk a lot of shite,' she says.

'That's why you loved me.'

'Yeah, well.'

He gives a sad laugh. 'So this Norman. What does he do?'

'He helps give people living in fear of their lives new identities.'

'Funny. What does he do, seriously.'

'I am serious.' And her face tells him she is.

'You mean he's a fucking cop?'

'Home Office.'

'And he . . . and you . . . Jesus. Isn't there something unethical about that?'

'He's not a doctor, Martin.'

'Nevertheless, I don't approve.'

'Martin, I'm long past the point of caring what you do or don't approve of.'

He nods sagely. 'It won't last,' he says.

'Yes it will.'

'How do you know that?'

'Because I love him.'

'I don't need to hear that.'

'Well, don't fucking ask then.'

Behind her another woman emerges from a doorway and looks across frostily before ringing a large bell in her hand, like something out of *Little House On The Prairie*. Some of the kids begin to go back inside, others linger by the slide and sandpit. Lianne says, 'I have to go.'

'OK. Lianne?'

'What?'

'Nothing.'

She sighs. 'Is everything OK?'

He nods.

The other woman in the playground rings the bell again, like round two is about to start. And it very easily could. He was always very good at winding up Lianne.

'Well, look after yourself.'

Well, look after yourself. That's what you say to someone you've no intention of seeing again. She could easily have said, give me a bell sometime, or here's my email if ever you need to . . . but no, look after yourself like he's an ex-boyfriend she's embarrassed to have met in the street.

How does he respond to look after yourself?

'Sure,' he says, 'I'll wrap up warm.'

And she looks at him oddly, then turns back to her nursery school, no lingering looks, no fingers touching through the wire, she just goes. Deranged husbands have stormed into nursery schools with machine pistols for less. He stands with his fingers on the wire, looking at the empty sandpit and the slide, and then up at the CCTV camera watching him. He gives it the fingers, which isn't very big of him, but understandable, under the circumstances.

8

He spends his days keeping an eye on Fond Farewells, his evenings hanging around the Crook and Staff. He plays two more gigs, Duffy slips him forty quid a time, the shows go down well enough, but Hatcher fails to show at either of them. Fair enough.

Patience is a virtue.

Hatcher runs five funeral homes in the north of the city, but spends most of his time at Fond Farewells, the largest and most austere looking of the lot. Luckily there's a decent amount of parking nearby, so Murphy sits in his van, just watching, occasionally lifting a pair of binoculars, but he doesn't see much. Mostly just sad people crying over loved ones, and the dark, morbid faces of Mitchell and Johnny crack into smiles when they're not looking. He catches glimpses of Annie at upstairs windows, on the phone. He sees her leave for lunch, once with Hatcher, but usually without. He thinks about bumping into her at the small pub she sometimes repairs to, but thinks better of it. He doesn't keep the photograph in the van of her making love to Hatcher, but sometimes he looks at it at night, hoping for inspiration for a song. He can't see her face in the photograph, but he sees her ankles, her legs, her ass. With the aid of a magnifying glass – honestly, I'm working – he sees that she has a small tattoo of a butterfly on one of her exquisitely rounded cheeks. He wonders idly if butterfly tattoos start out as caterpillars as well.

Murdoch calls to see how things are going, but he's fairly relaxed. He's pleased that their little drama worked out so well and can't wait for Murphy to attend the party. He's like a big kid, sometimes. Other times he's like a big fucking ogre. Marty laughs at the thought of it, then focuses his binoculars on Hatcher, shaking hands with the widower outside the church now, with the tear-stricken daughters; watches Mitchell guide the pallbearers, with a gentle assist here, a whispered encouragement there, as they slide the coffin into the back of the hearse; watches the priest nod and shake, nod and shake; he can't hear the words but knows the mourners are talking about how wonderful the dearly departed was, how he was taken before his time, or it was a blessed relief or how're you keeping yourself, Father. The priest smiles and—

'Holy mackerel.'

Murphy sits bolt upright in his seat.

No.

Yes.

No.

For fuck's sake.

He should leave it, he really should leave it, or put it in storage to be retrieved later, but he's so surprised that he can't resist the temptation to act on it. He'll be careful. He's always careful. He's a professional. Just a quick word.

The elderly woman has confessed all, though there wasn't much beyond a swearword in a moment of anger with her deaf husband and a couple of nips of sherry to stave off the cold. She's a Pioneer, see, thinks alcohol is the Devil's vomit. But she was tempted! Please forgive me. She says, 'Thank you very much again, Father McBride,' on the way out, happy now.

Father McBride sits back in the box and lifts the *Daily Mirror* again. He's been making his way through the problem page, but keeps getting interrupted. Then he hears the door going again and he sighs and folds the paper. Emma from Coventry who's being pressured by her boyfriend to get breast implants will just have to wait.

The voice says, 'I knew McBride when he used to rock 'n' roll.'

McBride looks startled, peers into the darkness. 'Who . . . is that?'

The Belfast accent, the intonation – abruptly it changes to stage Irish. 'Forgive me, Father, but it's been twenty years since my last confession – and boy, have I got some stories to tell . . .'

And McBride suddenly twigs and for a moment he's numb with shock and surprise, then he bounds out of his box and rips open the door of the confessional and there he is grinning impishly out.

'Martin? Martin! Christ Almighty!'

Murphy smiles back. 'Are you allowed to take the Lord's name in vain?'

McBride puts his hands on his hips. 'I wasn't. It was a little prayer. Marty . . . honest to God, where did you spring from?'

Murphy shrugs. They stand awkwardly looking at each other for several moments, then McBride comes forward and gives him a hug.

Murphy breaks away first. 'Jesus,' he says, 'that's a bit grown-up.'

McBride laughs and says, 'Well, one of us had to. Martin, Martin Murphy. Murphy. Martin.'

'Well, I think we've established what my name is. Now how about a wee drinky to celebrate?'

The priest is in his very late thirties. His hair is receding and he's baggy about the eyes and jowls. So changed from when they were together. Used to be slim as a rake. Footballer's legs and spiky hair, racing down to the newsagent to buy the *NME* on a Thursday, gigs, records, speed now and again, but mostly cider.

Every time I hear the word culture, I reach for my Strongbow.

They're in the pub now.

Father McBride hesitates for only the briefest moment – what if he's an alcoholic or drinks Babycham now? – before ordering Murphy a pint, and instinctively it's Harp, because that's what they always used to drink, but it costs extra over here because they have to import it. The pub's busy because of lunchtime, the noise levels up; there's a fruit machine by Murphy's shoulder: when they speak they almost have to shout, which makes it difficult to get really personal. They both know it and are embarrassed by it, but neither of them suggests leaving; it also protects them, a little bit, from saying too much.

'Twenty years,' says Father McBride. 'Oh dear, Marty, is it really that long?'

'Twenty years. The best punk band in Belfast.'

'Fatal Distraction. We were going to conquer the world.'

'We didn't even conquer Belfast.'

'We didn't even conquer our street.'

'We didn't even conquer your garage.'

They laugh.

'We were the most talentless bunch of wasters, weren't we? Those songs, they were really embarrassing,' says the priest.

'No they weren't, they were fine. Just . . . ahead of their time.'

'Oh balls, Martin, they were awful.'

'I'm still writing.'

'Songs?' Murphy nods. 'Seriously?'

'Semi-seriously.'

McBride smiles, but worried that he might have put his foot in it. Then he shakes his head. 'Jesus, Marty. How on earth did you find me? Are you living over here? What are you working at?'

'Chance, yes, and the same old stuff.'

'Really? Seriously?'

'I was just passing. Saw your face. Nearly had a friggin' heart attack.'

'Well, they say the Lord moves in mysterious ways.'

Murphy laughs quietly.

'What?' asks McBride.

'The Lord moves in mysterious ways – it's just hearing you say it, and look at you, in your priest get-up.'

'It's not a get-up.'

'You know what I mean.'

'And I'm sure you look just as ludicrous in your uniform.'

Murphy laughs again. 'Yeah. I suppose. But you, a priest, sure you nailed half the girls in Belfast.'

McBride shrugs, because he knows he didn't, really, he just talked about it a lot.

'I was just getting it out of my system,' he says. 'And look who's talking. You who ripped off half the car radios this side of the Lagan, now you're a peeler.' He takes a sip of his beer, then looks glumly at his old friend. 'I, ahm, must admit, I read about the . . . unpleasantness back home.'

'Yeah. It was very unpleasant.'

'I didn't mean – well, never was very good with words, you know that from our song lyrics.'

This time Murphy laughs aloud. 'I know. The only punk in Belfast who could get antiestablishmentarianism into the chorus of a pop song.' He drums his fingers on the table. He nods, as much to himself as to the priest. 'It was unpleasant. It was a long time ago. It's finished.'

Afterwards Murphy walks him back to his church. It's old, needs fixing up, there's a small graveyard which is badly overgrown. Outside a crumbling wall, London traffic heaves past. It's one of those grey London days when nothing feels right, when you want to pull the quilt up over your head. Murphy tells him that he's split up from Lianne, that they came to London to start again, but it just made things worse, away from friends and family, and that she's met someone else.

'What about you?'

'I meet interesting people from all walks of life, and I get to arrest them.'

The priest smiles, but he sees that Murphy's unsettled. His eyes are darting about the graveyard, looking at the faded inscriptions.

'We're a little overcrowded,' says McBride.

'One day,' Murphy says, 'the council is going to come along and dig all these up and relocate them somewhere.'

'Over my dead body,' says McBride.

They talk a bit about music. Murphy tells him he should think about taking up the guitar again, that maybe with age and experience they could write some decent songs together. He adds quickly: 'On the strict understanding that they don't contain the word antiestablishmentarianism or deal exclusively with God, Jesus or the Crucifixion.'

'Pity,' McBride says. 'I was thinking what a fine word transubstantiation is.' He smiles. He says he'll think about it.

'Do you still have your guitar?' Murphy asks.

McBride nods. 'I do some music with the kids in the church.'

'I can imagine.'

'It's not that bad.'

'I bet it is.'

'So where are you stationed?' he asks out of the blue.

'Round and about,' Murphy says.

McBride nods. 'I kind of guessed you probably weren't PC Plod.'

'You do what you do.'

McBride then says abruptly, as if he's suddenly remembered that he's a priest: 'If you want to talk about your loss, you can.' He nods sagely for a moment, then hastily adds: 'I haven't got all the answers.'

'Of course you have,' Murphy fires back, 'you're an instrument of God. And I hope you play it better than you played the guitar.' He laughs to himself, scuffs his shoes. 'That's all I want, Frank, three chords and the truth.'

As McBride's about to speak, there's a sudden electronic interruption, and the priest delves into his jacket. He removes a beeper and examines the number displayed on it.

'Sorry,' he says, 'I have to go. I'm on call for last rites.' When he sees Murphy's smirk, he feels obliged to explain. He thumbs back at the church. 'There's one church, but two parishes. It's like Wimbledon and Crystal Palace sharing a ground. Only we bury a few more than they do.'

He hurries away, leaving Murphy standing alone in the graveyard. He rubs his hands together and wonders whether he's done the right thing, talking to the priest.

9

He doesn't look on it as being reckless, just sowing the seeds of his future integration into the gang with no name.

He doesn't tell Murdoch, because even though he would understand, someone like Carter would just smirk and think it was funny that Murphy would choose to concentrate on the blonde, rather than say Johnny or Mitchell. He would say in his deeply sarky way, sure you haven't got the hots for her, Murphy? And then they'd fire abuse at each other and have a fist fight.

Deep down, Murphy knows that Carter, if he was ever to articulate such thoughts, would be right on the button. But he thinks, my life, my risk. If I'm going to be dealing with bad guys and bad girls, well, at least the bad girls might be more interesting.

He's been to her home, a two-bedroom townhouse not more than a mile from Fond Farewells. He has watched her cook a meal for herself. She doesn't bother to close the blinds. Not even in her bedroom. Twice he catches a glimpse of her in her underwear. And once he freezes as she looks out of her bedroom window and for a moment he's sure she's seen him, but he's in the darkness of a shop doorway and she's looking from light into dark through glass, which is never going to show you much.

He doesn't really mean to, but before he knows it he has been to her house four nights in a row.

Looking for clues.

Staking her out.

You have to be a bit obsessive to stake out people. It's not nine-to-five with an hour for lunch.

She goes out at exactly 9 p.m. one night, taking a taxi. He follows for a couple of miles, then loses her when she hops out and into a tube station. He curses and goes for a drink. He's not more than ninety minutes, but when he drives past her house again, the lights are on and she's in her bedroom brushing her hair for all the world to see, if all the world happened to be skulking across the road in a shop doorway.

He liked singing 'Annie's Song' to her.

Perhaps he will write another one about watching her, and her not being aware of it. The songs are so much better when you can inject them with a personality, rather than some vague notion of romance or love.

The following morning he follows her from home to a Safeways. He watches her get a trolley and enter the supermarket and he drums his fingers on the steering wheel and then thinks that he's actually quite low on frozen food at home and what harm could there be in stocking up now that he's actually at a supermarket, and sure if he happens to bump into her, it won't do his cover story any harm at all.

So he gets a trolley, hurries into the store, spots her, tracks her, observes what direction she's touring the aisles in and works out the best place for them to meet.

He stands by the bread, loaf in hand, and collars a gawky looking Assistant Manager.

'Here, mate,' he says, 'explain something to me.'

'Sir?' the Assistant Manager says, all smiles, like he's fresh out of training camp.

'This sell-by date, does it mean the bread's poisonous after that date?'

The Assistant Manager blinks for a moment, not sure whether the customer is serious or drunk.

Then he remembers that the customer is always right, even when they're barking.

'It's not a sell-by date, sir. It's a best-before date.'

'Ah. Right. So what does that mean then?'

'That the bread is at its freshest on or before that date.'

'Right. I see. So after that date, it's poisonous.'

'No, sir, it's not poisonous.'

'Fifteen minutes after midnight on that date, I'd be taking my life in my hands if I tried to make a sandwich. Or toast.'

'No, sir, I'm sure the bread would be perfectly fine fifteen minutes after midnight. It would be fine, I'm sure, for two or three days.'

'Well, why not put a different date on it? People must be throwing out perfectly fine bread all the time.'

'The bread is fine to eat, but it is best before the date on the bag.'

'You should put on it, poisonous after such and such a date.'

'Sir—'

'You should print labels that say, absolutely lethal after—'

'Sir, do you intend to buy that bread?'

Murphy looks at him, sees in the red cheeks and the slightly flared nostrils that the Assistant Manager is doing his best to keep his temper but that a couple more pushes and they'll be having a brawl in the bakery department. Murphy smiles then and says, 'Congratulations.'

'I'm sorry?'

'I'm from headquarters.' He gives him a conspiratorial wink. 'You handled that situation really well. Customers can be really annoying, but you dealt with me calmly and professionally. Keeping your temper, that's the key. You'll do well,' and he reads the name tag on his lapel, 'Ken. I'll put in a good word with Mr Walker.'

'Well . . . well, thank you, I do my best . . .'

'No problem.' Murphy winks again, thrusts the loaf into Ken's hands and walks on.

Ken blinks after him for several moments, flushed but elated. It will be at least an hour before he wonders who Mr Walker is.

Half of this exchange has been witnessed by Annie,

stopping surprised at first, then thinking about pushing on, ignoring this wind-up artist, she has enough to worry about, but then she finds herself laughing into her hand as Murphy continues to talk nonsense. As he walks away from the Assistant Manager she pushes up beside him.

'Hello,' she says. 'What was that all about?'

Murphy glances back and laughs. 'Just bored. Taking the piss.'

'Seemed like a lot of effort over a loaf of bread.'

'Well, you can't be too careful. Five more minutes and I would have been asking him about orgasmic food.' She smiles. 'Didn't know you lived round here.'

'Oh yeah, just around the corner. You?'

'Yeah. Not far.'

'That was a nice song the other night.'

'Well, thank you. Helps when you have someone to sing it to.'

He looks quite embarrassed, and she likes that.

'And you wield a mean axe.'

'I . . . ?'

And now she blushes. 'I mean, hitting that bloke with your guitar.'

He laughs. 'Oh yeah. Right. Just spur of the moment. You get over it OK?'

'Oh yeah. Fine. But scary, isn't it, what can happen when you're just out for a drink. He could have killed us without a second thought. You're still coming to Mr Hatcher's house for the party?'

'Wouldn't miss it, be the gig of the year.'

She smiles. 'So you're not off on tour anywhere.'

'I'm between tours right now.'

'Well.'

And then there's a lull, the kind of lull you get when you meet someone you don't know very well, someone you wouldn't mind standing talking to but you're racking your brain for something to say. She's about to push on when he says quickly, 'Do you fancy a cup of coffee?'

She blushes further and says, a little too quickly, 'No I can't.'

And he looks away and says just as quickly, 'I didn't mean—'

'No . . . I mean, I'm late for work. Just buying some essentials. Really, I'd better fly. Sure, see you at the party.'

He nods and she walks on and he goes in the other direction.

If it had been real life, he would be cursing himself for such a cack-handed performance, but this is undercover, this is infiltration by stealth, and he thinks he's done OK. She likes him, he knows that; he likes her, he's made that clear to her; nothing will happen, but she will feel sure of herself around him, she will assume that air of superiority that women get when they're aware of being coveted. She won't mention it to Hatcher. She won't say, that funny little man with the guitar made a pass at me. She'll just think how attractive she must be and isn't it great.

Pushing through the checkout with a fresh cream cake and a bag of sprouts, Murphy wonders why, if he's so astute about women, why the hell he can't sort something out with Lianne.

But no.

Don't go there.

But he will.

10

He's sitting in his car a little way up from Lianne's house, watching her kissing her man goodbye, then driving off to work. Norman's in a dressing gown and has a cup of tea or coffee in his hand. His hair, although not long, looks a bit wild, like he's just rolled out of bed. A bed head.

Murphy likes the phrase, bed head, and resolves to use it in a song.

Bed Head.

Last of the Bed Heads.

Return of the Bed Head.

Battle of the Bed Heads.

Titles are easy, content is hard.

He waits another ten minutes, listening to a repeat of *Desert Island Discs*. He has often fantasised about appearing on *Desert Island Discs* with Sue Lawley. He wonders if she is always the proper English lady, or goes into the studio in dressing gown and curlers. Or a Bed Head.

Marty Murphy – great songs, and a great face for radio.

He imagines her lovely, soft voice saying, now tell me why this song means so much to you, Martin? And he'll be a cheeky chappy in all his responses, but eventually she'll get to him in her soft investigative way – she'd make a great cop, would Sue, get a desk down in New Scotland Yard's Aristo Branch – and he'll break down and talk about his son and the horror of it all and she'll come across the studio and hug him and say, 'Don't worry, Martin, everything's going to be OK, and this is "The Birdy Song".'

He would choose Springsteen, and The Clash, and Van, and he'd rack his brains for something classical that wasn't a movie theme or the soundtrack to a commercial, because you've got to show you're a bit posh on *Desert Island Discs*, or even just sitting having a coffee with Sue, and then he'd also rack his brains for something recorded after about 1985 when he stopped trying to keep his finger on the pulse, and started trying to work out if he still had one.

And your one luxury item, Martin?

A box of Tetley Teabags, Sue.

Really?

No, Sue, actually a gun to blow my fucking head off.

Oh, all right then, and now for your final selection.

He switches the radio off, climbs out of his car, and crosses the road to Lianne's house. He rings the doorbell. There's a bit of a delay, and then the door opens and Norman's standing there tying a knot in his dressing gown, and his hair is askew in a totally different direction because he's gone back to bed and fallen asleep in the ten minutes Murphy has taken to listen to Sue and her guest this morning, the Right Honourable nonentity for somewhere obscure.

'Norman,' he says, 'how're you doin'?' like they're old mates.

But Norman has a face on him like a Lurgan spade. 'What do you want?'

Which isn't very old mate-ish.

'Lianne in?'

'No.'

'Oh. Just wanted to . . . well, doesn't matter. So. Settling in all right?' Norman just looks at him, then folds his arms impatiently. 'Sorry about the other night. Out of order. Too much wine. You know how it is.'

But there's something about Norman that suggests that no, he doesn't know how it is.

Norman looks up and down the street, then indicates with a twist of his head for Murphy to come in.

Murphy steps into the hall, Norman closes the door, then grabs Murphy by the lapels and thrusts him hard up against the wall. Framed photographs rattle.

'What the fuck do you want, Paddy?' Norman hisses into his face, his breath plaque sour, his stubble grey, his hair black. He dyes his hair, does Norman.

'Bacardi and Coke would be good.'

Norman slams him again.

'You do that once more, Norman,' Murphy says from his position of weakness, 'I'll break your fucking neck.'

'Yeah, you and whose army?'

Murphy raises an unruffled eyebrow. 'You are aware of what I do for a living, aren't you, Norman? What I'm trained in? One flick of my wrist and I could snap your head off.'

'And are you aware of the SAS, and what I'm trained in?'

'Lianne said you worked for the Home Office.'

'I do. But until about six months ago I was in the Regiment.'

'Well, what did you get drummed out for? Being a fat fucker?'

Norman howls and frees one hand so that he can punch Murphy's jaw. But Murphy brings his knee up into Norman's groin and Norman goes down like a tonne of bricks. Murphy stands over him, exultant and points down. 'Not so tough now, are you, Bravo Two Fucking Zero?'

But Norman's hand races out and grabs Murphy's ankle and pulls hard and then Murphy's on his back on the ground and fat Norman's sitting on him, pinning him down.

'What are you doing here?' he bellows. 'What do you want? I'm trying to keep Lianne safe and all you can do is hang around putting all of us at fucking risk!'

He raises his fist, and is about to pound Murphy's face, but then he hesitates, thinking of the consequences, not just for his work, but having to explain to Lianne. So he climbs off. He shakes his head sadly. 'What're you playing at, man?'

Murphy gets up slowly, straightening his jacket. 'I'm not playing at anything, I'm just checking on my wife.'

'Well, you don't need to. She's with me now.'

'That's what worries me.'

Norman sighs. 'You . . . you of all people should know the danger she's in. You're in.'

'That's all in the past.'

'That's crap, and you know it. You both put them away, and the whole fucking organisation put the hit out on you. They've forgotten most things, but they're not going to forget this.'

'And how would you know?'

'Don't you think I checked it out? Don't you think we looked into setting Lianne up back in Belfast before we went down the change-of-identity route. I'm telling you, you wouldn't last five minutes back in Belfast.'

Murphy shrugs. They stand awkwardly for several moments. Murphy looks up the stairs. 'My name's still on this house, you know.'

'I know.'

'You should be paying me rent.'

'Don't start.'

'Are you going to marry her?'

'It's none of your business.'

'You ever do anything to her, I'll fucking murder you.'

'I'll bear that in mind.'

They glare at each other. Then Murphy sighs. He extends his hand. 'I won't bother youse again.'

Norman nods, then extends his own hand.

Murphy grasps it, manages a smile, then yanks it hard towards him, jarring Norman off his feet.

Norman stumbles forward.

As he comes towards him, Murphy head-butts him.

Norman hits the ground hard, rolls, his hands going to his face. His nose is bleeding.

Murphy reaches down, pulls the loose knot in the dressing gown free, then grasps one side of the garment and pulls hard, rolling Norman onto his side. He's a big man, and it takes some effort.

'What the fuck are you . . .' Norman shouts, trying to balance himself, but Murphy's still pulling hard at the gown, flipping Norman onto his stomach.

Murphy yanks hard at it again, and the dressing gown comes away in his hands like he's a magician stripping a tablecloth from beneath plates, leaving Norman naked and vulnerable on the floor.

'Jesus!' he yells, trying to cover himself with his hands.

Murphy stands over him, and points a finger. Norman cowers down. 'You may have my wife, you fucking cunt, but you're not getting my fucking dressing gown as well.'

Then he turns and walks out of the house with it.

A completely pointless visit, but somehow very satisfying.

11

Murdoch drives the taxi which takes Murphy to Hatcher's house. Without the stinking parka, with the padding removed, the hair combed, he's a new man. If Hatcher was to look out the window he'd think Murdoch and the tramp were a different species entirely. The meter is running and Manhattan Transfer are singing 'Chanson D'Amour' on Radio 2, which is about as close as Murdoch gets to rock 'n' roll. He sings along with it for a while, then glances at his passenger. 'Have guitar, will travel,' he says.

'Aye,' says Murphy.

They've been stuck in traffic for a while but Murphy's not worried about being late for his gig. It's not that kind of an affair.

'You were never a pipe and slippers kind of a guy,' Murdoch says.

'No.'

'Neither was I. It just kind of creeps up on you. Now I kind of fancy slippers. Not so keen on the pipe.'

Murphy nods. He looks out of the window. It's another bright, cold autumnal day and he's off into no-good man's land without a safety net or a big gun to shoot people with. Murdoch has offered to put people outside the house in case he needs to be rescued, but there's no point. He's not going to try anything. He's just blending in. Getting to know them. Gaining trust. He'll sing some songs for the old man's birthday, he'll lead the singalong. Plenty of time to work his invidious moves yet. It'll all happen soon enough, then the bad guy will be in prison and he'll be free to become Holland, Dozier or Holland, although he'd probably settle for Jimmy Nail.

They pull into a driveway which is long for this part of London. A good sized house with a large garden. Not big enough for a swimming pool, but space for a hot tub, for rusty croquet hoops on the lawn and what appears to be a track worn by tractor or motorbike wheels circling the property inside the wall. There are eight or nine cars parked along the drive.

'He can afford this, what the hell does he want diamonds for?' Murdoch asks.

Murphy shrugs, then when he's climbing out makes a show of paying Murdoch for his trouble in case anyone's watching.

Murdoch counts his money and says, 'What about a tip?'

'Don't sleep in the subway,' Murphy replies, and then thinks that he needs to get some new lines. Maybe he should pay someone. He could be a singer and comedian, like Billy Connolly started out. Gradually the gaps between songs would get longer and then he'd be a fully fledged comedian.

Or maybe not. He turns for the house.

He's not nervous. He's not excited. He's a singer doing a gig and trying to make ends meet.

Terry Hatcher has the hots for Annie Guthrie. He could write that in steam on the kitchen windows. He looks at her, fixing her own drink in the kitchen, hair pulled back off her face, just a little make-up, and he knows that she knows that he's watching her, but she won't look. Confident. He likes that. His wife, damn her, she never had confidence. She wouldn't have fixed her own drink first. She wouldn't have ignored the pinging of the microwave. She wouldn't have said: 'Your titbits are ready, Mr Hatcher,' and swanned out of the kitchen to enjoy the party, leaving him to burn himself on the plate trying to get them out. 'Your titbits are ready, Mr Hatcher,' with as much style and sophistication and yes, dammit, sex, as . . . as . . . Sharon Stone – yeah, that's who she reminds me of, Sharon Stone. He wonders if she would ever have the balls to stab him in the back, and he thinks, yes, she probably would.

He moves around with the plate, a tea towel protecting his hand, offering the food to his guests. His family. Dad, God love him, there's not too many of his generation left, and of those that are, a lot don't want to know. Long memories. His dad was a bit of a bastard in his time.

Hatcher smiles. Like father like son, they'd probably say. But nothing wrong with being strong, with knowing what you want and going for it. Except his father, well, he knew what he wanted, but he gave up short of the summit, then slid back down. But he taught me well, and I won't be falling down. Top of the world, Ma!

There's a nice hum of conversation. The music in the background is fifties pop. Glittery letters spell out Happy Birthday Dad! on the wall. The old man, strategically placed in his wheelchair so he can see every coming and going, coughs and splutters into a handkerchief.

Johnny says, 'Y'all right, Mr Hatcher? Get you anything?'

'It's me chest, Johnny,' he manages between spits, 'nothing but phlegm and gristle.'

'Are you sure it's not just the sausage rolls?'

The old man waves him away.

Hatcher turns as the front doorbell goes and someone closer to it than him opens it. He sees who it is and cries, 'Music man!'

Murphy enters sheepishly, no point in dashing in and casing the joint; time, patience, relax. Hatcher comes towards him, a plate of sausage rolls in one hand, and a can of lager he lifts off a table in the other. He thrusts it at Murphy and says, 'There you go, mate, good to see you. And you got the old banjo with you.'

Murphy smiles and pops the can and says, 'Hope I'm not too late. Bloody traffic.'

'Bags of time,' Hatcher says. 'Listen,' he waves his free

hand proudly around the expansive ground floor, 'treat it like it was your own.'

'Really?' says Murphy, but Hatcher's away before he gets the joke.

It's crowded, smells of smoke and whisky. There are birthday banners Blu-tacked to walls. A man stands talking earnestly, his elbow over the top of a fish tank, waving his hand about and dropping ash into the water. Attached to the ceiling there's a Sony projector, on the wall an eight-foot screen hangs down and what he presumes is a DVD of Garth Brooks is playing, but the sound is turned down and there's too much light for the picture to be clear. There are several leather sofas. Half a dozen oriental vases. Plastic fruit in bowls. Framed photographs of Hatcher handing over cheques to local charities. Hatcher giving a new football strip to a boys' team. Hatcher senior is an old man, but there's surprisingly few of his generation here. Most of them are his son's age. Dressed smartly. Rolex and chains. Cigars. In one corner there's a jukebox.

Murphy makes a beeline for the buffet table, and it's not a surprise to him when he finds in amongst the sausage rolls, the John West salmon sandwiches and the vol-au-vents a generous supply of caviar. Have money, will burn it.

Murphy spoons it up greedily.

'You like caviar?'

He turns, mouth full, to find Annie standing beside him. He swallows quickly. 'No, but it's expensive.'

She rolls her eyes, then tries some herself. Her nose

crinkles up in disgust, but she swallows politely. Her eyes are bright. She looks like she's had a couple of drinks. Just a couple. Enough to make her more talkative than usual.

'So how long have you two been an item?' Murphy asks.

She gives a small, surprised laugh. 'Who?'

'You and Mr Hatcher.'

'Whatever gave you that impression?' He shrugs. 'I work for him. He's a director.'

'Film?'

'Funeral.'

He nods, like the penny has suddenly dropped. 'Really,' he says, drawing it out. Then he does what he thinks everyone would do. He gives a little shiver. 'Wouldn't have guessed. So what do you do?'

'I'm in strategic planning.'

'You mean you order the flowers?'

She gives him a sarcastic smile. 'So where's your wife?' she asks. 'Or don't you bring her to gigs?'

Ah, so that's what she was thinking the other day in the supermarket. That he was married or attached and chancing his arm.

'I haven't got a wife.'

'Of course you have. It's written all over you.'

'No, it's not.'

'Is she waiting in, what is it, Belfast for you?'

'No she isn't.'

'What did you do, promise her fame and fortune, the streets of London paved with gold?'

'No, I didn't.'

'Thought you were going to be Bob Dylan, and you ended up Bernie Flint.'

'There's no need to be cruel.'

Hatcher calls her across then to meet someone, and Murphy makes himself at home. He has three or four cans, he lingers on the edge of conversations, he talks to the old man about music, he tells him truthfully that he's seen Johnny Cash in concert three times, he wanders casually around the house. He uses the upstairs toilet only when the downstairs one is locked. He takes his coat off and puts it with the others in the master bedroom, and spots the door to an office lying slightly ajar just off it. Later, plenty of time later.

When it comes time to do some singing, Murphy finds a comfortable spot at the foot of the stairs. He plays much the same set as he did at the pub the night the old man was in, but just for variety, and to make a point so subtle that nobody gets it, he sings 'Heartbeat' and 'Chain Gang', or maybe Annie gets it, because he catches her eye a few times and though she doesn't smile there's recognition and maybe something more. He doesn't play her song, that would be too much.

Halfway through Roy Orbison's 'Crying', which is hard work, Hatcher stands abruptly and calls for silence. Murphy tries not to look too aggrieved. Everyone makes sure they have a drink then gathers round.

'Thank you, maestro!' he says and encourages them in a round of applause. 'Now,' he says, cutting that short as well, 'I'd like you all to raise your glasses, and drink a toast to a very special man. He's eighty-five years old, he's constantly telling us he's not going to last until the weekend . . .' Everyone laughs. Old man Hatcher raises his glass. 'But I'm telling you, he'll be here long after we're gone. I give you a man I love very much – my father!'

Murphy cuts in with the chords to Happy Birthday and leads the charge. He's singing it, but he's thinking, here I am, punk rocker, going to change the world, and I'm singing Happy Birthday at some old bloke's birthday. But all the greats start somewhere. The Beatles with the whores and the speed in Hamburg. Barry Manilow playing the piano for Barbra Streisand. Or was it Bette Midler?

The good thing is, after the singing, the cutting of the cake, the drink really starts to flow. By the time it's dark outside they're all pretty much rolling in it. Murphy takes the opportunity to slip upstairs. He goes along the hall and back into the master bedroom, and from there he steps deftly into Hatcher's office. He knows Hatcher's not going to be stupid enough to keep anything here. A quick glance around, light on, door nine-tenths closed, tells him there's no black bag with Swag written on the side. There's a small safe which he tries to open, but no luck. There are several filing cabinets, a phone, a mobile phone, a computer; he examines what he can but learns nothing apart from how expensive it can be to die.

Then there are voices on the stairs, then they're in the hall. He moves swiftly to switch off the office light; in virtually the same action he closes the door even further so that there's barely a hair's-breadth of light, just enough to see Hatcher come through the bedroom door with someone behind him. Hatcher locks the door. Murphy catches the merest glimpse of blonde hair, then both are past the crack and all he's left with is the sound of two bodies hitting a bed, two bodies tearing at each other's clothes, pants, pants and cries and yeses! and pounding and shouting and coming and within three minutes Murphy's the only one in the room with an erection.

After they go, Murphy stays in the room for a few minutes, checks out some more paperwork, then returns to the party. Annie's over talking to Mitchell and Noreen, not a hair out of place, Hatcher's trying to pick out a tune on Murphy's guitar.

Murphy goes over and says, 'Do you play the guitar?'

'I think it's bleedin' obvious that I don't. I'd love to learn to play some instrument though.'

'What sort?'

'Any sort.'

'I can get you a good deal on a tuba.'

Hatcher's brow furrows, he's not quite sure, then he smiles and says, 'You're a laugh a minute, aren't you, Murphy?'

Murphy shrugs. Hatcher laughs quietly, plucks another string or two, then hands the guitar back. He starts to walk off, then stops abruptly and turns back to him.

'Did you ever ride a quad bike, Murphy?'

12

No he hasn't, but Hatcher says what the hell difference does that make, and five minutes later the whole party is outside in the night air to watch Hatcher slide back double garage doors to reveal four – count 'em! – quad bikes sitting on the cold concrete.

Hatcher claps his hands together. 'Announcing the fourth annual tour-of-my-big-house quad bike race! May I have the competitors please!'

Annie can't stop herself from laughing at the surreality of it all. She hugs herself against the cold, her breath coming misty, and watches as Mitchell, Johnny, Hatcher and finally Murphy climb aboard the quads. There's a roar of engines, and the four of them, clearly drunk as skunks, ease the bikes out of the garage in a cloud of exhaust fumes.

Mitchell loves it.

It's like Formula 1!

It's like an aircraft carrier on the verge of war!

It's nothing like either but you can delude yourself about anything when you're pissed.

They line up in a loose parallel with the front door, then Noreen comes forward with a bottle of champagne and the moment it pops they're off, churning up mud and splattering the guests, who take a step or two back en masse, but cheering all the way. They've agreed three laps of the house, and by the time they hit the first corner Hatcher is already nudging ahead, Mitchell's behind, then Johnny. Murphy brings up the rear. Like his betting, Murphy's on the donkey. Hatcher, he's sure, is on the thoroughbred. He may just be good, more likely he's designed it that way. People like Hatcher don't like to lose.

Except, at the end of the first lap, right where everyone can see him, something happens with Hatcher's bike, the engine just splutters out and he can't do a damn thing about it. Mitchell roars past, laughing loudly, followed by Johnny and then, close behind, Murphy, who's starting to get the hang of it now, and maybe it isn't such a donkey. Hatcher smiles stupidly, embarrassed in front of his people, then climbs off. He pretends to kick the bike. They laugh. He hurries across to the crowd and says, 'My money's on Mitch.'

Good call, Hatcher. He's only freakin' first.

But wait, they come out from the dark side of the house at the end of the second lap and Mitch and Murphy are almost dead level and Johnny's nowhere to be seen. He's misjudged his cornering and gone ploughing off through a hedge and then over a low wall into the next door neighbour's garden. It says a lot about Johnny that nobody's overly concerned. Johnny's made of rubber, nothing hurts him.

Murphy's really enjoying this now. He's drunk, but Mitchell is plastered. Murphy comes up level and knows he can take him on the next corner, there's just enough space for him to squeeze past. As he comes up, Mitchell realises he's left a gap, he can easily slide across and block, but instead he pulls sharp left and cannons into the side of Murphy's quad, half forcing him out of his seat and pushing the bike hard against the rear wall of the house. Sparks fly off, half a dozen flowerpots are pulverised, but Murphy hangs on. Mitchell cackles; it's Ben-Hur! I'm Charlton Heston! Murphy is behind now, but still going straight; the rebound from the attack has taken Mitchell's quad wide. There's still a gap. Murphy guns the quad towards the final blindside corner. He hasn't quite got the speed to pass Mitchell but he has enough to pull a little right just before the corner, bringing his front tyre against Mitchell's back left; he barely touches it, but it's enough, with the speed and the mud, to knock Mitchell off course. Suddenly he's Stephen Boyd. He tries to bring the quad back under control, but now the drink has really kicked in and the co-ordination is finally gone; he flails helplessly at the controls, the quad spins off right, hits a small backyard wall and hurls Mitchell off and up into the air.

Murphy's first instinct is to go after him, check him, make sure he's OK, concern for a fallen comrade, but no – win the race, gain respect, then worry about him.

It's more than just a fun race. Statements are being made, and he has to get his message across.

Victory first, then consider the vanquished.

He speeds past the line to surprised applause, but as he pulls up, Noreen and half a dozen others are already hurrying down the steps and around the corner in search of Mitchell. Hatcher and Johnny, without a scratch, stay where they are. They already have fresh drinks. Murphy wanders across, smiling.

'Hey, Murphy, where'd you learn to drive like that?' Johnny asks.

'Being chased is a great incentive.'

'Ever caught?' asks Hatcher.

'In the end you always get caught. The secret is knowing when to quit.'

Hatcher blinks at him for several moments. 'You're very deep for someone who just won a quad bike race, aren't you?'

Murphy smiles again, but before he can say anything, Mitchell comes storming up, holding his arm, trailing his audience behind him. His face is red, both with the drink and with anger. He looks like he's been pulled through a hedge backwards, and indeed he has.

'You've broken my arm, you Paddy bastard.'

'Take it easy, Mitch,' says Hatcher, but Mitch isn't listening. He takes a swing at Murphy with his good arm, but Murphy leans back expertly, causing Mitchell to stumble past. Murphy doesn't quite know what to do now as Mitchell comes tearing back at him; again he sidesteps him and he crashes off the steps and down onto the churned-up track below. This time he doesn't get up. Noreen goes to him. There's a little laughter now from those watching Mitchell sprawled helpless and incoherent in the dirt.

Hatcher clamps his arm round Murphy's shoulders and says, 'Come on, we'll get you a drink.'

He leads him back inside, and the rest of the party follows, leaving Mitchell where he is, trying to get up, but being pushed back down by his wife.

Eventually, an hour later, Mitchell skulks back inside. He has mud on his knees and his shirt is hanging out of his trousers. Noreen has dirt on her dress and her eyes are drunkenly narrow.

He has sobered up, a little. Noreen wants him to go to the hospital, but he's putting it off, it's only a sprain. Most of the partygoers have left now, even Annie. The old man's away back to the nursing home, but there's still nine or ten drinking on; it's a lot more subdued.

Murphy comes from the kitchen and sees Hatcher talking to Mitchell and Johnny in the corner and knows that the next few minutes will be crucial. Mitchell is in an armchair, massaging his injury. Hatcher, sitting on the arm of the chair, waves Murphy over. Murphy nods, lifts a fresh can, then saunters across. He keeps his eyes on Hatcher.

'Mitch has something to say,' Hatcher says. 'Haven't you, Mitch?'

Mitch avoids eye contact. He stares at the floor. 'Terry thinks I was an arsehole,' he says quietly.

They wait several moments to see if anything will follow. Then Hatcher laughs and says, 'That the closest to an apology you're going to get. Might as well accept it.'

Murphy thinks for a moment, then nods. He extends his hand down to Mitchell, who finally looks up, nods curtly and extends his uninjured left hand; they shake awkwardly.

Johnny punches Murphy lightly on the arm, then does a little shimmy. 'Where'd you learn to move like that anyway?' he asks.

'I was with the Royal Ballet for three years.'

'Really?' Johnny's dead serious.

'No,' laughs Murphy, 'the army. Royal Irish Rangers.'

'Ever fire a shot in anger?' Hatcher asks.

'Anger? No.' He takes a sip. 'But there were a couple of guys talked during my encore once . . .'

Hatcher laughs. 'Where do we go to get a straight answer round here?'

There's a sudden sneeze and then laughter from two couples on the far side of the room, which makes them all turn for a moment, then they turn back and now Murphy finds himself the focus of an awkward silence; he's the odd one out, not part of the gang, he has entertained them, and now it's time to go. They will not talk freely with him there. But he has made an opening for himself, and he must take advantage of it, make it wider. Normally his is the patience game, but sometimes you just have to go for it, stick the foot in the door.

'I was looking at the house,' Murphy says. 'Very impressive. Wouldn't mind a piece of it.'

Hatcher looks at him oddly. 'You mean like timeshare?'

'That's right.' He takes another sip, then lets the jolly Irish entertainer mask slip. It really is a transformation; his face is suddenly blank and cold and his eyes grow icy. 'Unless I've read you all wrong, you're in a business where you need a good driver, and I'm not talking about taking stiffs to the cemetery.' He glances down at Mitchell. 'And you won't be driving anything for a while.'

'Don't worry about me, Paddy. I'll be fine.'

'It's not Paddy.'

They lock eyes.

Hatcher looks at Murphy with bemused detachment. 'Well, you're not backwards about coming forwards.'

'It doesn't pay to be.'

'Well, let me have a think.'

Mitchell pushes himself up ramrod straight in his seat. 'Hatch, I do the fucking driving!'

The remaining drinkers across the room glance around at the raised voice. Hatcher smiles over, then places his hand on Mitchell's injured arm and begins to stroke it.

'Just keep it down, Mitch,' he says.

Mitchell, instead, keeps it up. 'I do the—'

'Hush.' Mitchell stops, but he's seething. 'Just look at it sensibly,' Hatcher continues. 'You made an arse of yourself, you've nobody else to blame. Now, I need a driver, and it's patently clear to me that you won't be driving anything, apart from Noreen insane, for quite a while. Now do you understand?'

'I'm not letting that Paddy—'

Hatcher suddenly digs his fingers into Mitchell's wounded arm. Mitchell's face explodes in pain. *'Jesus!'*

Hatcher won't let go, he digs harder and harder, Mitchell bucking against him, crying out loud. Noreen, coming out of the kitchen with another drink, freezes there, not knowing what to do.

'Now,' says Hatcher, 'do you understand?'

'Yes!'

'And it's OK with you?'

'Yes . . . Jesus!'

Hatcher lets go of his arm, and Mitchell immediately clamps it to his chest and doubles over.

'There,' Hatcher says. 'First time I got a result from a one-armed bandit.'

There are a few awkward chuckles.

Murphy moves from one foot to the other. 'I'll, uh, maybe get a drink. But have a think, yeah?'

Hatcher nods at him and he moves towards the kitchen. Hatcher laughs to himself and then looks down at Mitchell. Noreen is on her knees before him, trying to soothe him; she looks up at Hatcher and cold hatred pours from her eyes. Hatcher puts his arm round Mitchell's shoulders and gives him a squeeze.

'You OK?' he says. Mitchell grunts something indistinct. 'Mitch, are you OK?'

'Yes,' Mitchell hisses.

'Well, before we go to the hospital, I was wondering if you had twenty minutes to spare.'

Mitchell's brow furrows. 'What do you mean?'

'Well, we don't let any old fucker waltz in and take your job, do we? C'mon, we'll go and sort Murphy out.'

13

It's raining heavily when Murphy leaves the house. He's made his pitch and now it's time to get out, let them chew it over. He pulls up his collar and walks down the drive and out onto the main road. He'll pick up a taxi somewhere along the way. He has his guitar over his shoulder, troubadour back on the road again, going from town to town earning a living, entertaining the folks with his soft country ballads; meeting a girl or two, enjoying a roll in the hay, then drinking the local moonshine till dawn. Maybe he'll hitch a lift on the back of a truck, sleep down in the hay.

This late, there's not much traffic, so he becomes aware very quickly that there's a car shadowing him and for a moment he's not quite sure what to do about it, run, ignore, hurl abuse. The decision is made for him when suddenly it pulls forward and splashes through a puddle to stop beside him. The back window purrs down, and there's Mitchell grinning out at him.

'Get in, Paddy,' he says.

Johnny's driving, Hatcher's in the front passenger seat. Mitchell moves over to make room for him, wincing a little as he moves his arm.

Nothing else for it.

'Decent of you,' Murphy says. 'Taxis this time of night are—'

'Shut the fuck up,' says Hatcher.

Murphy puts his guitar in the back, then slips in.

They drive for maybe ten minutes, sticking to the main road, nobody saying anything. Murphy's wondering why he didn't insist on back-up, and whether Murdoch or Carter or some Boy Scout might be back there anyway, looking out for him. Then Johnny pulls the car into a parking spot opposite a block of five or six shops. Hatcher turns from the front and he has a gun in his hand.

Murphy's thinking, how did they guess? And why do it here instead of some country lane? Except Hatcher turns the gun abruptly and hands it to him. 'OK, hotshot,' he says, 'you've talked the talk, now let's see you walk the walk.'

'What?'

Hatcher nods across the road at the row of shops. It's pretty late, so four out of five are shut, but there's the neon sign of an off-licence winking on and off. 'Go and do the drink shop,' Hatcher says.

Murphy, gun in hand, looks across the road to where a drunk is just staggering out of the front door.

'I said I was just a driver,' Murphy says.

'No such thing,' says Mitchell.

Murphy waits for a gap in the traffic, then darts across the road. The gun is zipped inside his jacket. He pauses for a moment in the doorway, takes a deep breath, then enters.

The off-licence is brightly lit. There are three aisles, one other customer, an elderly lady, and a man in his early thirties reading a newspaper behind the counter. Murphy pretends to examine some beer, slowly making his way along the first aisle, then when he's just about opposite the till he turns quickly, only to find that the woman has bustled up ahead of him and is buying a bottle of whisky. The man behind the counter glances at him as he steps up behind her, sees that he has no drink in his hand, then continues to wait on the woman as she laboriously counts out change from her purse.

'It's not for me, you understand,' she's saying, 'it's for my mother.'

The man nods, bored. He pushes a coin back to her. 'Spanish.'

'Really don't know how that got in there. Where would I get a Spanish coin from?'

Finally she completes her purchase and shuffles off. Murphy smiles as he approaches the counter. He squints down at the name badge on the man's chest. You are being served by Trevor.

'Tell me this, ahm, Trevor,' he says, 'did you ever see *Candid Camera*?'

'Candy what?'

'*Candid Camera*. It was a TV show back in the, I

don't know, seventies.' Trevor looks at him blankly. 'Unsuspecting members of the public were set up in embarrassing situations, without knowing they were being filmed. It was dead funny.'

'Sorry,' says Trevor, 'you've lost me.'

Murphy sighs. 'Right. OK. Bear with me.' He drums his fingers for a moment on the counter, then bends in closer to Trevor. He drops his voice to a conspiratorial whisper. 'Without looking . . . there's a car across the road that's filming your every move.'

'My . . . ?' Trevor's head juts to his right.

'I said don't look.'

'I know, but sorry, the Volvo, is it?'

'Yes, the Volvo, but don't look again, please. If it looks like you've spotted them they'll just pack up and move on and you'll lose out on all this free advertising. It's ITV Network television, y'know. Be on right after the new series of *Morse*.'

'I thought Morse was—'

'Commercial television reaches beyond the grave. Now pay attention. This could be your big break. In about five seconds I'm going to take a fake gun out of my pocket and point it at you.'

'You're—'

'The important word to focus on is fake. A *fake* gun. Do you understand?'

'Y-yes . . .'

'It has to be fake. Our insurers wouldn't allow us to use a real gun, even with blanks. Look what happened to Brandon Lee.'

'Who?'

'The son of Bruce, he—' Suddenly Murphy reaches up to his ear, then nods, and says, 'Yes, sorry,' to the air. He rolls his eyes at Trevor. 'Sorry, they think I'm wasting time. OK, now, you're listening?'

'Y-yes . . . of course.'

'Good. Now stay with me. I promise there's nothing to worry about.' He takes out the gun and points it at Trevor, who breathes in sharply. 'Trick gun, OK?' Trevor's eyes dart nervously about, then he nods. 'Now open the till.' There's only a moment's hesitation, then he opens it. 'How much you got in there?'

'About two hundred.'

'OK. Doesn't matter how much. Now, while you're taking that out and sliding it across the counter, what I'm gonna do, Trevor, out of sight of the TV viewers, is take about two hundred and fifty out of my other pocket, that's the two hundred I'm going to take from you plus fifty for your trouble, and just drop it on the floor here for you to pick up when I'm gone. Does that sound fair enough?'

Trevor nods, reaches down, extracts the money, and then pushes it across gingerly. Murphy removes what notes he has – though he knows it falls somewhat short of £250 – from his back pocket, and makes sure Trevor can see him dropping the little bundle on the ground. He winks at Trevor and whispers, 'You're doing fine,' then picks up his cash from the counter. 'You're a natural,' he says. 'Now just keep smiling until I get to the door, then I'll pop back in a moment and get you to sign your release forms, OK?'

'OK.'

Murphy turns for the door. He's halfway there when Trevor calls after him. 'Hey, mister?'

Murphy spins angrily. 'I told you not to—'

Except the grinning innocent is no more. Trevor's standing there with a shotgun levelled at Murphy, his eyes suddenly bulging wide.

'What sort of a fucking idiot do you think I am?' Trevor shouts.

Murphy tries to brazen it out. 'Now this is what I call Method act—'

Before he can finish, Trevor raises the gun expertly to his shoulder and lets fly with both barrels. Murphy dives through a pyramid of Carlsberg cans which expode a fraction of a second after he passes. He lands in a heap, beer spraying over him, then rolls away quickly along the aisle.

Trevor presses a button beneath the counter, and an ear-splitting alarm begins to wail.

'Scum like you aren't going to drive me out, do you hear?' he wails above it.

He presses a second button and immediately metal security shutters begin to descend across the front of the shop.

Trevor steps out from behind the counter, slipping two new shells into the shotgun.

'I've had it with you bastards!'

He sees movement and shoots immediately. Murphy hits the deck as bottles of wine erupt all around him. He picks himself up off the floor, then dives right into aisle three as he sees Trevor appear suddenly at the far end of aisle two. He has his own gun out now. He glances back down the shop and sees that the security grille is more than halfway down already.

Trevor reloads as he moves closer. 'I'm sick and tired of this night after night!' he yells.

Murphy jumps up and shoots twice, deliberately to Trevor's left. Trevor ducks down. Murphy starts running hard down the aisle. Two more shells explode after him as he dives at the security grille. He just manages to squeeze under. A moment later it slams into the floor and locks into place.

Murphy lies on the footpath for several moments, breathing hard. He looks up to find a well-to-do couple, out walking their dog, looking down at him apprehensively. He shields the gun and thumbs back at the off-licence. 'They're really strict about closing time,' he says, smiling.

They edge away around him, and the dog snarls.

'Bastards,' Murphy says as he climbs into the car. They erupt into laughter.

Johnny pulls out, tyres screeching, and they bomb away down the road.

'Bastards,' Murphy says again and they laugh even harder.

Before they're more than a few hundred yards away a police car comes racing up from the other direction, but it's too little, too late. Murphy unzips his jacket and takes out the two hundred quid Trevor gave him. He tries to pass it forward to Hatcher, but he waves him away.

'Keep it,' he says. 'You've earned it.'

'Guy's name is Trevor Moore,' Mitchell says beside Murphy. 'Used to be a cop. He's run that place for five years, had something like nineteen hold-ups in that time, and nineteen arrests. Doesn't take no prisoners, our Trevor. It's known as the Fortress. Or it was.' He smiles at Murphy, then extends his uninjured hand. 'Put it there,' he says.

Murphy doesn't hesitate. He grips Mitchell's hand hard, and they shake.

Hatcher nods back at him in the mirror. 'Consider yourself hired,' he says.

'Well,' says Murphy, 'I suppose we should celebrate then.' From his jacket pocket he produces a fist full of purloined cigars and holds them up. 'Care to join me?' he says.

14

At the gym, Father McBride is on to his sixth mile on the treadmill when he happens to glance up and see Murphy standing with his arms folded, watching him.

'I'll bet you're gaspin' for a fag,' Murphy says.

McBride manages a half smile then drips sweat over the controls as he knocks the speed down to almost nothing. 'You're late,' he says breathlessly, gripping the bars for the first time.

'I was early,' Murphy says. 'I just couldn't get the door open.'

McBride manages an appreciative nod as he steps down off the track. 'I . . . should get . . . changed,' he says.

Murphy nods. 'I'll wait for you in the bar.'

'Juice bar,' McBride corrects.

'Is there any other sort?'

The gym is packed with sweaty flesh. It inspires Murphy to pat the cigarettes in his pocket lovingly. He can't remember the last time he was even in a gym. He can't remember the last time he took serious exercise, or even humorous exercise. He must have had to prove something to get into the cops in the first place, and he definitely passed out of the training barracks back in Enniskillen with flying colours, but since then – well, he's been too busy. He could be as buffed and bronzed as the next man, if he tried. Honest. Sometimes he tries to convince himself that scientists are on the brink of announcing exercise is bad for you, stop immediately, you're doing yourselves terrible damage, here, have a fag.

He takes a seat in the juice bar and a tracksuited waitress comes up to take his order.

'Mineral water,' he says, 'fresh from a mountain stream.'

'Ice?'

'Is it also fresh from a mountain stream?'

'Tap, I think.'

He thinks for a moment, then shakes his head. 'Just give it to me straight. Oh, and an orange juice for my friend.' She looks at the empty seat beside him. He winks at her and says, 'He thinks he's invisible.'

She nods uncertainly, and turns back to the bar. Murphy laughs to himself and reaches for his cigarettes. He puts them on the table then looks around for an ashtray. When she brings the drinks he says, 'Is there an ashtray, love?'

She looks at him mildly shocked. 'Of course not. You can't smoke in here. It's a health club.'

'Oh, right.'

'Sorry.'

'What about drugs? Can I do drugs?'

She shrugs. 'As long as you don't smoke them.'

'So when do you do your smoking, lunchtimes?'

'I don't smoke.'

'Yes you do.'

'I don't, really.'

He smiles at her, and takes a sip of his water. He nods approvingly. She rolls her eyes and waits for him to pay. She's very pretty. He doesn't make any move to get his money out. She folds her arms and looks at him quizzically.

'What's your game?' she says. '*Candid Camera* or something?'

'You remember that, do you?'

'My dad tells me about it.'

'Ouch,' says Murphy. He drums his fingers on the table. 'I'll tell you what,' he says, 'I'll tell you three things about yourself that you don't want anyone to know, and if I'm right you pay for the drinks.'

'What are you, Uri Geller?'

'He bends spoons. I'm not big into cutlery.'

She has a why-am-I-wasting-time-with-this-chancer look on her, but at the same time she can't resist it. 'Try me,' she says.

Murphy nods slowly. 'Well,' he says, 'we've already established that you're a heavy smoker.'

'No we haven't.'

'Oh, sorry. Well, we'll take that as one of the three, and then let's see, we'll add the fact that you've suddenly become quite self-confident, and thirdly that you've had a near death experience.'

She looks at him oddly. 'Who've you been talking to? You from the dole?'

He laughs. 'No. Relax. I just observe.'

'You mean you're a stalker or something?'

'No. Just since I came in.'

'Well, how could you . . .'

He takes another sip of his water. 'OK,' he says. 'You won't get offended?'

'No, I—'

'You've had your teeth capped, front six, correct?'

Her hand begins to go involuntarily to her mouth. 'Y-yes . . .'

'And they look great, they really do.'

'But . . .'

'Well, they're not white, are they?' She goes to say something, but he holds up his hand. 'They're kind of a creamy, off-white, aren't they? They're the kind dentists tend to give you if the teeth they have to match up with are stained, and I'm willing to bet that when you smile widely I'll see a hint of nicotine staining on some of those other teeth, won't I?' She tries to say something again. 'So you've had a thing about your teeth, they probably weren't that bad at all, but people are strange. It's a self-confidence thing. So I get to thinking maybe it's not just the teeth—'

'Listen,' she says quickly, 'I really—'

'Give me a chance.'

She sighs. 'Right. Go on. If you must.'

'I see the way you deliberately push your hair behind your ear, but it's not so long or annoying that it has to be there, it's more like you're showing the actual ear off. So I see that the ear itself, the inside of it, doesn't look quite right, maybe a trifle swollen still, so the plastic surgery to mend the sticky-out ear nobody but yourself would think was sticky-out couldn't have been that long ago. I might also notice the fact that although you aren't encouraged to wear make-up in a health club, what with all the steam and sweat, you are wearing quite a lot, and it does seem to be noticeably thicker around the bridge of your nose, which I must say is looking sleek and lovely. So I suppose that could be because we had some very nice sunny weather a few weeks ago, but because your nose was bruised and swollen from the operation – you've had it straightened, haven't you? – you wore quite a lot of make-up to cover the bruising so you didn't get the same tan over your whole face. There's only a tiny discrepancy in the skin colour, honestly, it's only because I'm looking for it.' He sits back a little in his chair. 'How am I doing?'

'What about the near death experience?' she says a little frostily. Her arms are still folded and one foot is balanced impatiently behind the other.

'Are you sure you want me to continue?'

'Oh yes.'

'Well, I would say that someone like yourself, perhaps turning their lives around, wouldn't be caught dead wearing that cheap and nasty piece of jewellery hanging round your neck. From that I would surmise that you probably had both operations at the same time, they probably cut you a deal of some sort; plastic surgery is expensive and maybe you couldn't get all the time off work that you needed. So I think you went to have them both done at the same time, except you forgot to tell them that you were a bleeder, or maybe you didn't know. Anyway, you were on the operating table and they couldn't get the blood to stop and they nearly had a freakin' heart attack themselves. It was touch and go for a while, they thought maybe they'd lost you, but they pulled it round in the end. When you finally woke up they were really upset, they said you could have died, so they gave you that locket you're wearing, it contains the information that you're a bleeder and probably allergic to penicillin, so that if you have an accident and have to go to hospital they'll know to look in there first to see about your condition.'

Murphy folds his own arms and smiles up at her.

The smile is not returned.

'For your information,' she says sharply, 'the teeth were just crap, too many sweets as a kid, so I got them capped, nothing to do with bloody smoking. Secondly, I got hit on the ear with a hockey ball last month so it's only now going down. Thirdly, I happen to like wearing make-up to work, it doesn't mean I've had a nose job. And this cheap and nasty piece of jewellery was given to me by my mother, on her deathbed.'

Murphy nods to himself. 'So,' he says, 'I was pretty close.'

'That'll be three-fifty for the drinks.'

He counts the money out onto the table.

'Plus tip.'

He gives her an extra fifty pence.

'Thanks, Richard Branson,' she says as she scrapes it off the Formica into the palm of her hand. 'You must be a nightmare to go out with,' she says.

Murphy nods ruefully. 'It has been said.'

She wheels away, and almost collides with McBride. She blows exasperated air out of her cheeks and hurries away.

McBride, still looking red-faced, sets his gym bag down and says, 'What's up with her?'

Murphy shrugs and pulls McBride's chair back. As he sits down, Murphy says: 'I was thinking about what you said. About if I ever wanted to talk.'

McBride nods, takes a sip of his juice.

'They try to get me to talk about it all the time down at work. I don't want to talk to someone whose job it is to talk to me, who'll write a report, who'll pass it up the food chain. I want to talk to someone because they care, someone who'll advise me what's best based on what they genuinely feel rather than on what the party line is. Do you know what I mean?'

'I do.'

'You can be my father confessor, it'll be between you, me and the man with the beard upstairs.'

'OK, Marty, I'd be glad to help.'

'I can make it official if you want. Let them know I'm seeing someone. They might even pay you. We could work out some deal on the paperwork, share the money fifty-fifty.'

'Marty, I—'

'Only joking.'

The waitress appears back at their table, bearing two plates, a huge slice of carrot cake on each one, and sets them down before them.

'OK,' she says, 'so you were half right. These are on the house. But no one likes a smarty-pants, you know?'

With that she turns away. Father McBride looks quizzically at Murphy who shrugs again and says, 'There are so many weirdos in this town.'

They skirt around it.

Murphy thinks it will probably take a while because although they were the best of friends, they went their separate ways years ago. It will take a while for them to talk easily with each other. They can talk about childhood escapades for hours, but anything in the past ten years causes their conversation to descend into half-finished sentences and shrugs.

'So how come you left Belfast?' Murphy asks him.

'Oh, new horizons, new challenge. You know how it is.'

Murphy raises an eyebrow. 'Let me rephrase the question. What the hell are you doing in London? You loved Belfast. You used to get homesick when we went down to Bangor for a gig.'

'I matured.'

'Yeah. Right.'

McBride scuffs his shoes on the ground. 'I got out for the same reason you did. Had to get out. Although obviously when I say same as you, I don't exactly mean same as you. But nevertheless.'

They're walking through a park. Kids are playing on the grass.

'I hope your sermons are a bit more coherent,' Murphy says, 'because you're telling me nothing.'

'I had . . . issues . . . with the hierarchy.'

'You mean God issues, does he exist, was the virgin birth literal, getting transubstantiation into the chorus of a song?'

'No, nothing like that.'

Murphy stops. He raises an eyebrow. McBride looks away.

'You didn't . . .'

McBride blows air out of his cheeks. 'I did.'

'Boys?'

'No – for fuck's sake, Murphy!'

'Girls?'

'Yes. No! Not girls. Women, I mean. I mean woman.'

'You were messing around with a wee doll?'

'Yes. No. I mean, nothing really happened. But it could have. I got transferred.'

'You dirty stop out.'

'It was just a bit messy. I didn't really do anything wrong. It was London or Patagonia, basically.'

'God. But fair play to you. Here was me thinking you'd gone all fruity or something. They should have given you some sort of medal, the only heterosexual priest in the Catholic Church. Not drum you out.'

'You're not funny, Murphy. And they didn't drum me out.'

Murphy shrugs. 'Christ, I'm going to end up giving you counselling rather than the other way round.'

It's not a big park by any means. There's broken glass on the tarmac path that leads through it.

'Do you think,' the priest asks, 'if you had your life to live over again, you'd make the same choices?'

'Are you talking about my son or your girlfriend?'

'Neither. Either.'

'Would I still try to save sixty people while fully aware of the possibility that I was sacrificing my family in the process?'

McBride nods.

'I don't know. I think they were always going to kill my family, whether I helped them or not. They were teaching me a lesson. But given a choice now of sixty people lined up with a machine gun against those trees, and the life of my son, I'd choose my son.'

McBride just looks at him.

'Why, you want to ask.'

'Why?' McBride asks.

'Because, right or wrong, the sixty odd people who would have died in that police station, whether they were in uniform or did the cleaning, all made the choice to join up and fight the IRA. They were always aware of the risks. My son was only aware that his daddy didn't spend enough time with him. He was only aware of laughter and Teletubbies. He wasn't aware of all the shit in the world.'

They're silent then for several minutes, walking along, birds singing in the trees, traffic a low rumble beyond. Murphy doesn't look at the children playing on the grass. Several women pass by and say hello to Father McBride.

'So,' Murphy says, 'the vow of celibacy, it's a lot of crap really.'

Father McBride nods. 'You just have to be careful.'

15

First day at work he has to give his national insurance number. Really.

There's no problem, of course, it's all set up in advance, just he's never been asked for it before.

Then there's the problem of what to wear, and what exactly his duties are, and does he get overtime or time off in lieu, is there a pension fund or paternity leave. All the standard hood questions.

The answers to these are: black suit, what we tell you, no, no, no and fuck off.

He goes around saying good morning to everyone in the office, and practising his morbid expressions. He won't be dealing with customers directly, but there is a certain ambience expected of funeral parlours. Nobody wants a cheeky chappy in the undertakers.

He had not imagined that life as a driver for a murdering armed robber would all be speeding cars and hails of bullets, but neither had he expected his new employment to be quite so mind-numbingly boring. Too much hanging around while Hatcher deals with dead business. On his second morning of reporting for work at Fond Farewells he brings his acoustic guitar with him to play in between driving jobs, but he's barely through the door before Mitchell snaps it off him and locks it away in a cupboard.

'It's a fucking funeral home, have some fucking respect.'

'The French horn is out of the question then?'

'Very funny, Paddy.'

'It's not Paddy.'

In keeping with his surroundings, Murphy is obliged to wear a dark suit, white shirt and black tie. He also has to shave and get his hair cut. It doesn't do a lot for him. He kind of suits scruffy. He looks at himself in the mirror and it reminds him of that joke. What do you call a Scouser in a suit? The Liverpool team.

Annie puts her head round the door while he's looking at himself. 'Why, Elvis has joined the army,' she says, then gives a sarcastic wolf whistle. He rolls his eyes. Then Hatcher comes out of his private office, the door behind him whirring and locking as he taps in the code for the security system on a key pad attached to the wall. Annie hurriedly moves on. Murphy stands expectantly; Hatcher doesn't seem to notice his change in appearance, he merely nods at the door then stands for a moment to allow Murphy to lead the way downstairs to the car. Along the way Mitchell and Johnny join them.

'So,' Murphy says, as they all climb in, 'what's the plan for today?'

'The plan is,' Mitchell says, 'we tell you where to go, you do as you're told. Think you can cope with that?'

Murphy nods.

Pubs, mostly. Wednesday is collection day, so they spend it travelling between fifteen different pubs, mostly in north London. Murphy stays in the car with Mitchell while Hatcher and Johnny pick up the money. They are rarely gone for more than five minutes, and when they return they scarcely look any different, not obviously weighed down by huge amounts of cash. No bags of Swag.

Mitchell doesn't say much while they wait. Murphy turns on the radio, Mitchell turns it off. Murphy hits the electric window, Mitchell zips it up again. Murphy lights a fag, Mitchell shakes his head. Murphy climbs out to smoke it, Mitchell makes him get back in. Murphy fears that they are not destined to be friends. Yet for the good of the cause, he must make the effort.

'How's your arm?' he asks.

'Bleeding obvious.'

Noreen has drawn a heart on the plaster. Annie has written Get Well Soon. Johnny tells Mitchell it's really a masturbation injury, but when he comes to write something smart on the plaster he can't remember whether masturbation is spelt with a 'u' or 'e', so writes Wanker instead, then laughs about it for at least an hour. Mitchell has the arm of his jacket pulled fully down over the plaster so that the customers won't be offended. You don't want to see the word wanker at a funeral.

'Do you want me to sign it, Mitch?'

'No.'

'How long do you have to keep it on?'

'Six weeks. Then you'll be looking for a job.'

'What if I turn out to be the most fantastic driver he's ever had?'

'You'll still be looking for a job.'

'You haven't really warmed to me yet, have you?'

'You could say that.'

'Yet I'm kind, considerate, I can provide a shoulder to—'

'Will you shut the fuck up?'

By the time of their eighth collection of the day, Murphy is bored to distraction. 'I should have stuck to country and western,' he says. 'It was more exciting.'

When Hatcher gets back in the car with Johnny, Mitchell says, 'Paddy's bored.'

Hatcher looks at him. 'Are you?'

'Yeah.'

'My heart bleeds. Try a crossword.'

But at the next stop, Hatcher says, 'OK, Action Man, this time you can come with us.'

He's out of the car quick as a flash, straightening his suit, pulling his shoulders back, trying to look tough and menacing.

The bar is called the Fallen Eagle. It's big and cavernous with a domed ceiling. On the way in Johnny says it used to be a bank. It's four in the afternoon, there are maybe half a dozen people drinking inside. There's a jukebox playing Michael Jackson's 'Billie Jean', a cigarette machine, food is served all day, but it still feels like a bank. It lacks atmosphere, the decor is poorly maintained, the carpet vaguely sticky, so that he couldn't moonwalk across it even if he knew how.

The barman, leaning on the counter, reading a paper, gives them a bored look as they enter, then returns his attention to the 3 AM girls. He's wiry and his fingers are stained brown. He waits until they're standing at the bar before he closes and folds the paper, then says, 'Yes, gentlemen, what'll you be having?' which earns a smirk from Johnny.

'Where's the boss?' Hatcher asks.

'Called in sick.'

'Call him for me.'

'Sorry, no can do.'

'Did he leave anything for me?'

'I don't know. Who are you when you're at home?'

'My name's Hatcher. Terry Hatcher.'

The name clearly means nothing to him. 'Sorry, mate. What was it, something you left behind? Keys or a coat or something? There's an acoustic guitar back there someone left.'

Murphy says nothing.

Hatcher says, 'No, it was more in the nature of hard cash.'

The barman clearly hears it, but he still doesn't understand. 'You left—'

Johnny grabs him by the hair and trails him right over

the top of the bar and down onto the carpet. The guy is so shocked he doesn't say anything, doesn't even make a noise or say, Jesus Christ, I'm only trying to earn a living, he just lies there panting, staring up as Hatcher stares down and Michael Jackson sings 'Billie Jean is not my lover'.

'How long have you been working here?'

'Three days.'

'Your boss said nothing about a collection?'

'No. I'm sorry, I don't know anything about it. I'm from an agency.'

'You're completely innocent in this, I understand. Nevertheless.' Hatcher turns and nods at Johnny, who aims his boot hard into the barman's chest. Ribs will be broken, Murphy's sure of that. Johnny turns to him then and says, 'All right, cowboy, your turn.'

Murphy looks at the poor sod, coughing up blood on the floor. Then he picks up a stool and heaves it over the bar into the shelves of bottles. They explode loudly, spraying everything with drink and glass. The customers, who've thus far managed to ignore the whole situation, run for cover. As Murphy lifts a second stool, Johnny grabs it angrily away from him.

'What the fuck do you think you're doing?' Johnny snaps.

'I—'

'Outside,' hisses Hatcher. To emphasise the point, Johnny gives Murphy a shove, then turns and puts the boot into the barman for the second time. Murphy, approaching the door, definitely hears something snap.

Hatcher crouches down beside him. 'You phone your boss, he gets the money to me by midnight, or I'll have him dead and buried by Friday. Understand?'

A blood bubble comes out of the barman's mouth. He manages to nod his head. Hatcher pats him on the shoulder, then stands and walks out of the bar.

When they're back out in the brightness and Murphy's moving towards the driver's door, Johnny catches hold of his arm and drags him back. He thrusts Murphy hard up against the wall of the bar, knocking the wind from him. Hatcher stands just to his right, shaking his head. 'Murphy, what did I ask you to do?'

'You told me to—'

'I told you to give the guy a kick. I didn't ask you to trash the place.'

'Sorry, I thought—'

'Don't think! It's not about damage, it's about threat! You don't intimidate property, you intimidate people. You can't put the fear of God into a bottle of vodka. How're they supposed to make enough money to pay me if they're closed for repairs?'

'Don't know,' is the best he can manage. 'Sorry. Guess I fucked up.'

Hatcher sighs. 'Please, where this line of work is concerned, don't use your initiative, OK? Leave that to me.' Murphy nods. Hatcher pats his cheek. 'There's a good lad, then we'll all get on famously.'

Johnny lets him off the wall. Murphy straightens his suit.

As Hatcher crosses to the car, he sees Mitchell leaning

on the bonnet, smirking. 'What's so fucking funny?' he snaps.

'Nothing, boss,' Mitchell says.

And so it goes, extreme boredom, interspersed with some small-scale protection and occasional bursts of violence. Murphy gets to act the heavy. Now he can eyeball with the best of them. But it's all loose change, really, it's not what he's there for. Murdoch points this out. He's not happy.

'Results!' he tells Murphy. 'We need results!'

'What do you want me to do?'

'Get results!'

'You want me to encourage them to go on a killing spree or something?'

'I want you to encourage them to do something. I have to go to my boss and show him how much this is costing and then justify it.'

'What is it costing? My wages?'

'It's more than your wages, Murphy.'

'Do you want me to start collecting receipts or something? Would that help?'

'Sarcasm is the lowest form of wit.'

'Then give me a chance. It's only been a couple of weeks.'

'A couple of weeks is a fucking eternity in this business.'

'It didn't used to be.'

Murdoch rings his hands together and sighs. 'Times change, Murphy. Used to be we could take the time, build a strong case. Now it's instant gratification, instant results. Going undercover is a dying business, Murphy. It's all going electronic. You said it before, you are the last of the Mohicans.'

'It can't all be done by electronics.'

'Tell them that. You should go private.'

'You mean like a private dick.'

'Private like we buy in your services when required. You can charge what you want.'

'Are you serious?'

'No. But it'll come to that. Marty, they're breathing down my neck. They didn't want you in the first place, and now they've got you on videotape raiding an off-licence and an asthmatic with broken ribs but twenty-twenty vision who did the best artist's impression of his assailants I've ever seen. So far, you're in the minus points, Marty, you've given us nothing. Nothing.'

'What're you saying? That I'm not trying?'

'No.'

'It's not easy.'

'I didn't say it was.'

'I'm in, aren't I? I'm driving them, aren't I? What do you want, blood?'

'Perhaps I haven't made myself clear. RESULTS.'

Murphy shakes his head. He can walk away from this shit any time he wants. Then his mobile goes – the one Hatcher gave him, the one Hatcher pays for – and it's Hatcher wanting to be picked up. Murphy listens for a moment then says, 'OK, boss, be there in five.' He cuts the line and looks at his other boss and says, 'I'm wanted.'

'Well for some. Look at you. You're happier than you have been in months.'

'Doesn't mean I'm going to take seven types of shit from you.'

Murphy gets out and goes back to his own car. Murdoch slips his Mantovani tape out of the glove compartment.

16

This time, when Ken the Assistant Manager sees him, Ken the Assistant Manager makes a beeline for the staff toilets. Mr Walker – huh. They don't pay him enough to deal with nuts like that guy.

Murphy sees Ken the Assistant Manager scuttle away, smiles to himself, puts a tin of beans in his basket, then moves round the corner of the aisle and catches Annie bending over a freezer.

'Let me guess,' he says, coming up behind her, 'research into cryogenic freezing.'

She glances back. 'That's right, Murphy.' She straightens, with a large bag of frozen peas in her hands.

'That's a big bag of peas,' he says.

'Well, they don't sell singles.'

'You must find shopping therapeutic. It must calm you down before you have to go deal with the stiffs.'

'Are you stalking me or something?'

'No, actually, I have a life. And that involves eating. And I might ask the same of you.'

'That's right, Murphy. I'm stalking you. Game's up.'

'Well,' he says, 'see you at work.'

She nods. He walks on. She calls after him. 'You want that cup of coffee?'

He shakes his head. Then quickly adds. 'But tea would be good.'

There's a cafe just around the corner. They have tea and a KitKat each.

'So,' she says, 'how have you found Fond Farewells?'

'Well, it's a living.'

'And what about Terry. Mr Hatcher. What do you make of him?'

'Well, I don't think we'll ever be best mates. But he's OK.'

'You've no qualms about his – other interests.'

'He buries people all day, he deserves some light relief.'

'You mean protection money and armed robberies.'

'Is that what he does? I'm glad I wore these wires.'

She smiles and stirs her tea. 'I think he's a dangerous man.'

'So am I.'

'Murphy, you're about as dangerous as a muffin.'

'Don't be deceived by this happy-go-lucky exterior. Inside lurks . . . someone really, really mean.'

'Yeah. Right.'

'You're sleeping with him, aren't you?'

'What?'

'You're sleeping with him. It's pretty obvious.'

Annie blows air out of her cheeks. 'What has this got to do with you?'

'Nothing.'

'Well, for your information, no, I'm not sleeping with him.'

He raises an eyebrow.

'Christ,' she says.

'Sorry, I just thought—'

'Don't think too much, Murphy, you might do yourself an injury. Or maybe I will.'

'Is that a threat?'

'No, it's a promise.' She shakes her head. 'You're . . .' she begins, 'you're the sort of guy who just makes a ridiculous statement in the hope that you'll get some sort of reaction. You think you'll prompt me into telling you about my love life by making that kind of a wild accusation, like I'd be stupid enough to sleep with the boss.'

'Well, who are you sleeping with?'

'See! There you go. It's none of your business.'

'So you're not sleeping with anyone.'

'It's none of your bloody business.'

'So what're you doing having coffee here with me?'

'I felt sorry for you. And it's tea.'

'No need to feel sorry for me. I like the single life. What about you?'

She laughs aloud this time. 'I'm not telling you. Christ, this is like an interview.'

'Got me,' Murphy says. 'I'm Special Branch.'

She shakes her head. 'You're incorrigible.'

'Cute, though.'

She stands. 'Whoever told you that needs their head examined.'

He stands. 'You told me it.'

'I never said a word.'

'It's in the eyes. I can always tell.'

'That's right, Murphy. You can always tell. We're late for work.'

'Perhaps we should arrive separately. In case people talk.'

'No, Murphy, we can arrive together. Because people would never believe it in a million years.'

She stalks out of the cafe. He stays behind to pay, which is the story of his life.

17

'You really don't like coffins, do you?'

Murphy's at the wheel, Johnny's beside him. They're making a delivery to one of Fond Farewells' other branches across town. It's like a car rental agency that way, you can deposit your body at one, have it picked up at another. Only you have to pay extra for the valeting, though you save on the insurance. Bit late for that.

Because they're not officially on funeral duty they drive with the windows down, elbows out, and the radio on. Van Morrison has a new album out, his third this year. But Van's the Man and Murphy can listen to him till the cows come home.

He glances back at the coffin. 'No,' he says bluntly.

'You get used to it.'

'It's not the coffins, it's the bodies.'

'They're dead. What harm can they do?'

'You never been to the movies?'

'Murphy, movies aren't real life.'

'Of course they are.'

'You never had a pet rabbit as a kid?'

'No.'

'Mice, dog, cat?'

'No.'

'You never had a pet die on you and you buried it in the garden then you dug it up a few months later to see what it looked like?'

'No.'

'Well, if you had, you'd know there's nothing scary about a dead body.'

'No, there's nothing scary about a dead mouse. I could juggle with dead rabbits. But there's lots of things scary about a dead human being.'

'Well, you better get used to it.'

Murphy shrugs, keeps his eye on the traffic. 'You worked for Hatcher long?'

'Ten years.'

'Long time.'

'Yeah, well, we're mates. We go back. Grew up together.'

'Right. And you could see how this might be his career plan, it being the family business'n all, but—'

'Wasn't suited for nothing else. Tried, didn't work out.'

'What did you try?'

'Mobile phones.'

'Selling?'

'Nickin'. Two years, I got.'

Murphy sighs.

'What's wrong?'

'Nothing,' he says. 'Just didn't realise mobile phones had been around that long. It's depressing.'

'Here . . . take a left here.'

'Wouldn't it be—'

'Here.'

Murphy turns into a side street. Johnny directs him up to the end, then left, then left again.

'Pull in here.'

They're outside a semi. There's a nameplate that says 'Happy Lodge'.

'What're you doing, homers?' Murphy asks.

Johnny smiles sheepishly. 'Nah, just fancied a spot of lunch. Come and meet my old lady.'

Johnny leads him up the drive, puts a key in the door. A large woman in her mid-fifties, her grey hair tied back in a bun, an apron round her voluminous waist, comes out of the kitchen to see who it is. Her face lights up when she sees him.

'Johnny,' she says.

'Brought someone for lunch,' Johnny says, going down the hall and kissing her on the cheek. 'This is Marty Murphy. He's Irish. But it's OK, he knows how to use a knife and fork.' He winks back at Murphy, then follows her into the kitchen. 'You have enough to go round?'

'Course I do, Johnny. Come in, Marty, sit yourself down. I have a nice steak 'n' kidney pie. That'll do, won't it?'

'Marvellous,' Johnny says.

Murphy sits. Johnny sees that he's troubled by something. 'What's wrong?'

'You're just going to leave the deceased outside?'

'Why, you want me to invite him in for dinner?'

'No, I—'

'Relax. He's going nowhere.'

The kitchen is smart, modern, top of the range. Johnny and his mum keep up a lively banter all through the meal. When he finally finds a gap, Murphy jumps in with: 'So did you know Terry Hatcher when he was a kid?'

'Oh yeah, a right little tearaway. Used to get up to all sorts of mischief.'

'This was when his dad was inside?'

Johnny finishes chewing and says, 'What is this, *This Is Your Life*?'

'Shush, Johnny, he's just interested. Who wouldn't be? Yeah, his dad was banged up. Thought Terry would turn into a right head case, but he got himself together. And now look at him. Fine example of a man like Terry, done us proud. You should meet his dad, he's just mean through and through. Terry's tough enough, but kind too, been very good to us, has Terry, but that old bugger never did a kind thing in his life.'

'He's not well, I hear.'

'Yeah, well, serves him right.'

'Don't say that,' Johnny says. 'Old Mr Hatcher's OK.'

'Well, you're entitled to your opinion, but I think he was always mean. Mean-spirited. Not like Terry, he's paid for holidays for us. And you should see his Christmas presents. It's embarrassing sometimes, because he won't let us buy him nothing.'

'He never been married?'

'Terry? When he was a kid, sure. Plenty of girls since, too.'

'But none of them lasted the pace,' Johnny says. 'You should see Terry with a wine list, knows more than most waiters, I reckon. And he's the same about women, appreciates a bit of quality. Just like me.' Johnny laughs. His mother laughs. Murphy laughs, although he's not sure why.

Johnny goes off to the toilet upstairs while Murphy carries the dishes across from the table. 'I'll do them,' he says. 'Lovely meal.'

'Stick them in the dishwasher, Marty. I haven't scrubbed a dish in seven years. He treats me well, Johnny does.'

'Well, it's nice to have a son like that.'

She stops suddenly, like she's been slapped. 'What did you say?'

'I . . . well . . . you must be proud of him.'

'Proud of who?'

'Johnny.'

'That's not what you said.'

'Yes it is.'

'No it isn't. Tell me what you said.'

'Listen . . . Mrs . . . I'm sorry, I didn't . . .'

'You said I should be proud of my son.'

'Yes.'

'I don't have a son. Johnny's my husband.' She sits down heavily at the kitchen table. She starts to cry.

'I'm . . . sorry.'

Like mistaking a fat woman for a pregnant woman, he's got mother for wife. Doesn't know where to look. Anything he says will make it worse.

Johnny comes back through the door. He sees her tears and his mouth drops a little. Then he spins on Murphy.

'What'd you say to her?'

'Nothin'.'

'Well, what's she cryin' for then?'

'It's all right, Johnny,' the wife says.

'What did he fucking say? What did you fucking say?'

'I didn't do anything. I . . . don't know my arse from my elbow. Thanks for the lunch Mrs . . . I'll . . . check on the stiff.'

Murphy hurries out of the kitchen, down the hall, and only breathes a sigh of relief when he's back sitting in the hearse.

Johnny comes out ten minutes later. He slams the door. Murphy starts the engine. They pull out into the traffic.

'I—'

'Shut it and drive.'

He shuts it and drives.

A short way down the road Johnny says: 'She was thirty-five, I was seventeen.'

'Your business, Johnny.'

'I love her to bits. Can't help getting old.'

'No one can.'

18

'Fucking hate this place,' Hatcher says as they walk up. 'Like the waiting room to hell.'

'That's rich coming from a funeral director,' Murphy says.

'It's different. By the time they get to my place they're just dead meat. All I do is window-dressing. Cake decoration for the newly departed. This . . . I just hate this place.'

Johnny and Mitchell have been dropped back at the funeral home to attend to business. Meanwhile Hatcher and Murphy are going through the doors of the Sunshine Nursing Home, and it's predictably dark and dreary. Dozens of the living dead sit vacantly about, waiting and dribbling. Smell of damp and boiled vegetables.

As they walk down the corridor Hatcher says, 'But he's better off here, couldn't manage him at home, even with a live-in nurse or something. They know what they're doing here. They're great really.'

Murphy had said he was happy to wait in the car, but Hatcher wouldn't have it. 'Dad thinks you're great, Murphy, do him good to see you.' Great. 'Though he's obviously no judge of character.'

Murphy waits in the doorway while Hatcher checks the old man out. Murphy's relieved to see that he's asleep. Hatcher examines three birthday cards sitting on the top of a locker, then leans over his father and kisses him on the forehead. There's no response. Hatcher stands back, looks down, shakes his head. He turns to Murphy and raises his eyebrows.

'Out for the count,' he says.

Murphy nods. 'He looks very peaceful.'

'Yeah.' But then he tuts, shakes his head at the emaciated figure. 'How the mighty have fallen, eh?' He looks at Murphy and gives a sad laugh. 'Comes to us all, this, but when he was younger, Jesus . . .'

He trails off. But maybe with a little prompting . . . 'What line was he in?'

'Like son, like father. Anything that would make some money. Protection, mostly. He ran a few things out Highbury way. That's where he bought his first funeral home, it used to put the fear of God into people. Still does. You see, Murphy, you don't fuck with funeral directors, we have the ways and means of making you disappear.' He keeps his eyes on Murphy for a moment more than is comfortable, then shakes his head. 'And now look at him. He's scared of the dark.'

'It's just old age.'

'No. It's more. Fear of dying. Been like that for years.'

'What brought it on?'

'Prison. Prison fucked him up. He did some time, more than he should have. He came out, no one knew who he was, the world had moved on. He should have done something bold, something to make everyone sit up, give him a bit of respect back, but he just kind of gave up. Lost interest.'

'Maybe he just wanted to go straight.' Hatcher shrugs. Murphy pushes for more. 'How did you feel about him giving up?'

'What are you, Murphy, a fucking psychiatrist?'

'Just interested.'

'Well, for your information, what I felt about it was, hey, fuck, didn't we used to have some money, didn't we used to get the best, I never used to get fucking smacked around the head in school when my dad was on form.'

'And there and then you resolved to get it all back, and this time hold on to it.'

'Yeah, maybe something like that. What the fuck, each onto their own, you know? Far as I'm concerned, for whatever reason, he had no ambition left. But in any business, you just have to keep moving forward, like a shark, otherwise you drown.'

Murphy lets it sit for a few moments, nodding thoughtfully.

'What?' Hatcher asks.

'So when are we going to do the shark thing?'

Hatcher smiles. 'You're very impatient, aren't you?'

'Well, life's too short to fuck around all day.'

Hatcher shakes his head. 'You eat steak every night of the week, it soon loses its appeal, you know what I mean? This job, the funeral business, the protection, it's our bread and butter, you know. And every once in a while we have our steak. We appreciate it much more then.'

'I'm just peckish,' Murphy says.

And then there's another voice, calm, relaxed, enjoying itself. 'If you're going to talk about me,' his dad says, opening one eye, 'could you at least keep the bad language to a minimum? There's no need for it.'

Hatcher laughs. 'We weren't talking about you, Dad. Murphy here wants the whole world, right now.'

'So did I once,' old man Hatcher says, 'but I settled for Fulham.'

Then he cackles and coughs.

Murphy glances at the man with the look of death in his eyes.

Then he returns his attention to old man Hatcher.

19

Fond Farewells has six branches, all of them in north London. Forty-two full-time employees, twenty others on a part time-basis. Murphy hasn't been working for Hatcher very long before he discovers the con with the plastic coffins. Johnny lets it slip over a liquid lunch on a day when Hatcher is away on business – what business, what fucking business, Murphy, you're supposed to be his driver! But he can't find out. Johnny lets it slip in a chummy, all mates together kind of way, but before Murphy can pump him for more, steer him around to plans and diamonds, Mitchell arrives in the bar to join them and Johnny instinctively shuts the fuck up.

Plastic coffins. He can only presume that they're all in on it, every single employee, because how else could it be pulled off? And if they are, how many other frauds must they be involved in? Even if the half of them are only turning a blind eye, they still know. Pehaps they're all on a percentage. Perhaps they're all second, third or fourth generation low-lifes in a business that suits them right down into the ground, a business of the underworld, for the underworld. The quick-fingered and the dead.

Perhaps it will be the way they get him eventually, the way they got Al Capone over his tax. Murphy will get nothing on the diamonds, but put him inside for crimes against late humanity.

Even Annie, standing by the window watching another funeral leave, like a beautiful guardian angel, she more than most of them will be aware of the fraud Hatcher is perpetrating. Strategic planning. What could that be other than ordering the cheap plastic coffins?

Usually, when he's at Fond Farewells, he stays clear of this room, the showroom. All of those coffins on display, and especially the tiny white one in the corner. He can't bear to look there. It brings tears to his eyes. So he stands in the doorway without entering and says, 'Penny for your thoughts?'

At first he thinks she doesn't hear him. Then she turns slowly, as if she's in a dream and says vaguely, 'Sorry?'

'I said, penny for your thoughts.'

She shakes herself out of her fog and says, 'Sorry,' again. 'Miles away.'

'Do you think,' Murphy asks, 'there's life after death?'

'Excuse me?'

'Is there somewhere we go after we're dead?'

'You mean apart from the cemetery?' He nods. 'I try not to think about it.'

'Yet everyone who comes here for help is thinking about nothing else.'

'Yeah. I suppose.'

'It's weird that, isn't it? If you weren't feeling well and went to a doctor and explained your symptoms and he said he hadn't a clue, you'd think he was crap. But you come here looking for reassurance and you're basically told, who knows?'

'That's life, Murphy.' She smiles weakly. 'What's got you coming over so morbid?'

He nods around the showroom. 'Well, hazard a guess.'

'You should try working here, instead of hanging around looking gormless.'

'I am here merely to be at my master's beck and call. As for being gormless, I don't feel that is entirely deserved.'

'You should try looking in a mirror.' Her mobile rings. 'Excuse me,' she says. She takes it from inside her jacket pocket. Murphy remains in the doorway while she turns to face the window and says, 'OK,' into the receiver. Then she speaks in tongues.

Well, tongue, to be precise. Japanese, he's almost certain.

She snaps the phone closed again and turns to walk out of the room. He moves out of the doorway to let her pass.

'Very impressive,' he says as she goes through the door, and then begins to walk down the corridor. 'Though you could have been talking gibberish for all I know.' She has one hand on the banister. 'Was it Japanese?'

'I worked as a translator in Tokyo,' she calls back, 'just for a couple of years.'

'How the mighty have fallen.'

'Look who's talking, gofer.'

She turns up the stairs.

That afternoon a fella from one of the other branches of Fond Farewells is dropping some paperwork off when he hears Murphy talking to Mitchell. When Mitchell turns away, the fella comes up to him and says, 'Hey, mate, you from Belfast?'

Murphy nods. The fella's of a roughly similar age, thinning hair, moustache, earring in his right ear, brown cords, black bomber jacket.

'So am I. What part?'

'Belfast West.'

'So am I. Whereabouts?'

'Harcourt Street.'

'Shit. So am I. What number?'

'Thirty-two.'

The fella blinks at him. If you were looking at Murphy, you'd think he was dead calm, but there is sweat dripping down his back. He doesn't dare glance back to see if Mitchell or anyone is listening to this.

Then the other fella laughs abruptly. 'You should see your face.' He sticks out a hand. 'Declan Coombes, left Belfast when I was sixteen, too much death and destruction, so I end up over here working in a fucking undertakers, what about that for a laugh?'

Murphy laughs.

'So, what're you doing over here?'

'Ah, pretty much the same. Y'know. Gotta earn a livin' and there was bugger all back home.'

'Aye, I know what you mean. But sure it's all changed now. We could go back home now and be welcomed like lost sheep. Carried shoulder high through the streets.'

'Somehow I doubt that.'

Declan laughs. 'Yeah, got enemies back there myself. Fancy a pint sometime?'

'Yeah. Dead on.'

Declan winks and goes off to complete his paperwork. Murphy goes down to the men's toilet and hides there until Declan leaves. He washes his face, wipes it on a paper towel. He looks at his reflection in the mirror.

Is Declan too much of a risk? Is he likely to run into him again? Will he start asking questions? Today was a bit of a laugh, but what if he starts to get curious? He could call Murdoch, have Declan hauled in, questioned about terrorism, or connect him with some sex crime, enough to get him sacked out of the Fond Farewells operation.

Murphy sighs. No. He was just being friendly. Polite. He has no intention of meeting up with me again for a drink. He has his own life. Forget it. Continue as normal. You will probably never see him again.

He goes back to work.

Later in the day, without raising a finger, he threatens to kill someone, and they hand over the money, no problem.

'You're gettin' the hang of this, kiddo,' Hatcher says.

'I've been watching the master,' Murphy says.

'And licking his arse,' Mitchell adds and Johnny nearly chokes on his cigarette.

Murphy spends as little time in his apartment as he can. When he's there he keeps the TV on, and his guitar handy. Distractions. Mostly he's trying to avoid the cupboard.

He keeps two dangerous things in his apartment: one, a gun, is taped under his bed for easy access. The other, a video cassette, is in a cardboard box in a cupboard under the sink.

He made the mistake of telling the police shrink about the tape and she advised him to get rid of it.

His wife knows about the tape. He offered her a copy and she said no, get rid of it.

It's nothing incriminating, it's nothing pornographic. It is worth nothing more than an old videotape is worth.

And he knows that without the distractions he forces upon himself, he would spend all day watching it.

The tape lasts for twelve minutes. His wife made it. It shows Murphy playing with his son. The last two minutes of it show him putting him to bed the night before he died. He begins by singing 'You are my sunshine, my only sunshine,' and Michael joins in with 'You make me happy, when times are blue.'

He loves the tape with all his heart, and it destroys him every time he watches it.

20

He's parked outside Monza's restaurant in Chelsea. Minimalist food. Extravagant lighting. Inside, Hatcher and Annie are at their table, drinking wine, the attention of half a dozen waiters, hovering like flies. Murphy's trying to think of lyrics again, but it's getting harder and harder to come up with new ways of saying his heart's been broken.

When he was growing up in Belfast there were two punk bands who ruled. Stiff Little Fingers, with their agit-prop lyrics, handily written for them by a local journalist, and Rudi, who produced perfect pop but never made it big. The first song Murphy ever heard played live was Rudi's only venture into social comment – 'We Hate The Cops', which had an opening and closing chant of 'SS-RUC!' which Murphy would happily join in with because it was all about the cops beating up a crowd of punks waiting to see The Clash at the Ulster Hall rather than a comment on the political situation in the Province. The chant was soon hijacked by the hoods and became political, so Rudi stopped playing it. Murphy wonders when he stopped being an anarchist, and started thinking about joining the cops. Right about the time he met Lianne and needed the money, probably, no bigger reason. No crusading need to bring peace to the Province. Just a job. But it sucks you in. They give you a gun and you go all kind of wanky with it for a while, thinking you're the bee's knees, throwing your weight around and walking with that RUC swagger, and then after you've had friends killed on you, blown up, decapitated, you go through a Death Wish phase when all you can think is how to stick it to the rebel bastards, and if you're lucky you come through the other side and turn into a proper cop, not concerned about green or orange, but black and white.

A guy in a pre-eighties duffel selling *The Big Issue* comes up and taps on his window. Murphy looks away and holds up a no thanks hand at the same time.

The guy taps the window, Murphy waves him away again.

He taps for the third time and this time the window comes down. 'Why don't you just take no for an answer and fuck away off?' Murphy says.

'That's not very nice, Murph,' the man says.

Murphy looks closer, then says, 'Holy fuck. It's Carter the Unstoppable Sex Machine.'

'How are you doing?'

'OK. OK. Sorry the police thing didn't work out. Still, I'm glad to see you've found something more attuned to your talents.'

Carter looks at him drily. 'Very funny,' he says.

Murphy keeps one eye on the restaurant as he speaks. 'What brings you out on a night like this? Your bridge evening cancelled?'

'Just keeping a friendly eye out for you, Paddy.'

'I need your friendly eye like I need a hole in the head.'

'One day you might appreciate me being here.'

'You stick out like a sore thumb, Carter, you could really fuck this up. Now why don't you just fuck off.'

'Murdoch wants results.'

'Yes, I do believe he's made that clear already. What're you, the carbon copy?'

'Time is running out.'

'Time isn't going anywhere. Time is what it is. People are just impatient.'

'The higher echelons are impatient.'

'I don't give a flying fuck about the upper echelons. I'm just trying to get on with the job.'

'It's a matter of fiscal responsibility, Murphy. There's only a finite amount available to pursue unconventional strands of investiga—'

'You're the one standing there like a fucking bag lady, Carter. Now, why don't you try taking the marbles out of your—'

There's movement behind him, and there's Hatcher and Annie coming out of the restaurant.

'Oh, swell,' Murphy says quietly. Carter doesn't turn to look.

Murphy's not a chauffeur, so he doesn't get out to open

the rear doors for them. Hatcher looks at Carter and then at Murphy. 'Go on, Murphy,' he chides gently, 'give the man a break.'

Murphy fishes a pound out of his pocket and gives it to Carter. Carter hands him *The Big Issue* with the actor Edward Norton on the front.

'Thanks, guv, you're a real gent,' Carter says, like he's out of *Oliver Twist* or something. Hatcher doesn't seem to notice. His eyes are for Annie.

'Have a nice life,' Murphy says.

Carter hurries away to confront another couple coming out of the restaurant.

Murphy starts the engine. 'Where to, boss?'

'My place,' Annie says.

He pulls out into traffic. He glances in the mirror as much as he can. Annie's sitting against the door, Hatcher close beside her. Twice he sees Hatcher try to kiss her, twice she turns her face away.

A tiff.

When they pull up outside her town house, she climbs out quickly. She looks back in at Hatcher and says, 'See you tomorrow.'

He nods gruffly.

When they're pulling away, Murphy says again, 'Where to, boss?'

'First base would be nice.'

And they both laugh.

'Take you home?'

'Yeah.' And then a moment later: 'No. Drop me at the Kensington Hilton. Then you go on.'

'I can wait if you want.'

Hatcher catches his eye in the mirror.

'I'll just go on,' Murphy says.

He watches as Hatcher crosses the road to the hotel, crosses the lobby and enters an elevator. No walking up to reception to ask for someone, no asking for a key, he just knows exactly where he's going.

Murphy sits outside for half an hour, debating what to do. He could slip across and charm the info out of reception, he could call into HQ and access the computers and find out the name of everyone staying in the hotel. He could maybe even use a passing satellite to pinpoint the exact room and photograph the exact shit that was going down.

He could.

It's all going electronic.

The last of the Mohicans.

Fuck them. He'll sit here and he'll watch and he'll learn and he'll show them it takes more than a fucking degree in electronics to bust open an arsehole like Terry Hatcher.

Well, he sits there for about forty minutes until he gets bored and cold, so he drives around to a McDonald's and buys all sorts of shit to keep him going, and then on to a newsagent where he has to push through the late-night men looking for comfort from the top shelf in order to get at the *Q* and the *Mojo*. Then he sits and stuffs his face and depresses himself reading about songwriters who have made it and lost it and won it back again, when he can't even make it for the first time. He settles in across the road and down a little from the hotel, close enough to keep an eye, far enough away not to be spotted. Burgers. Mmmmm. He was a vegetarian for about a week in 1979.

He dreams about Michael.

On their last day together, possibly for weeks, in reality for ever, he was due to go undercover again. He took Michael out to McDonald's and then the movies and that evening they went to a football match. Lianne didn't like him spoiling Michael like that, one out of three would have been enough, but Marty liked to make his days out with his son really memorable. He had a low threshold for boredom, back then. Always up and about. Now he could bore for the world. Cans of beer and a guitar, paper and a pen.

So they went to McDonald's, and Michael insisted on sitting on the tiny kids' chairs, so Murphy had to sit beside him, like it was Land of the Giants or something. Then they went to see a Disney film and Michael was too young for it, really, so it held his attention for about ten minutes and then he was charging up and down the aisle annoying everyone. And then finally they went to Windsor Park to see Northern Ireland play the Republic in a World Cup qualifier. He'd had to really pull in some favours to get the tickets, it was a big game and Belfast was out in force, so he felt really great taking his first son to it even though he knew Michael was far too young for international football. But you craft your son in your image. And one day he'd be able to say to his friends, he was there the night the North beat the South and qualified for the World Cup, even if they didn't. Michael slept through the second half, even with all the abuse being yelled at the invaders. But he got his son a programme, and swore to keep it for him for twenty years. Except, in the dream, Michael is all grown up and talking to his daddy in McDonald's, but Daddy's ancient beyond years, confined to a wheelchair, barely able to chew his burger but pathetically happy at the toy he's got with his Happy Meal. The movie is a fantastic cacophony of colours, it reminds him of *Yellow Submarine*. And at the match Murphy is parked in the disabled enclosure, but proud as punch because his boy is out on the field, rising to head home a cross from George Best that will take his country to the World Cup finals . . .

. . . there's a hammering on the windscreen and Murphy, peppered with McDonald's salt, jumps up awake to see a traffic warden gesticulating at him to move his vehicle. Flustered, Murphy waves at her, and starts the engine. Just as he does, he glances across at the Kensington Hilton and sees Hatcher coming out of it, and there's a woman with him and they're laughing together. They stop and kiss passionately. Then they both climb into a taxi and drive off.

There's always a blonde.

After a nickname, there's always a blonde.

But he hadn't expected her to be Noreen, Mitchell's wife.

He gives a low whistle. The jigsaw thickens.

21

Most days of the week, because Mitchell can't drive with his arm in plaster, Noreen drops him at work, but this morning there's a problem with the car, so Mitchell phones Murphy and tells him to come and pick him up.

'Yeah, like I'm your slave,' Murphy says.

'You listen to me, Paddy, you fu—'

'Only winding you up, Mitchell. What's the address?'

He arrives in about twenty minutes and rings the bell. It's an apartment on the fourth floor of quite a nice looking block. Noreen opens the door, smiles at him, then nods behind her. 'Sooner he gets that bloody plaster off the better,' she says. 'He's driving me mad.'

'Shut your face,' Mitchell shouts from the bathroom. But he doesn't sound all that mad. 'I'll be out in a minute, Paddy.'

'It's not Paddy,' Murphy calls back.

Mitchell curses.

'Fancy a coffee?' Noreen asks.

Murphy nods and follows her into the kitchen. She's wearing a silk dressing gown, loosely tied so that he sees a fair amount of breast and a fairer amount of leg. She's aware of it, of course. She must be. Lianne was never like that. Whenever someone came to the door and she wasn't fully dressed, she'd make them wait until she was. Murphy too, sometimes.

There's a breakfast bar, from which she's removing two plates and the remains of a fry. There are pans in the sink which haven't been washed in a while. There are three empty white wine bottles sitting on the shiny Formica top. An ashtray filled to the brim.

There's a fridge with children's stickers and superhero character magnets stuck all over the front.

'I didn't realise you had kids,' Murphy says.

'We don't.'

Murphy nods at the fridge.

She follows his gaze, then laughs sadly. 'And Mitch has Trivial Pursuits, doesn't mean he's a bloody genius.' She runs her hand over the stickers on the fridge. 'It's second-hand,' she says. 'Couldn't get the bloody stickers off. We can't have kids.'

Murphy nods. A conversation killer if ever there was one.

'Nice area,' Murphy says.

She puts the coffee in front of him. She has one for herself. 'So how're you settling in? You like working in that dump?'

Murphy shrugs. 'It's a job. And the overtime can be quite rewarding, or so I'm told.'

She shakes her head. 'Yeah. Rewarding enough to get me a dodgy fridge.'

'Well, I suppose you can't be too ostentatious. You suddenly go out wearing a diamond tiara, people might talk.'

She laughs. 'One day, maybe.'

She looks kind of sad and wistful. The way he would probably feel if he had to sleep in the same bed as Mitchell. Although he would add terrified to that list as well.

'So, what do you do with yourself all day?' he asks.

'Not much. I've a part-time job nights. Nurse.'

'Oh. Right. Whereabouts?'

'Agency. So I can be anywhere, you know? Gets me out of the house, mind. Hours are a bit crap though. Have to sleep over twice a week.'

Murphy nods. Yeah, sure.

'You from Belfast?'

'Well spotted.'

'All quiet is it there now?'

'It has its moments.'

'I have friends in Dublin.'

He nods. She nods. They both search around for something to say. After an awkward silence suddenly she pipes up with: 'That was some quad bike race the other night. I thought you'd broken his bloody neck. Pity you didn't.' She laughs. 'Do you hear that, Mitch!'

'Do I hear what?' he shouts from the bathroom.

'I said it's a pity he didn't break your bloody neck in that race.'

'Yeah, right,' Mitch shouts back.

'Trouble with him,' Noreen says, 'is he always charges into things without thinking about them. Should be more like you, take your time and then sneak up from the back, catch them unawares.'

Murphy smiles.

'You like coming from behind, do you, love?' she asks.

To which there is really no answer.

'So, you married, love?'

'Nah.'

'Good-looking boy like you, not married?'

'Haven't met the right one.'

'You're not fruity, are you?'

'No. I'm not fruity.'

'Mitch hates fruits.'

'I imagine Mitch hates a lot of things.'

'What does Mitch hate?' Mitch says, coming into the kitchen, dabbing at his face with a towel.

'My,' Murphy says, 'you're looking handsome this morning.'

Mitchell's brow furrows; Noreen smothers a laugh.

'What the fuck are you talking about, Murphy?'

'Nothin', mate, only rakin'. You ready to go?'

Mitch looks from Murphy to Noreen and back.

'Oh, lighten up, Mitch,' Noreen says.

Mitch tuts, then lifts her coffee and takes a drink of it. She shakes her head and lights a cigarette.

'Let's go, Paddy,' Mitchell says.

Murphy raises an eyebrow at Noreen, gets a smile

in return, then stands and follows him to the front door.

'Oh, Mitch,' Noreen calls after him. 'I'm working tonight. I'll see you in the morning.'

'Yeah, whatever,' Mitch says, opening the door.

'Oh, and Mitch?'

'What?'

'Missing you already.'

'Yeah, yeah.'

He ushers Murphy out, then pulls the door closed. He glares at Murphy. 'What're you laughing at.'

'Nothing,' Murphy says. Then when they're going down the steps: 'You're not really a morning person, are you?'

'Fuck up, Murphy.'

22

The Crook and Staff is crowded. It's karaoke night. They've done some advertising and Duffy is hopeful of big things. Hatcher said he had some out-of-town clients coming in and could Duffy put on a night of typical English entertainment to impress them. Short of setting up a couple of strippers, Duffy hasn't much of a clue until Murphy volunteers the karaoke idea. Minimum expense, it'll pull the punters in, and it'll be a good laugh.

'It's not exactly tradish, is it?'

'It's new tradish. Like new country. Best of the old and mix it with the new. It's Knees Up Mother Brown meets hi-tech.'

Duffy doesn't know what the hell he's talking about, but any port in a storm. 'That's all fine, Murphy, as long as you host it.'

'I don't host karaoke. I'm an artist.'

Murphy playing hard to get again. 'One hundred and fifty.'

'I'm a serious artist.'

'One seventy-five plus drinks.'

'Plus drinks and crisps, you have a deal.'

'You drive a hard bargain, Murphy.'

'Aye. That's right.'

Duffy laughs. And is still laughing, because it really does pull the punters in and what's more, they're drinking too. Murphy does a few songs first to get them going, then he starts inviting people up. Some of them aren't bad either, some of them are bloody awful. After about an hour of reasonably civilised entertainment, Big Irene, a regular at the bar, all hair extensions and tattoos, half cut already, jumps the queue by the simple method of storming the stage and demanding that she be taken next. Murphy asks the audience for their opinion, which is overwhelmingly in Big Irene's favour.

Murphy takes a long look at her. 'On your own head be it,' he tells the audience, and asks what she wants to sing. He says, 'I should have guessed,' when she selects Patsy Cline's 'Crazy'.

Duffy watches as Murphy sets the song up and begins to cue her in, then his attention is taken away from the stage by the group of Chinks crossing the floor of the bar. Smart looking guys in business suits, but incongruous in this place, which is strictly spit and sawdust. He wonders how they got past the doormen but then sees Hatcher's bit of stuff is with them, and fuck me if she isn't jabbering away to them in whatever the fuck language it is they speak. So much for the dumb blonde.

So that's what he's up to, Duffy thinks, bringing the Chinks in to have a laugh at our expense. What else could it be? If you have a meeting with fucking businessmen, you take them to some flash restaurant up the West End then on to *Phantom of the Opera*, not to some dodgy north end boozer where the fucking toilets don't work.

Nevertheless, Duffy goes across to them and does what he thinks is right under the circumstances. He shakes hands with Annie, he bows to the Chinks.

If only he could understand what they say.

One says, 'What's with all this bowing shit?'

'What does he think this is, fucking Charlie Chan?'

'Relax,' says another, 'just keep smiling. Stereotypes can be useful.'

The first one isn't convinced. 'We're at a karaoke night. Now that is stereotypical.'

'But we're here with an ulterior motive, that's post-modernist stereotyping in a karaoke context.'

The first guy shakes his head and looks to Big Irene murdering Patsy on the stage. 'Karoake lost its edge when it broke out of the ghetto,' he says ruefully.

Annie smiles along with them, then turns in time to see Hatcher emerging from the kitchens with Johnny and Mitchell on either side of him. He nods. Annie leans across to Han, the slightest of the Japanese, but also the man in charge, and whispers in his ear. He looks up, sees Hatcher, nods, then gets up, says something quietly to his companions then follows Annie across the floor. Duffy sees that the Chink is holding a briefcase, but what he really sees is that it's linked by a chain to his arm.

Fucking Hatcher bringing Chinks in here to do his dirty deals.

Hatcher and Han shake hands, then Hatcher turns and leads them up the stairs towards Duffy's private office.

Duffy scowls after them. He spent an hour up there this afternoon tidying his private snake pit, removing the girly calendars, emptying the overflowing ashtrays, making sure the real accounts, the ones that show how much he's skimming off the top, making sure they were offside.

Murphy has spotted the Japanese and the briefcase as well; he watches as Annie, Hatcher and Han ascend to the office. Mitchell and Johnny take up positions at the foot of the stairs. Big Irene comes to the end of her song to a chorus of boos. Murphy crosses the stage, calming the audience with his hands, then he raises them in a faux Jolson pose and shouts: 'You ain't seen nuthin' yet!' and immediately he presses another set of numbers. 'Hit it, Irene!' he yells, then sharply quits the stage as Irene bulldozes her way into 'Don't It Make Your Brown Eyes Blue'.

He gets a drink from the bar, then saunters across to where Mitchell and Johnny are standing.

'Hey, boys,' he says, 'I think we're on a winner tonight. You should get Hatcher down for a listen.'

'He's busy,' Johnny says.

'Sure I'll pop up and let him know.' He tries to push past them, but they block him.

'I said, he's busy, Paddy,' says Mitchell.

'No, he said it,' Murphy corrects, nodding at Johnny, who shakes his head in exasperation.

'Either way, he's busy.'

'And you'd be better sorting out that witch,' says Johnny, nodding at the stage.

If 'Crazy' was crazy, 'Brown Eyes' is murder and the punters really are now starting to rebel. Beer mats are skimming across the stage, showering around Irene like cardboard moths attracted by a bright, lethal light. Irene, who is built of cement and cinders, is affected not in the least. In fact, she ups the volume. From the back, somebody throws a bottle. Then half a pork pie.

Murphy turns back to the stage.

In the middle of the floor, the Japanese are really starting to get into it.

'Now this is what it used to be like in the ghetto,' one of them says and flicks off his table's supply of beer mats while Murphy battles through and up onto the stage where he cuts the karaoke machine dead to a roar of approval.

'Ladies and gentlemen,' he says, 'I apologise for the interruption to normal service; it will be resumed after Big Irene has been removed to a home for the terminally tone deaf.' He looks out to the audience. 'Gentlemen, the butterfly nets, please.'

She chases him across the stage.

The audience laps this all up, like it's part of the cabaret. And maybe it is.

Duffy watches from the sidelines. He thinks Murphy's

a bit of a star. He should reward him. Maybe give him a title, like Head of Entertainment. And extra crisps, of course.

The night passes, the crowd thins out. Han returns from his meeting with Hatcher, who tells Duffy to bring half a dozen bottles of champagne to the Japanese table. The first of the Japanese has been up on stage by now, belting out a pretty good version of 'The Green, Green Grass Of Home', and as the drink flows they really start to get into it. Hatcher sits with them for a while, then disappears upstairs with Duffy. Annie sits on, talking in a relaxed manner in Japanese. One by one they take the stage; they have a particular liking for 'I Just Called To Say I Love You' which they sing three times. All of them, including Annie, get up for 'I Should Be So Lucky'. She laughs happily and Murphy wonders if she has any idea at all that Hatcher is screwing Mitchell's wife. Han is the last of the Japanese to be persuaded to take the stage, but once he's up, there's no stopping him. He's loosened his tie, he's clicking his fingers like Frank Sinatra.

As closing time approaches, Murphy tries to switch off the machine. Han protests, Annie says no, let him sing, he's enjoying himself. So they sit through 'Rivers Of Babylon', 'Tiger Feet', 'Angie Baby' and half a dozen others. The shutters on the bar are down, Han is sitting drunkenly on a chair on the stage, microphone clamped tight in his fist, refusing to budge while his companions urge him to come home.

Annie speaks to him in Japanese, in English, but he's so pissed he doesn't care.

'More music, more music!' he shouts.

One of his companions says to Annie, in English. 'His . . . father, will be . . .'

'I know, I know.' Annie speaks to Han again, his companions remonstrate with him again, but this time he responds by waving his fist and shouting in English. 'Go on! Get lost! Go home, chickens!'

They exchange glances and speak in urgent whispers. One says to Annie, 'We are concerned—'

'It's OK,' Annie says. 'He's just drunk.'

'He has to return to the hotel.'

'I'll make sure he gets home OK,' Annie says. 'He just wants to enjoy himself. I will take full responsibility.'

The Japanese look at her, torn.

'Honestly, he'll be fine. Our meeting went very well, he's just celebrating. He should be allowed to enjoy himself.'

'His father will be . . .'

She raises her hands to pacify them.

Han launches into what Murphy presumes is another tirade of abuse, and this serves to make up their minds for them. They retreat, with much handshaking and many smiles for Annie.

As they leave, Han lurches across the floor and jabs the buttons of the karaoke machine himself. He screams along to 'I Left My Heart In San Francisco'. Annie and Murphy stand shaking their heads helplessly while the staff upturn chairs on tables and mop the floor.

'You better do something,' Annie says.

'What, do I look like a bouncer? Call in the heavies, they can beat him to a pulp.'

'Yeah, that would be good for business.'

She doesn't say what business.

Hatcher, Mitchell and Johnny appear downstairs at last, with Duffy tagging along behind, muttering about his licence and the noise and the neighbours. Han, thoughtfully, slumps back down on his chair, falls silent, then throws up. He manages to avoid his expensive shoes, but covers the wiring for the in-house PA system.

'Right, Annie,' Hatcher says, 'you played a blinder tonight.' He winks at her. 'Now we're going into extra time. Make sure he gets back to his hotel, and make sure he doesn't get talkative.' Annie nods and stands. Hatcher tosses keys to Murphy. 'If he looks like he's gonna be sick, hit the ejector seat.'

Murphy smiles.

It wouldn't surprise him if Hatcher did have an ejector seat.

23

Han vomits on the way to the car, and then again as he hangs out of the back window. He moans and groans. His briefcase is clamped between his legs. Annie passes him tissues and tries to stop herself from being sick.

They cross town, bound for the Hyatt Regency.

Murphy glances at Annie in the mirror. 'So what's the story with yer man?' he says. 'Coffins made out of bonsai trees, is it?'

'That's right.'

He gives her a pained expression. 'C'mon, talk to me. I'm interested.'

'I'm sure you are,' she says, then sighs. 'It's just a deal. Concentrate on the driving.'

When they get to the hotel they give Han five minutes in the underground car park to sort himself out, but he's all over the place. Before he takes half a dozen steps he keels over and is sick on the ground. He says in Japanese, 'I can't raise my head.'

Murphy has to help him up, then support him into a lift which they take up to reception. Annie makes apologetic noises to the girls on the desk and manages to get a replacement for the key card they haven't been able to locate about Han's person. They travel up in silence to the eighth floor, then Murphy rests Han against the door while Annie fits the key card. When the door opens, Annie pushes the handle down, and Han falls through it and lands flat on his face. The briefcase rebounds off the floor and cracks him on the back of the head. Han groans again.

They both look at him for a moment, then Annie says, 'Well, duty done.'

'We can't leave him like this.'

'Why not?'

'What if he chokes to death on his own vomit? Or someone else's for that matter.'

Murphy steps around Han into the room. Annie hesitates a moment, rolls her eyes, then follows. Murphy puts his hands under Han's arms and drags him forward, then pushes the door closed behind them with his foot.

He glances quickly about the room, then without letting Han down says: 'OK, I'll toss him in the shower, you fix the drinks.'

'I—'

'Go on, this might take a while. Mine's a vodka and white.'

She glares at him for a moment, then sighs, even offers half a smile. 'Right,' she says, then looks about for the mini-bar. 'Vodka and white, you say?'

'Yeah,' says Murphy, now dragging Han across the floor and into the bathroom. 'White lemonade. Seven-Up if you want to be vulgar.'

'Sprite,' Annie says, 'if you want to join the twentieth century.'

Murphy smiles back. He sets Han, now snoring, down against the shower door, then looks back out at Annie. 'I'll be as quick as I can,' he says, then closes the bathroom door. He crosses to the shower and pulls the door open. Han keels over. Murphy turns the shower on, but makes no attempt to put the sleeping Japanese inside. Instead he kneels beside his briefcase. He lifts it, examines the lock, the chain and its connection to Han's wrist. He sets the briefcase down again and goes through Han's pockets looking for a key, but there's nothing. He finds a passport and examines it briefly. He memorizes the relevant information, and the fact that he's clearly a well-travelled young Han. He searches again for the key, but still nothing. He curses to himself.

'Drink's ready,' Annie calls through the door.

'There in a minute,' Murphy calls back.

He lifts the case again. He glances at Han, still out cold. He decides to chance it. He cracks the lock against the edge of the sink.

No good.

He cracks it again.

Still nothing.

Annie drums her fingers on the door. 'You're not having a shower with him, are you, Murphy?'

'That's exactly what I'm doing,' Murphy shouts back. 'I think I'm in love.'

She laughs.

He cracks it a third time, harder, and this time the lock yings off, the top of the case flaps open and a fine powder explodes out of it. And over him.

'Shit!' Murphy says.

He drops the case and rubs his sleeve across the steamed up bathroom mirror and examines his white-caked reflection. He looks like a clown. Coco.

'Shit,' he says again.

As he turns from the mirror he sees that Annie is now standing in the open doorway, her mouth slightly open, her eyes on fire. 'What the bloody hell do you think you're doing?'

Murphy looks from Annie to the case to the freshly powdered but still sleeping Han, to his own speckled clothes and finally back to Annie. 'He slipped,' he says weakly.

Annie raises a finger, about to hurl abuse at him, but instead she turns swiftly, she's heard something that has been masked from Murphy by the shower. She steps fully into the bathroom and closes the door. Then she carefully, quietly locks it. As Murphy's about to speak, she puts a finger to her lips. She rests back against the door. He joins her, listening. They hear hushed Japanese voices. The bathroom door handle is cautiously depressed. The resistance of the lock is met, the handle is tried again, then there's a low, urgent tapping. Han's name is whispered, then hissed. It goes quiet for a few moments. Then they both jump as the door behind them is suddenly pummelled by angry fists; now they're angrily shouting Han's name, and more.

Murphy starts to whisper something, but she shushes him. Instead she whispers something in Japanese to him.

'What?'

'Say this,' and she repeats it. He looks confused. She thumbs beyond the door. 'Say it.' She repeats it for a third time. 'I'm in the shower,' she adds.

He cups his hand over his mouth and does his best to mimic Annie's pronunciation.

A long tirade of Japanese is fired back. When there is no response from Han, a final fist rattles the door, then angry voices trail away. After a few moments they hear the room door close.

Without realising it, they have moved very close together. They're both breathing hard from the effort of not breathing at all. Their eyes meet.

'So,' Murphy says quietly, his voice a little huskier than normal, 'what was that all about?'

Annie's voice is hesitant. She should move away, now, but she doesn't. 'His comrades from the bar. They said he couldn't hold his drink, that he was an embarrassment to them, and especially to his father. Basically, they called him a wanker.'

They gaze at each other, close up.

Then she remembers herself and pushes away from the

door. She looks at him, at the state of his clothes. 'Now explain to me why you're not a wanker as well.'

Murphy gives a little shrug. 'You mean explain why I'm covered in heroin?'

Murphy finishes tucking Han into his bed, the briefcase hanging over the side, closed and locked again, then turns back to Annie, standing by the window, drink in hand, looking out over the city. She glances back at him as he approaches, and then away again.

'Don't give me that disapproving look,' she says.

'I didn't give you a disapproving look.'

She sighs. 'So diamonds are OK in your book, but you look down your nose at drugs.'

'I never said a thing. If you ask me, you're suffering from some deep-seated insecurities about what you're doing for a living. And I'm not talking about the stiffs.'

She takes a long drink. It makes her cough a little, and she half smiles, embarrassed, puts the glass down on the windowsill and turns to him. She puts a hand on his jacket. He's not sure how to react. It's not seduction, exactly, but it's that kind of subtle pressure, let me tell you a secret, then we'll both be on the same side. 'Look,' she says, 'I'm a translator, and I'm now a businesswoman, OK?'

'OK.'

'I've been involved in perfectly legitimate deals worth billions of pounds. I've made those deals and I've saved them – but what do I get out of it? Some tiny little fee that wouldn't get you a decent holiday. So maybe it's time for me to make some money as well. You only live once, Murphy, you know?'

'So it's heroin.'

'It's money. Heroin is an equal opportunities employer, Murphy. If you can raise the money, doesn't matter whether you're male or female, black, white or yellow, you're in the game.'

'So that's what the diamonds are about. Just a way of raising money so youse can sit down with Han Solo here.' He glances back at the bed.

Annie gives a short laugh. 'No, not Han. He does the negotiating for his dad. He's not exactly the brightest bulb in the shop, but at least he can trust him. Though clearly not to go out drinking.'

Now she puts the other hand on his jacket. That's two hands.

'One more job, Murphy,' she says, 'and it'll give us enough to sit down at the table. After that, the sky's the limit.'

'In that case,' he replies, 'we'd better fasten our seatbelts.'

He moves towards her to kiss her, and their lips meet for the merest instant before she turns her head away.

'Don't be a stupid bugger,' she says.

'Stupid is as stupid does,' Murphy says. She snorts and walks off.

24

Here he is in the car outside the Hyatt Regency – different car, of course – watching as Han leaves the hotel, head down, surrounded by his comrades. There's a stretch limo parked in the bay. A uniformed driver opens one of the rear doors and a middle-aged Japanese man emerges. The approaching group stops at a respectful distance, but Han continues to walk forward. He bows. The man does not return the bow.

'I'd say your friend Han is in deep shit,' Carter says from the back seat.

'Right, Sherlock,' Murphy replies.

Murdoch is holding a fax in his hands, comparing the somewhat blurred photograph on it with the man inspiring all the respect. 'His name is . . . well, I can't pronounce that for a start.'

He shows it to Murphy, who shrugs, then hands it back to Carter, for whom it won't be a problem.

'Fujimoto Kawaisara. Known as Fuji.'

'Well, thank Christ for that,' Murdoch says.

'Japanese origin, but operates out of the Golden Triangle.'

'Always liked that song,' Murphy says.

'What song?' asks Murdoch.

'"Golden Triangle".'

'You mean "Bermuda Triangle",' Murdoch says.

Murphy nods. 'I was thinking of "Golden Shower".'

Fuji ushers Han into the back of the limo, and it pulls away, leaving the others standing unsure of themselves outside the hotel.

'Are we following?' Murphy asks.

'May as well,' says Murdoch.

'Fucking heroin,' Murphy says as he pulls the car out into the traffic. One thing, a limo that size, and white to boot, he's hardly going to lose it. 'Fucking heroin,' he repeats. 'This is going to get worse instead of better, isn't it?'

Carter leans forward between the seats. Murphy catches a subtle hint of aftershave off him. Subtle. Carter all over. While Murdoch smells like a whore's handbag.

'Drugs are like any other business,' Carter says with an authority calculated to impress Murdoch and educate Murphy. 'There are cartels, monopolies, franchises, contracts. Every once in a while one of those franchises comes up for renewal. Now, if you're right—'

'I am right.'

'If you're right, and Hatcher wants in, well, it's good news for us, isn't it? We stay with this, we can not only take Hatcher, but Fuji as well. With one stroke we could decimate a whole supply chain. You've done very well, Martin.'

'Thank you, Popeye Doyle.' He glances across at Murdoch, then returns his attention to the limo, four cars up, waiting for a roundabout to clear. 'We're after Hatcher. We know he has one more diamond job coming up. That's where we end it. We take him, we put him away. If we start following the drugs, it'll go on for ever. Fulham Palace one day, I'll be up to my oxters in a poppy field singing "Golden Triangle" the next.'

'"Bermuda",' says Murdoch, 'and we can't just ignore Fuji.'

'I can.'

'Murphy.'

'It's too big. You'd have to bring in half a dozen other agencies, there'd be people swarming all over the place. It's too big. It's not the way I work. I work alone. All I ever hear is we haven't the budget, we haven't the manpower, we haven't the time, we haven't the inclination. Now Fuji shows his head and you're prepared to throw everything I've worked for out the window.'

'We're not throwing anything out the window,' says Murdoch. 'We'll just extend the operation and provide extra cover for you.'

'We'll keep it all under tight control,' Carter adds. 'Do it our way, your way. I completely agree with your assessment, Martin. If we bring in outside help, there'll be too many chiefs, not enough—'

'He's right, Murph, we'll do it our way, but we have to do it. I mean, why settle for Hess when you could have Hitler?'

'Why settle for one dead civilian when you could have half a dozen?'

'Well, that's your call.'

'Meaning?'

'You go with us on this, you stay with the operation, you let Hatcher carry out the next heist, you use your influence, make sure nobody gets killed, and you work towards bagging us Hatcher and Fuji and the whole bloody lot of them.'

'The alternative being?'

'You never eat lunch in this town again. Marty, c'mon, we've worked together for—'

'Don't.'

Carter tries his best. 'If I may give my two—'

'Shut the fuck up, Popeye.'

He has him.

'What gives you the fucking right to—'

'OK! All right!' Murdoch explodes. 'Just settle down.' He drums his fingers on the dash. 'I need to think.'

Murphy looks back venomously at Carter, who returns it in spades. They drive in silence for five minutes. Murphy is becoming aware that Fuji's driver is taking a somewhat circuitous route back to the Hyatt Regency Hotel.

'OK,' Murdoch says eventually, 'I'll do you a deal.'

'I can't wait to hear.'

'You stick with Hatcher, but you pursue Fuji through

him as your ultimate goal. And I'll send Carter back to Traffic Branch. How's that sound?'

Carter sits back, momentarily dumbfounded.

Murphy laughs aloud. 'Now you're talking,' he says.

25

He's lying on his bed, propped up on one elbow, half watching an early evening soap on his portable when there's a knock on his front door which momentarily freezes him. He never, ever has visitors. The knocking comes again, more urgently, and he rolls off the bed. He puts the photograph of Hatcher and Noreen, or possibly Hatcher and Annie – it's still impossible to tell – making love, which he has been half examining in the commercial breaks, under the mattress and removes instead his gun.

No visitors, ever.

He approaches the door, although not face on. 'Who is it?' he calls.

'The ghost of Christmas past.'

Lianne. Unmistakably, Lianne.

He lets out a sigh of relief and opens the door.

She smiles at him awkwardly in the shadowed doorway. He sees that she has a suitcase at her feet.

He says, 'I knew you'd come back to me eventually.'

'Yeah, Marty,' she says, 'that's just what I'm doing.'

She lifts the suitcase and he stands aside. She walks in, takes up a position in the middle of the room, and looks around.

'It could do with a tidy.'

'Yeah, well.'

She sighs. Now that he can see her properly he realises that her eyes are moist and red-rimmed.

'What's the matter?' he says.

'Nothing.'

'Did he throw you out?'

'No, of course not.'

'You left of your own accord?'

'No, I haven't left, Martin. I'm still with Norman. In fact, he's waiting outside.'

'Oh. It would be stupid of me to ask then how you managed to find me. Seeing as how I'm at work and nobody is meant to know where I live.'

'Norman knows people.'

'Yeah, I'll bet he does.' He stands fuming. The bastard. Outside. He should go and throw rocks at him. 'So,' he says instead, 'can I get you a drink?' She shakes her head. 'Cup of tea? Jam sandwich?'

'No, Martin.'

Finally she sets the case down. It is small and he sees now that there are several small stickers on it – not stickers which show that it has successfully returned from myriad foreign destinations, but stickers which show spacemen involved in a laser battle.

Suddenly Murphy feels sick to his stomach.

'I'm moving, Marty, getting out of London.'

'What's Norman doing, giving you a lift to the station?'

'No, he's coming with me.'

'Oh. Right.'

'We're going to start again, up north. Or south. Or east . . . Do you know what I'm saying?'

'You're leaving and you don't want to see hide nor hair of me again.'

'That's about it.'

'Right then.'

She comes to him then, grabs him by his shirt, then kisses him hard on the lips. He is surprised, to say the least. He tries to kiss her back, but she pulls away a few inches. 'You are the most annoying man on the planet, and a tiny bit of me still loves you, but there's been too much shit, Martin, I need to start my life over again and I think I can make it with Norman. I need to go somewhere, be with someone, where I'm not constantly looking over my shoulder, somewhere where I can forget . . .' Her voice is starting to break.

He looks down at the case, and back at his ex-wife. His voice is cold. 'You think this will do it for you, leaving the case?'

'No it won't, but it's a start. It's either that or burn it. And I couldn't do that. If you want to do it, feel free, but that's why I brought it.'

He nods. His face is white.

'Oh Martin,' she says, and she buries her head against

his chest and cries. He stands immobile and fails to put consoling arms round her. She realises this, looks up, wipes at her eyes. 'I never blamed you, Martin.'

He shrugs.

She sighs, then turns for the door. She opens it, then hesitates. She looks back and gives him half a smile. 'When's the old Martin going to come back, eh?'

'The minute our son walks through that door and we're a family again.'

It's like a cold knife that jabs between her ribs.

It's like going down under the ice for the final time.

Any trace of humour and life in her face is expunged. 'It's done enough damage,' she says. 'Don't let it destroy you.'

'No,' he says, equally dead. 'Sure I'll be as right as rain tomorrow.'

She bites at her lip, and then she goes.

He watches her climb into the car. She hugs Norman for what seems like a long time. Then the car pulls away and Murphy's alone in his apartment with his TV and his guitar and his dodgy lyrics and a suitcase full of his dead child's clothes.

26

He searches the kitchen for alcohol, but can only find a bottle of Irish whiskey, a Christmas present from . . . he has no idea. It is not usually his drink of choice, but needs must. He gets Michael's tape out of its box and slips it into the video recorder. He slumps down into his chair in front of the telly and presses play on the remote.

You are my sunshine.

You were my sunshine.

You are my sunshine.

Michael, what would you be now?

He had an agreement with Lianne when she was pregnant that if they had a girl, she would tell her the facts of life, but if it was a boy, it was his job. They had teased each other about it, because though he was never shy about coming forward, the thought of describing the facts of life to his own son was already filling him with utter terror, and he didn't even know if it was to be a son.

'And no taking the easy way out,' Lianne had said.

'What easy way out?'

'Buying a porn video.'

He had laughed, and then thought, and then asked, 'What about renting?'

He sighs. They used to be so great together.

Two, and then three, and then two, and then one. Life as mathematics.

And before that when his son was being born: she was in labour for twelve hours and then they asked him if he wanted to cut the umbilical cord and he dropped the scissors he was that nervous.

A boy, a baby boy.

He blinks at the screen again. His son. Innocence. No comprehension at all of what is about to happen.

Before he's a third of the way down the bottle the tears are rolling down his cheeks.

Gets him every time.

He knows he's sad and pathetic, but nobody understands. Nobody really understands. Not Lianne, not Father McBride, not fucking Dr Coates.

They should have killed him, not the child.

It was cruelty beyond cruelty, and one day he will have them.

He knows that, deep down.

That even if he's seventy and losing it, he will recognise them in the street, and he will kill them.

No war crimes trial for them.

Execution.

He gets like this when he's drinking. This is why it is

good that he's in London and not in Belfast. In Belfast he'd be roaming the streets with a gun.

He doesn't remember finishing the bottle, but when he wakes an hour later he's lying on top of his bed and it's dark outside and the only light in the apartment is the glow from the television in the other room. He lies blinking through the thick fog of drink that is slowly morphing into a hangover – and then he hears it . . . feels it . . . movement from the other room.

He reaches under his bed and removes his gun for the second time.

Wait for a bus for ages, then two come along at once.

He rolls off the bed, gun in hand, and moves cautiously towards the half-open door. He waits on the dark side of it for a moment, then edges very slightly forward. There is football showing on the TV, and the green sheen off the screen and movement of the camera and players is throwing odd shadows across the rest of the apartment. For a moment he thinks he's just being paranoid, and then it comes again, definite movement, heavy breathing, a grunt, and a shape moves on the far side of the kitchen. Fucking burglar. Fucking kids downstairs. Hatcher. The boys from home. Shoot first, ask questions later. It's something large – on the ground, but now rising, getting bigger, moving towards him . . .

Shoot.

Can't.

He raises his gun.

'Move a fucking muscle and I'll blow your fucking head off.'

The figure stops.

'Are you trying to be funny?' asks a querulous voice.

Murphy keeps the gun trained, but drops one hand from it and feels along the wall for the light.

He switches it on.

Father McBride.

'What the fuck are you playing at?' Murphy spits.

'What the fuck are you playing at?' McBride spits back.

Murphy lowers his gun and shakes his head groggily. 'What . . . what are you even doing here?'

'You invited me round for the football, you clampett.'

'I . . .'

'United, you tube. Arrive here, the door's on the snib and you're sleeping like a friggin' baby. What's an instrument of God to do? By the time I'd got home I'd have missed the first half. So I make myself at home and let you sleep it off. Then you try to shoot me.'

Murphy sighs.

'Here,' McBride says. 'I was foraging for food, best I could find.' He shakes a box of Quality Street at him. 'Although I claim all the orange ones.'

'No, no thanks . . . I'm sorry . . .' He looks at the gun. 'I'll . . . just put this away.'

He goes back into his bedroom to re-secure the gun. He sits on the bed, shakes his head, then feels beneath.

'United are two up already,' McBride calls, back sitting now in front of the telly.

'Sorry, mate,' Murphy says. 'Completely forgot . . .'

'Never worry. Didn't know when you were going to wake up, so I taped it for you.'

'Cheers.'

And he has the gun in place, but something isn't right and he can't quite put his finger on it and he sits on the bed for several long moments while McBride gives a running commentary from the other room.

'That Beckham's something else, isn't he? Reminds me a bit of meself when I was—'

Then it comes to him and he dashes from the room and slides to his knees in front of the telly.

'Marty! I can't see—'

'Shut the fuck up!'

He stops the tape. He turns to McBride. 'The controls, give me the fucking controls.'

'All right, keep your hair on.'

McBride hands him the controls. Murphy fumbles them, picks them up, rewinds the tape just a fraction then presses play.

'Marty, what's—'

The live football is replaced on screen by that of a few seconds before – and then the picture dissolves to not more than a second of Michael smiling at his father, and then it dissolves again to some television programme of five years ago.

Murphy stops the tape. He looks back at McBride. 'You taped over my son.'

McBride's mouth drops open. 'Your . . . oh . . . Martin. I had no idea.'

'You taped over my fucking son.'

'Martin . . . I was just trying to help.'

'You taped over my fucking son!'

Murphy is up on his feet now, grabbing the priest by his shirt and dragging him to his feet. He shakes him hard. 'My son! I've lost my son! Because of you and your fucking football!'

'Martin . . . don't . . . Martin . . .'

'What the fuck were you playing at!'

'Martin . . .'

'Fuck!'

He throws McBride back down into his chair and reels away.

'Fuck!'

He kicks out and sends another chair flying. He smashes a lamp.

'Fuck!'

'Martin . . .'

'Fuck up! What the fuck are you doing here anyway? Who do you think you are? I fucking know you, McBride, you're about as much a priest as I fucking am! What the fuck do you know about God or death or anything? You just fucking listen and nod, listen and nod like one of those fucking little nodding fucking dogs in the back of fucking cars.' Murphy sighs deeply. 'Oh shit,' he says.

Then he stands there shaking.

'Martin . . . do you want to talk about it?'

'No!'

'Do you want to watch the rest of the match?'

'For fuck sake! Don't you understand?'

'I know . . . I'm sorry . . . Do you want me to go?'

'Yes! Just fuck off and leave me alone.'

McBride nods. He climbs out of the chair. He takes a handful of Quality Street from the box and puts them into his pocket. Then he walks to the door. He hesitates before opening it. 'Martin . . .'

'Just fuck off.'

'I . . . I didn't mean to tape over your son. I was only trying to be helpful. I didn't mean to destroy it.'

Murphy stares at the floor as McBride leaves, closing the door softly behind him.

27

Not a good night, then.

He stays up drinking late, and tries to write a song, but he keeps thinking about his son, and doesn't want it to come across all Eric Clapton.

There's a poor excuse for a veranda outside and he sits there into the early hours, quietly strumming, but as the sound of the traffic fades, so his guitar starts to annoy the neighbours.

The cow next door raps on her window, and he waves back at her.

The welder on the other side opens his veranda door and says, ''Ere, keep it down, mate, tryin' to sleep.'

Murphy gives him the thumbs up.

Twenty minutes later the old bat is back and this time she opens her veranda door and shouts, 'I'm gonna call the cops on you!' then slams it shut when he laughs and sings, 'It's only rock 'n' roll, man, but I like it.'

But he knocks it on the head, because he's the Singing Detective, and there's no point in looking for trouble.

He stays out in the cold, guitar by his side, smoking more than drinking now. Thinking about Lianne and how he met her.

Typically, it was her friend he was after, but she wasn't interested and stalked off, leaving him standing in the middle of a bar with Lianne, both of them not knowing where to look. When she spoke, he thought she sounded like Rod Stewart, but then she explained she'd just had her tonsils out and he said oh, and then she held up a bottle of beer and said, I'm not supposed to be drinking, antibiotics, I'll probably get really pissed, and do something I regret, and he said, let me buy you another and they both laughed at that, and really they didn't stop laughing for a lot of years after that, until the awful thing happened and there was no laughter at all, just a lot of tears and curses.

They slept together that first night, and she basically was never away from him after that. When he woke, the next morning, she was cleaning his house.

'There's no need to do that,' he said.

'Yes there is. There was a spider's web in the kettle.'

'I don't use the kitchen much.'

He'd only been living by himself for six months. His parents hadn't really trained him to live alone. He took his washing home. She moved in after about two weeks. He only thought of asking her if she was on the pill after about six months and she said no, I'm going to have your baby.

He didn't know whether to laugh or cry or apply for planning permission.

And a month after that she was pregnant, and a month after that they were married.

And now she's away into the wild blue yonder with Fat Norman.

He wonders if Norman told her about the dressing gown.

He probably didn't.

Probably said he lost it or threw it out or ate it as a snack before lunch.

Norman.

How to get Norman into the lyrics of a song.

Norman. Norman. You're such a wanker . . .

Not much radio play for that one.

In the morning, with his head heavy and his throat dry as a fossil, it takes him about half an hour to drag himself across the bed to answer the phone. He says hello so gruffly that Hatcher doesn't recognise his voice. 'Is that . . . Murphy?'

Murphy clears his throat. 'Mr Hatcher.'

There's a low rumble of laughter. 'Bad throat, or on the sauce?'

'Hazard a guess.'

'I need you here in thirty minutes.'

'I . . .' he rubs at his brow, trying to get through the fog. 'I . . . thought I had the day—'

'You do. But I just thought I'd let you know it's also National Shirley Bassey Day.'

With that Hatcher puts the phone down.

Murphy lies back on the bed and closes his eyes for thirty seconds. His head is pounding so hard he's almost willing to believe that he imagined the call.

Shirley Bassey Day.

Shirley Bassey Day.

Thin. Big hair. Coloured. Hey Big Spender. Welsh. Diamonds Are Forever.

He sits up abruptly. Diamonds.

It's on.

It's bloody on.

He hurries to the kitchen and quickly washes down half a dozen paracetamol with the aid of half a can of flat Sprite. He has slept in his clothes, so no preparation there. He looks at his son's clothes, spread out crumpled on the bed, and decides to leave them. He'll tidy them away later when he has time to do it properly. He crumples up what might have been a suicide note/lyrics, replaces his gun beneath the mattress – what the fuck was I doing with that out again? – then steps out of his apartment.

The old cow in the hall says, 'Bloody ridiculous,' as he passes.

'Yeah, yeah,' he says.

'I'm reporting you, it's not right.'

'Like I give a flying fuck.'

'You're disgusting.'

'Ah, fuck off.'

'Irish,' she calls after him, 'you're all the fucking same.'

On the way to Fond Farewells, he calls Murdoch on his mobile.

Murdoch answers. There's a lot of noise in the background, like he's on a plane. 'What was that?' he says.

'It's Murphy. It's on. The thing. The thing we talked about is on.'

'Oh. Christ.'

'I'm due there in ten minutes.'

'What was that?'

'I said I'm due there in ten minutes. Where the fuck are you?'

'I'm at the hairdresser's. My hair's soaking. Ten minutes, you say?'

'I've nothing else to give you. No location, no time, but it's on.'

Murphy hears a door open, then the sounds of traffic; Murdoch's voice becomes clearer. 'Well, don't worry, we'll be with you every step of the way. But we won't interfere unless it's absolutely necessary, OK?'

'OK. Oh, and by the way, I like the hair.'

'Oh right, thanks . . . fuck off, Murphy.'

Murphy grins as he snaps the phone shut.

How does he feel?

A weird mix of depression and elation.

His son, dead and gone.

His wife, might as well be.

Her memories of their son deposited in left luggage.

In the middle of the night he did not want to live any more, but fell asleep before he could pull the trigger.

He will have to give up his night drinking if he's ever going to be sober enough to kill himself. But he does not feel like killing himself now. The adrenaline is pumping, chased around his body by the paracetamol. He's going into action. He's alive. Why would he ever want to die? What would it achieve? Playing in a field of wheat with his son for eternity?

Go get the bad guys, Murphy.

Sort them out.

He thinks about the security guard in the morgue, and his bubbled, melted skin.

That's Terry Hatcher.

Remember that.

Murphy parks around the corner from Fond Farewells – staff aren't allowed to park their own cars in the actual car park, it's reserved for customers, alive and dead – then hurries into the building. He knows now that the smell is that of embalming fluid. There is a tape of 'The Lord Is My Shepherd' being played on a Bontempi electric organ.

Murphy moves along the hall past the showroom, on across the kitchen to a small door which leads him into a large garage space which normally houses three hearses, but which today boasts only one, plus one electric-blue people carrier. Mitchell and Johnny are just climbing on board. They're dressed casually, jeans and T-shirts and zip-up jackets. Mitchell has the sleeve of his jacket pulled down over his plaster.

'Oh look,' Mitchell says, 'it's Emerson Fittipaldi.'

'Oh look,' Murphy responds, 'it's the one-armed bandit. Are you along for amoral support or are you actually going to do anything?'

Before Mitchell can respond, or compute, there's movement behind and Murphy sees Hatcher coming through the door, smiling and clapping his hands together.

'OK, boys,' he says, 'let's get this show on the road.'

Murphy climbs behind the wheel. The keys are already in the ignition. He tuts. 'It's not exactly built for speed,' he says. 'You get better manoeuvrability in a fork-lift truck. And more speed.'

'How fuckin' stupid do you think we are?' Johnny asks.

'There's no answer to that,' Murphy says. He glances back at Johnny and adds, 'How about closing the door?'

Johnny grins at him. 'Hold on to your horses.' He winks at Murphy, then nods back to the doorway.

Annie steps through, carrying a holdall.

Murphy looks at Hatcher, who's shifting over to make room for her. 'What is it?' he asks. 'A Japanese bank or something?'

'Everyone earns their keep around here, Murphy,' Hatcher says.

Annie climbs on board, then Johnny slides the door shut. The garage doors open automatically as Murphy moves the vehicle forward.

'Some direction here would be good,' he says as he crosses the car park.

'Left, left, then left again,' Johnny says, and they all laugh.

'Don't worry, Paddy,' says Mitchell, 'we'll keep you right.'

'Or left,' Johnny says, and they all laugh again.

* * *

When they're out on the open road, Murphy spots the tailing car in his mirror. It's a long way back, there are seven or eight other cars between them. Johnny's looking out of the back window, but he doesn't know what he's looking for. Murphy's a little confused. Under normal circumstances – as normal as any kind of a heist can be – a tense silence would have fallen upon the gang by now. They would be primed, ready for action; there would be sweat; their lips would be moving, rehearsing lines, saying prayers, checking the action on their guns. But this – it's only slightly tense, it feels a little too relaxed. Can they be that confident? That it's just a Sunday afternoon stroll in the park for them?

Hatcher tells him to pull in. Murphy's eyes flit left, right, left, looking for the target, and the best he can come up with is a branch of Mothercare.

He parks the people carrier and they climb out. While he locks up, Johnny puts coins into a parking meter. Well, a first time for everything. Mothercare and a parking meter. But then he falls into step as Hatcher leads them across the road. As he reaches the other side, the tailing car moves slowly past and he catches sight of Carter, hands clamped to the wheel, studiously avoiding looking in any direction but straight ahead.

They follow Hatcher around the corner – away from Mothercare – and all becomes clear. There's the Underground sign. They hurry down steps into Highgate tube station; Hatcher first, then Annie, Murphy, with Mitchell and Johnny bringing up the rear. As they reach the turnstiles, Hatcher produces a clutch of tickets from his pocket and hands them out. Murphy somehow doubts that the man himself went out that morning to purchase them. Johnny, probably. It seems so ridiculous, being given a ticket for the Underground like this, they should leap over the turnstiles, kick ass, but then nobody ever goes to the toilet in cowboy movies either. Real life.

But still, Underground tickets. What next, a packed lunch?

When they reach the platform, the electronic noticeboard says the next train is due in three minutes. There are about twenty other people waiting for it.

Murphy says to Annie, 'How are you feeling?'

'Fine,' Annie says.

'Any idea where the picnic is?'

'Shhhh,' Hatcher says.

Murphy smiles, and glances back at Mitchell, who is watching Carter and another man emerge from the steps onto the platform. He studies them intently, then looks away. Then he looks back.

Murphy moves up beside Mitchell and says, 'So how's the treatment for paranoia coming along?'

Mitchell shakes his head. 'Don't get in my way today, Paddy,' he says. He scans the rest of the travellers. Carter and his companion walk past behind them and take up a position a few yards along. Carter whispers something in his companion's ear, and then they both laugh aloud. They don't look anywhere near Murphy.

The train arrives and the gang steps on board. Their carriage is packed, so the five of them are forced to stand at one end, holding on to the poles. Just as the doors are closing, Carter and his companion step on board.

They're just inches away.

Murphy sees a bead of sweat run down Mitchell's brow. Now it's starting to get to him. At last, a sign of some tension. They've done nothing so far but ride on the Underground, but Mitchell is spooked. He's been around. He can tell. He's not paranoid. Or if he is, even paranoids are right some of the time. Hatcher told him that once, and he thought it was very clever, once he worked it out. But now there's this cop a fist length from his face, he knows it, he can smell it, but what's he going to do?

Then the 'cop' turns to his companion and says something in German, and the other guy says something back also in German, they both laugh. They continue to chat in German, and Mitchell at last relaxes. At the next stop the Germans get out.

Carter watches the Tube pull away, and a moment later he has his phone to his ear and he's calling Murdoch. 'We had to let them go,' Carter says.

'Fuck,' says Murdoch.

28

Reginald Wilkinson has the distinction of being one of only a handful of people to have been christened Reginald in the past thirty years. Reginald is the most unfashionable name in England. Reginald as a name has a peculiar between-the-wars ring to it. Think of Reginald and you think of a middle-aged tax inspector, or a traffic warden or security guard, a deeply dull, deeply respectable, drab, undemonstrative man with a knotted handkerchief on his head in summer, who only paddles in the sea, trousers rolled up to his knees, who continually cleans his glasses; Reginald who has thinning hair, small piggy eyes, a superior look but from an inferior background.

This Reginald Wilkinson isn't like that at all. Not really.

Reginald Wilkinson deeply regrets being called Reginald, and prefers to be known by his middle name of Arthur, which is not, truthfully, a huge improvement. But at work, here at Beshauf International Diamonds, he is still known as Reginald, at least to his peers. To those below him – he's head of security and it is a multimillion pound concern, so there are many below him – he's Mr Wilkinson, and that's much more like it. Wilkinson. Like Wilkinson's Sword. The cut and thrust. That's him all over. Cut and thrust. He's no dowdy Reginald, he's the rapier-like wit of a Wilkinson, a dashing blade, and a grand uniform to go with it.

Self-image is a funny old thing.

Reginald Wilkinson is only twenty-nine, but he's doing OK. Married to his childhood sweetheart, he has reached a position of importance by climbing the career ladder rather than transferring into it from a loftier perch – the army or the police, like most of them do. What it gives Reginald Wilkinson is a respect for the job, for aspiring to do it properly, not like the blow-ins who see it as a cosy way to snuggle into retirement.

Reg the blade Wilkinson takes his job seriously. There hasn't been a single successful robbery at BID in the three years he's been in charge of security. It's not that they're that hi-tech, they're not, but they're thorough. Every conceivable criminal avenue of approach has been identified, and theoretically nullified. They have rehearsed countless scenarios, from full-on armed robbery to blackmail to assault by computer virus, but no one has thought until now about love, and what it will do to a man.

Reginald Wilkinson loves his wife.

'Do you hear that sound, Reginald?' Hatcher asks on the

phone. 'That's the sound your wife makes when she's about to die. Like it?'

'Who—?'

'Just follow my instructions, and she'll be fine.'

'I—'

'Deviate a fraction and I'll cut her fucking head off.'

He's absolutely terrified now. 'What . . . do you want?' he stammers.

'I want you to win an Oscar.'

Reginald stumbles out of his office, white as a ghost and clutching at his chest. He staggers against Rosie's desk, and his secretary looks up aghast.

'Mr Wilkinson, are you . . . ?'

Stupid bloody question.

He grasps for words, but they won't come, his eyes roll back and he flops down onto the carpet.

'Mr Wilkinson!'

He's on the floor and he's foaming at the mouth and having some kind of a weird fit and Rosie doesn't know what the hell to do except scream, and that brings them running.

Good old Reggie – Mr Wilkinson, they correct themselves – such a young man to have a heart attack, but he works like a demon. Should take more time to himself and that young wife. When's the last time he had a holiday?

The admin staff congregate about the main office, joined by jewellers from upstairs. The woman designated as First Aid officer is in a blind panic and can't remember what to do, so one of the guards from downstairs steps in and performs CPR. The First Aid officer arrives with towels and hot water, although it's clear Mr Wilkinson isn't about to give birth.

'Where is it?' Rosie shouts into the phone. 'Where's the bloody ambulance!'

'It's caught in traffic,' the controller says testily. 'Won't be more than ten minutes.'

But he doesn't know his arse from his elbow because Rosie can hear the siren already. She darts downstairs. The security guards are already opening the gates.

The ambulance steams in and the siren dies. Two crew jump down from the back in their smart green jumpsuits and baseball caps and Rosie shouts, 'This way, please!' and they hurry after her. Her heart is pumping so fast, though not nearly as fast as Mr Wilkinson's, lying dying on the Axminster.

Oh, I thought he was looking peeky.

Up the stairs, three at a time. 'Oh, please God, I hope you're in time!' Rosie shouts.

'Don't panic,' says the paramedic. 'I'm sure he'll be fine.'

They hurry into the main reception area upstairs and the crowd grouped around poor Mr Wilkinson instinctively moves back to give the paramedics room. They kneel down beside him, open their medical bags.

And it takes several moments for the employees of Beshauf International Diamonds to appreciate that the life-saving devices the paramedics conjure from their bags are exactly the opposite.

Hatcher stands first, followed a moment later by Mitchell.

'Right,' Hatcher bellows, raising his shotgun, 'who the fuck wants to go to hospital?'

Shocked and stunned, the employees can only stand there with their mouths open and enough colour draining from their faces to dye the carpet red.

On that carpet Wilkinson rolls over onto his side and puts his hands to his face. 'I'm sorry,' he mumbles.

'Don't be sorry,' says Hatcher. 'You were brilliant.'

There's a commotion at the door and three security guards are herded through by Murphy, Annie and Johnny, each with a shotgun, each with a transparent plastic mask pulled down over their faces.

Mask.

Masque.

The Masque of the Red Death.

Murphy's two parts terrified, one part exhilarated. He has permission to do this, though he'll probably never get it in writing. He's robbing a jewellery warehouse, he has a shotgun in his hand, he's yelling along with the rest of the gang for the jewellers to deposit their wares into a series of cloth pouches. His mission is to steal diamonds, preserve life. He has one guy down on the ground, a shotgun to his throat while he scoops up the diamonds. His finger is on the trigger.

Sometimes there's a temptation, to just . . . pull . . .

When you're told as a child, don't touch that, it's dangerous, the thing you most want to do in all the world is touch that thing.

'Give me the diamonds!' Murphy bellows. 'Give me the fucking diamonds!'

Hatcher is smooth and exudes strength and terror, Mitchell's the shouter, Johnny's just cold and efficient. Annie is shouting as well, her voice up a notch, and rising as the woman with the tight grey perm and the wedding ring and the elderly round glasses point-blank refuses to hand over her tray of diamonds.

'Give it over!' Annie shrieks.

But the woman just holds tight, her hands panic-frozen into place.

'I swear to God!' Annie yells.

But no movement.

'Let her have it!' Mitchell shouts, meaning both barrels, but in the noise and confusion Annie thinks maybe he's shouting at the woman to let go of the tray.

She holds tight. Backing away now, pulling the tray out of Annie's grasp so that now Annie's got no alternative but to raise the gun and take proper aim.

'Give me the tray,' Annie says.

Murphy looks across, tightening his bag of diamonds, his assigned row all cleared out in record time.

'Shoot her!' Hatcher shouts.

Annie exhales, which for a moment steams up the inside of her plastic mask. It clears in a second. The woman has stumbled over her own handbag now and is on the floor with the tray of diamonds clutched to her chest, trying to scramble backwards.

'Drop it!' Annie yells, gun to shoulder, but nudging it at the woman as if she's preparing to throw a spear. But the woman has closed down. She wouldn't give it up to Jesus on the Second, Third or Fourth Coming. Her diamonds. Her diamonds. Her . . .

Annie's finger's on the trigger, but she hesitates.

'Shoot the fucker!' Hatcher yells, and still Annie doesn't pull, and now Hatcher's turning and striding across and Murphy knows surer than hell that if Annie won't, Hatcher will.

Murphy steps sharply between the aisles of diamond cutters and brings his shotgun round on the woman on the floor; she has her eyes closed now and is uttering an urgent prayer, but her fingers are closed as tight as ever.

Murphy puts the two eternal black holes at the end of his shotgun barrels against the floor a foot from the woman's head and pulls the trigger. There's a blast and screams and smoke and splinters and the woman automatically lets go of the tray. Murphy scoops it up, has a brief glimpse through the hole of a shattered water cooler on the floor below, then thrusts the tray against Annie's chest. She nods and turns.

'OK!' Hatcher shouts. 'Let's get out of here!'

As they hurry towards the door, Wilkinson finally makes it to his knees. 'My wife . . .' he says. 'Please . . . my wife . . .'

Johnny laughs and whacks him in passing. The wife is fine, doing wife things.

The ambulance wails through the streets, Murphy behind the wheel. Traffic makes room for them. A woman waiting at traffic lights crosses herself as they pass.

In the back they're laughing and giving high fives – Hatcher, Johnny, Mitchell, but Annie's more subdued.

They park inside the skeleton of an old brewery plastered with signs proclaiming London's most prestigious new apartment complex. While Johnny sprays the ambulance with petrol, Hatcher collects the diamonds and transfers them into one bag. He weighs it in his hands, his face all smiles. He gives Annie a hug then moves round the back to talk to Mitchell. On the way he tells Murphy to collect the weapons and stow them in a golf bag he pulls out of the back of the ambulance. They're going to take the tube home, same way as they came. Annie says she's busting for a pee and heads off behind a wall. Mitchell watches her go – but not go, clearly – then shakes his head and looks at Hatcher. He doesn't have to say it.

'I know,' Hatcher says.

'Coulda got us all shot,' Mitchell says.

'So what were you like the first time?' Johnny says.

'Didn't fucking wet myself,' Mitchell snaps.

'She did OK,' Hatcher says. 'She needed to be blooded. But that's it. Next time she'll stay home and make the sandwiches, OK?'

Mitchell gives a sarcastic, 'Yeah, yeah.'

Hatcher clamps an arm round him. 'We have the diamonds, that's the end of it, OK?'

Mitchell nods. Hatcher turns to Murphy. 'Well done, Murphy,' he says, 'you old pro.'

'Par for the course,' Murphy says, lifting the golf bag.

Annie comes back, changed out of her paramedic gear.

'OK,' Hatcher says, 'burn it.'

Johnny flips a match and the ambulance goes up. They stand for a moment, watching it; the siren goes off of its own accord, just for a few seconds, then melts. Hatcher laughs and then turns and leads them out of the brewery and up the road towards the tube.

'All right,' he says on the way, 'who's for a quiet night in?'

29

They're in the Crook and Staff, celebrating like mad. The karaoke machine has taken root and Big Irene by pure chance is belting out 'Things Can Only Get Better', which is their theme for the evening. Hatcher, Mitchell and Johnny have their arms round each other, singing along, their feet pounding the floor in time to the music. The rest of the patrons have caught the party atmosphere. Even Duffy has a smile on his face. Murphy stands by himself at the bar, drinking. Annie comes up and orders her own drink. It's all on the slate, of course, so Murphy doesn't offer to buy. She smiles and says so what are you up to, up here all by yourself.

'Just wondering how to place a small explosive device in the karaoke machine,' Murphy says.

Annie laughs, then turns and stands with her back to the bar, watching Irene.

'I was thinking of something like a neutron bomb,

something that will destroy people but leave buildings and expensive electronic equipment intact. Not even people. Just Irene.'

Annie smiles again, then looks appraisingly at Murphy. She nods thoughtfully.

'What?' he asks.

'You're quite the stereotypical Irishman, aren't you?'

He raises an eyebrow. 'Meaning?'

'Meaning that you're all basically the same. You sing at the drop of a hat. You think your twinkly eyes and your gift of the gab's enough to charm the knickers off everything that moves. Given half the chance you'd drink yourself into oblivion every night of the week, then you'd crash into your pit at some godforsaken hour of the morning, sleep till lunchtime and then you'd drag yourself back to the pub to start all over again.'

Murphy ponders this for a moment. Then nods. 'Yeah, it's great, isn't it?'

She shakes her head. She glances at Hatcher, still singing happily. She gives Murphy a slightly embarrassed smile. 'Thanks for today,' she says quietly.

Murphy shrugs. 'All part of the service.'

'I couldn't—'

'It's fine.'

'Did you hear Mitchell?'

Murphy shakes his head.

'She's a poor little rich girl looking for kicks and she'll be the death of us. Don't drag us down over a bit of tail, Hatch.'

'That's a pretty good impression.'

She looks at him then, and her eyes grow a little cooler. 'You agree with him, don't you?'

He takes a drink. A little shrug. 'Just don't understand why you would want to do it. I can't, for example, picture Mitchell's wife doing it. Noreen.'

They both look towards Noreen, who's gazing at Hatcher.

'Mind your own business, Murphy.'

'I object to people playing one-upmanship with guns.'

'Piss off,' Annie snaps, and strides away across the bar.

Murphy laughs, then calls after her: 'Sure don't pay any attention to me, aren't I just the mischievous Irish tinker?'

She ignores him, and approaches Hatcher's table. He smiles at her and moves along his seat, forcing Mitchell and Johnny to move as well, to make room for her. She sidles in, aware of Noreen's glare, but ignoring it. She takes a long drink of champagne and then coughs at the bubbles.

Twenty minutes later she's up dancing with Mitchell, really rubbing salt in Noreen's wounds. But Noreen knows better than to start something, so instead she storms off home complaining of a sore head. Murphy's enjoying all this when Hatcher comes up beside him.

'What're you doing up here, Murphy, all by your lonesome?'

'Just watching the world go by.'

Hatcher sees that he's watching Annie and Mitchell dance. Irene's been booted off, finally, and there's a quite decent fella doing some Motown classic. Annie's looking pretty drunk now, dancing with her eyes closed, singing along to the song. Mitchell looks a bit lost.

'Look at her,' Hatcher says. 'Isn't she beautiful.'

It's a statement, not a question. Nevertheless Murphy nods appreciatively.

'If you ever try anything with her, I'll kill you,' Hatcher says.

'Fair enough,' Murphy responds after several moments of due contemplation . . .

30

Annie's sitting in the cafe waiting for him. It's pouring outside, cold and miserable and he's been walking without a hood so that his hair is slicked down straight on his head and his light green canvas trousers show every spot of rain. He's actually been watching her for the past five minutes, outside the cafe, off to one side where he can see her and she can't see him. She fixes her hair, she checks her make-up, but the whole time never removes her sunglasses. Blondes, cool as ice. She takes a call on her mobile, then she replenishes her lipstick. They don't even bother with the pretence of going shopping any more. They meet in the cafe, they drink tea, they gossip. Nothing more. It would be the kiss of death for both of them, they know that.

It's a fine line for Murphy. If he really went for it . . .

It's *When Harry Met Sally*.

Can you be friends with someone without fancying them?

Or stalking them?

Cool movie.

Great music.

Sometimes Murphy fancies himself as a kind of Irish Harry Connick Jnr.

It had to be you . . .

When his trousers have dried sufficiently, so that he no longer looks like he's splashed himself in the toilets, he enters the cafe his usual breezy self, despite the monstrous hangover drilling through his brain. But it's the morning after the night before for her as well, and despite the war paint she's sitting somewhat stooped over her table, trying to keep her head up, and to make things worse she's glaring at him through her shades as he takes his seat and pours himself a cup from the pot on the table. She's already eaten her full English breakfast; it hasn't helped her much, and its remains make Murphy feel even queasier.

'You were out of order last night,' she snaps almost immediately.

'I was pissed.'

'You were still out of order. What's it got to do with you who I'm involved with?'

'Nothing. Sure you're my sister.'

'And what's that supposed to mean?'

'We meet up like brother and sister.'

'We meet for a coffee before work.'

'Tea. And I'm sure Terry wouldn't look on it like that.'

'Terry's got nothing to do with it.'

'Yeah, sure. He'd cut our heads off and stick them on a pike.'

She stirs her tea. 'I just . . . although you're a total arse most of the time, I feel I can trust you.'

'Is that what you call a backhanded compliment?'

She smiles. 'I . . . don't know. I just . . . well, I can never really relax with Terry. And I'd rather stick needles in my eyes than confide in Mitch or Johnny.'

'Haven't you any proper friends?'

'Not who would understand this.'

'Fair point. What is it you want to confide?'

'Nothing . . . I mean, I can relax with you. We're mates, aren't we?'

'Is this leading up to something?'

She sits back a little. 'No. Of course not. We're just chatting.'

'What is it then? Guilty conscience about the heroin trade?'

'No, of course not. I just worry sometimes. About people getting killed. Like the other day. You went out of your way to stop anyone being killed. Terry would have been quite happy to blast them all.'

'Well, that's why he's a leader and I polish the car.'

'He is quite, quite ruthless.'

'Do you worry what'll happen when he dumps you for Noreen?'

'He won't dump me for Noreen, because there's nothing going on between us.'

'You want to be all friendly with me, but you won't admit the bleeding obvious.'

'It's not the bleeding obvious, that's why.'

'Fresh pot?' the waitress says, not in a kindly way, but with an accusatory look. They've been sitting over this one tiny teapot for too long.

'No thanks,' Annie says.

'Yes, we will, thanks,' says Murphy, and he pushes the dirty plate towards her as well.

'We'll be late.'

'So will they. Hangovers.'

'You don't know Terry like I do.'

'That's exactly what I've been saying.'

She sighs. The waitress lifts the plate and goes to fetch the pot.

'Can I ask you a personal question?' Murphy says.

'If I can ask you one.'

'Me? What have you got to ask me about?'

'Your girlfriend.'

'What girlfriend?'

'You're moving someone in, aren't you?'

'What?'

'Terry says there was a girl arrived at your apartment the other night with a suitcase.'

Murphy looks into his empty teacup. 'Is he watching me?'

Annie smiles. 'He watches everyone. From time to time. Like spot checks, you know.'

The waitress puts the fresh teapot on the table.

'So who is she, Mr Dark Horse?'

'Kate.'

'Kate?'

'Kate Moss.'

'Murphy.'

'None of your business.'

'Come on.'

'She's not my girlfriend. My ex-girlfriend. Just leaving some of my stuff back. She's away off out of the country somewhere now. New fella.'

'Yeah, Terry said there was someone. He followed them as far as Nottingham, do you know that? He's a bit obsessive that way.'

Murphy pours them both tea. 'What'd he think they were, Feds or something?'

'Some other gang, I think. I mean, we all have connections, don't we?'

Murphy shrugs.

'So,' she says, 'what did you want to ask me?'

'I've been dreaming about you.'

'What?'

'I don't mean on purpose. Just sometimes you dream about people you meet, you know, all this stuff you experience goes into your brain and then it all comes out in your dream, but usually all whacked around. At least, I think it's you in my dream, except I can't see your face. What do you think that means?'

'Apart from the fact that you're off your rocker?'

Murphy nods. 'I like analysing them. See if I can learn anything about myself.'

Annie laughs. 'Each onto their own.' Then adds more soberly, 'What am I doing in your dream? No, wait. What the hell am I asking? I don't want to know.'

'You're sunbathing.'

'Well, I'll be doing plenty of that once we make this deal.'

'I thought that might be the connection. But I'm still not entirely sure it's you. You're lying face down. But tell me this.'

He pauses and looks at her.

'Tell you what?'

'Do you have a butterfly tattoo on your arse?'

She bursts into laughter, a big loud guffaw which causes half the other customers to turn and look at her.

'Sorry,' she says, 'but mind your own fucking business.'

Murphy shrugs. 'Fair enough,' he says.

And then, not whim, not instinct, but with the clink of a penny dropping, he reaches across and takes off her sunglasses. She tries to stop him, but too late.

'Fuck,' he says, when he sees the state of her eye.

'I—'

'Walked into a door. Slipped on ice. Don't bullshit me.'

She sits, she shrugs.

'Tell me.'

'It's none of your business.'

But she's crying gently now.

'Please. I'll buy you a bun.'

She smiles through the tears.

'He was just drunk.'

'Terry.'

'No, the Bishop of Durham. Yes of course.'

'Christ.'

'Don't worry about it. It was just an accident.'

He raises an eyebrow.

'He was pissed, OK? He got a taxi home with me. I didn't want him to come in in that state, but he . . . he insisted, you know how he is. And then he tried to, and I wasn't having any of it, so he whacked me one.'

'And did he . . . ?'

'I Maced him.'

'You . . . Isn't that illegal?'

'A girl gotta protect herself, Murphy,' she says in faux Bronx. 'Bought it in the States. Didn't know what hit him. He was crying all over the carpet, couldn't see a thing. And I couldn't see a thing because of my eye, so it was the blind rapist leading the blind.'

'It's not funny,' Murphy says.

'Yes it is, in the cold light of day. It was terrifying at the time, but today . . .' She trails off, then sighs. 'OK. So maybe I'm putting a brave face on it. What should I do, run off to Women's Aid or something and forget about the money? I don't think so. He was very contrite when he sobered up.'

'Well, that's OK then.'

'Don't be sarcastic with me, Murphy.'

'Yeah, right.'

'When you drive with the devil, you have to accept that occasionally you get whiplash. And your time will come.'

Murphy blows air out of his cheeks. 'So you go back to work, like nothing happened.'

'Nothing did happen.'

'Most jobs, the boss tried something like that, they'd lock him up and throw away the key and give you about a squillion compensation and a medal.'

'Well, this is hardly most jobs, is it? Look, it's over. All I'm saying is, we're . . . mates . . . and I just don't think you realise how little he can be trusted. All of them, for that matter.'

'You think I'm not aware of that?'

'They're using you because they need a driver, but if you think they're going to divvy up an equal share . . .'

'That was the agreement.'

'Yeah, and that's worth the paper it's not written on.'

He nods quietly. 'And you think you'll get yours, if he doesn't beat you to death first?'

'He loves me, doesn't he?'

'Does he?'

She nods.

'Well, that's good,' Murphy says, 'because love conquers all.'

'What I'm saying, Martin, is that you have to know who you can trust.'

'You have to know which side your bread's buttered on.'

'Yes. Something like that.'

'Are you proposing an alliance?'

'I'm not proposing anything. I'm just saying, watch your back, or find someone who can.'

'I'll watch yours if you'll watch mine, is that it?'

She shrugs.

'Is it not "scratch", rather than "watch"?' he asks.

'Cats scratch,' Annie says.

'That's what I was thinking.'

She gives him a sarcastic smile, and replaces her sunglasses.

31

On the surface, he's calm as you like, but underneath, Murphy's jumping. Anytime now, he's sure of it. The diamonds are in place, what reason is there for any delay?

He's hanging around Fond Farewells so much even Hatcher says, 'You got no home to go to?'

'Sure I have,' Murphy says, laughing it off, 'but at least here I get to hang out with the stiffs.'

'The dearly departed, if you please.'

'Yeah, them as well.'

Nobody has mentioned Annie's eye in Hatcher's presence, even though it sticks out like a sore eye.

If she says she banged it, then she banged it.

'So,' Murphy says, 'did you see the state of Annie's eye?'

Hatcher doesn't even look up from his paperwork. 'What about it?'

'Nothing. Just looks like she took a whack on it. Banged it on a door, I don't think.'

'Murphy – is it any of your business?'

'Well, y'know, all for one, one for all. We're in the threatenin' trade, maybe we should threaten whoever done it.'

'Murphy, business is business, we're not running some sort of hit squad for the Samaritans.'

'I know, just she—'

'I'm sure she'll be touched by your concern. Now if you don't mind?'

Murphy shrugs and walks off.

When he does venture outside the undertakers, Murdoch pops up and hassles him. Where? When? Who? How much? How many? And all Murphy can say is be patient, any time soon, real soon. Murdoch says he can't keep men on high alert for ever and Murphy says why, are we running over budget? Bet they don't have budgets in the fucking Bermuda Triangle.

'"Golden Triangle",' Murdoch corrects, needlessly. Then adds: 'Excellent robbery, by the way.'

'Thank you.'

'Praise where praise is due. Handled it like a professional. It's in all the papers.'

'I know. I'm such a star. Soon I'll need a press agent.'

'And nobody much injured.'

'I used my influence. Like you said.'

'Boss is getting jittery, he's taking a pounding because the papers say this gang can just rob diamonds whenever they feel like it.'

'I always said we should stick to the diamonds. Not my idea to do the drugs. If he's wavering, he should make his fucking mind up. The longer I stay in there, the more dangerous it is.'

'He knows that and he appreciates what you're doing.'

'Well, that warms the cockles of my heart.'

'We will get them, Murphy, Hatcher and Fuji. Get them together. It will be like *The French Connection*.'

'Well, as long as I'm around for the sequel, that's all I ask.'

'You'll always be around, Murphy. More lives than a freakin' cat.'

Then Hatcher comes hurtling out of his office, bellowing, 'Murphy, let's go,' and for a moment Murphy thinks it's on and he hasn't had a chance to tip them off, but no, they're set for the Crook and Staff.

'Bit early for lunch,' Murphy says.

'Not if you're Hannibal the Cannibal,' Mitchell says, joining them on the stairs.

'Why, what's—'

'Just get the friggin' keys, Murphy.'

They race round to the Crook and Staff and it's barely open, but they're across the bar and up the stairs to Duffy's private office without pausing to enjoy the ambience.

Duffy's sitting with his feet up on the desk and the phone behind his ear, laughing with someone, a cigarette in his mouth with an inch of ash on it, which promptly dives off in fright as Hatcher storms through the door.

'Mr Hatcher—'

But Hatcher reaches across the desk and yanks Duffy out of his chair. He pulls him across the desk, throws him on the floor and kicks him hard.

'Hello? Hello?' comes distantly from the phone, which is now on the floor.

'Mr . . . Hatcher . . . I . . .'

Hatcher kneels beside him. 'You been ripping me off, you sleazy little cunt, ain't ya?'

'No—'

Hatcher aims a fist into the small of his back. Duffy flexes, yelps, coughs, spits. 'Mr Hatcher—'

'Don't fucking lie to me.'

'I wouldn't—'

'Shut up, I know you, I fucking employ you, don't you think I know when someone's got their hand in the fucking till?'

'I swear—'

He hits him again, same place, same strength, same reaction.

'I know you, you're an organised little fucker, so if you're creamin' it off, you've kept a fucking note of it. Now fucking show me.'

'I haven't—'

Hatcher twists, scans what's left on top of Duffy's desk, then lifts a heavy round paperweight, like a shell out of an ancient cannon.

'Fucking show me or by Christ I'll cave your skull in.'

He holds the shell above Duffy's face, so close that it looks ten times bigger than it is. Duffy moves his head a fraction, so that his own wide eyes can see the raw intensity of Hatcher's, can see the spit-flecked mouth and the flared nostrils, and he knows that if he wants to live he's going to have to tell the truth.

'In . . . the bottom drawer . . . inside the photo album . . . but Mr Hatcher, I swear to God, I would have paid it back . . . I just—'

'Shut the fuck up.'

Murphy moves behind the desk, opens the bottom drawer, and takes out a small photo album. He flicks through it. Family photos. Duffy with a wife and child. On a beach. He had no idea Duffy had a life beyond the bar. And at the back a small notebook, filled with figures. He passes it across to Hatcher.

'I . . . make it up from month to month . . . honest, Mr Hatcher . . . I just borrow a little—'

'One man's little,' Mitchell hisses from the door, 'is another man's . . . a lot.'

Hatcher shakes his head at his old chum, even grants the smallest smile, then he looks down at Duffy, crying and blubbering now about his family.

'Well,' Hatcher says, 'at least you told me.'

'I swear to God it won't happen again.'

'Well, as long as I have your word.'

Duffy doesn't get the sarcasm of it, he manages a hopeful smile, which is bad timing, because Hatcher plunges the paperweight down onto his teeth, shattering the top row and busting his jaw.

Duffy can't even scream properly because his mouth is full of teeth and blood, just manages a pathetic wail.

Hatcher sets the paperweight back on the desk.

Then he grabs Duffy by the collar, drags him out of the office along the floor, takes him to the top of the stairs, pulls him to his feet even though he's got no strength left in his legs. Then he hurls him down the stairs.

Duffy rolls and bounces, spraying blood all the way, then cracks off the banister near the bottom and lands in a heap.

Two cleaners stand looking at him, stunned.

Hatcher points a finger at them. 'And that's what happens to the next fucker who asks about a pension scheme.'

Mitchell laughs behind him.

'Let's go,' Hatcher says.

Murphy falls into step behind them, going down the stairs. He notes that Mitchell has lifted the gory paperweight off Duffy's desk and is wrapping it in a handkerchief.

When they reach the bottom, Hatcher rolls Duffy over with his foot. Duffy lets out a low groan and raises his hands to his face to protect himself from further damage.

'Whatever the money is, you have it paid back by Friday. And then you disappear off the face of the earth, do you understand? Otherwise you'll be needing more than a fucking dentist.'

His response is difficult to understand, but Hatcher seems satisfied. He kneels down, checks Duffy's pockets, then pulls out a set of keys. He turns to the nearest cleaner, a young Scottish guy called McMurdo Murphy's chatted to a couple of times. He tosses the keys to him, and he catches them against his chest.

'Here,' Hatcher says, 'you're the new manager. Get rid of this fucking scumbag.'

McMurdo's mouth drops a fraction in surprise, but his eyes light up. 'Right away, Mr Hatcher, sir,' he says.

Then Hatcher leads them out of the swing doors into the morning sunlight. Not more than five minutes have passed since they entered. He takes a deep breath of fresh air. 'Right,' he says, 'now I'm hungry.'

32

Mitchell throws the paperweight into the river on the drive back to Fond Farewells. Murphy curses silently to himself at the evidence going for a burton, and tots up everything they could have Hatcher for – the protection, the diamond heist, the attack on Duffy, the plastic coffins, conspiracy for a whole raft of things, but no, they're holding off for the heroin deal. Murphy wants to phone Murdoch and scream – 'Take him now, he's a fucking maniac!' but he knows what the response will be.

Patience.

There's a bigger picture now.

Yeah, like your promotion.

Local stuff doesn't mean anything any more, they've all got their eyes on the main prize, Hatcher and Murdoch both. He should just drive him now through the gates of the nearest police station, call a newspaper on the way and say here's your man, take him now before he damages anyone else.

He should, but he just drives.

'See his teeth?' Johnny says.

'Fucking amazing,' says Mitchell.

'Maybe they weren't his own. Maybe they were crowns. Maybe he'll be able to stick them back in.'

'Have to fucking find them first.'

'He always was a sleazy little git anyhow. Never did like him.'

'Wife's nice. You meet her? Looks like she needs some keeping. Maybe that's why he took it.'

'Maybe we should go see her. Duffy won't be kissin' her for a while, will he?'

'Or he'll be givin' her a real gummy one. A real suck face.'

They're laughing. Of course they are. All in a day's work. Only Hatcher remains poker-faced.

They go to an Italian restaurant. Hatcher's broody through the meal, sipping a glass of wine, while Murphy, Mitchell and Johnny consume a bottle each. It's on the house, of course. The waiter flits around them, offering exaggerated service; the sweaty-browed owner watches from the kitchen door. Even when Hatcher gets up to go to the toilet, the waiter faffs around him till eventually Hatcher snaps: 'Just leave me.'

'Look at them,' Mitchell says while he's gone. 'They'd kiss Terry's ring if he asked them.'

'Is that legal?' Johnny quips and the two of them dissolve into giggles.

'If I ever get that sucky,' Johnny says eventually, 'please shoot me.'

'Shoot Murphy, that's what he's like, always leachin' around Terry's arse. Aren't you, Paddy?'

'That's right, Mitch, just keeping it warm for you, till your wanking hand recovers.'

He can see the temper glowing in Mitchell's eyes, but Hatcher is coming back across the restaurant.

'Be warned,' Murphy says, 'if the owner's doing that much bowing and scraping out the front, he probably has the chef pissing in the soup out the back.'

Johnny laughs. 'No, they wouldn't,' he says.

'Oh yeah, you're sure?'

'I am actually. Because one time in this other restaurant the boss thought they were, and he took the soup away with him and had it tested. And they were. And they were on the boat back to fuck knows where by the end of the week, and the boss was the owner of a nice new restaurant. No one in these parts would dare try it again.'

Hatcher's taking his seat now. 'Johnny polishing my reputation, is he?'

Murphy nods. 'Well, he's polishing something.'

And they all laugh at that.

Hatcher spends the early afternoon doing paperwork in his office. Murphy lounges around. No burials today. Maybe trade is drying up. Maybe there's nobody left to bury because Hatcher's killed them all.

He stops in the doorway of Annie's office. 'How's the old eye?'

'Fine, thank you.' Very formal, barely looking up from her paperwork.

'Old days they used to put a steak against it. At least they did in *The Dandy*.'

'Before my time, Murphy.' And then she looks up properly and says, 'Can I help you with something?'

He glances behind him, back down the corridor, nothing moving, then says: 'My dream. You sunbathing. Is that the plan, to disappear permanently abroad, or just to take a sunshine break and then come back and take over the drug trade?'

'I don't know.'

'I thought you did strategy and forward planning.'

'Yes I do. And I don't know is another way of saying mind your own business.'

Murphy nods. 'I thought we were mates.'

'Whatever gave you that impression?'

He shakes his head. 'You're one foxy lady.'

She laughs. 'That's right, Mr Shaft.'

Then a call comes from the old people's home where they've stashed old man Hatcher, and suddenly it looks like he's on the way out for real this time. They go clattering out of the office together, burst through a group of newly bereaved just arriving to book a funeral, and out into the car park.

'Hang on,' Hatcher says to himself, 'hang on, Dad.'

Murphy drives at speed, Hatcher in the back, pulling at his tie, then drumming his fingers awkwardly on the side window.

'What did they say?' Murphy asks.

'That this might be it. God love him, he fights and he fights, maybe this time he'll let go.' He sighs. 'You have family, Murphy?'

'Wife. Ex-wife.'

'See much of her?'

'Nah. Well, I did for a while, but she's met some bloke, moved up north.'

Hatcher nods in the mirror. 'Sad.'

Always on guard, never sure whether it's a polite enquiry or an attempt to catch him out. He studies Hatcher in the mirror. Killer. Armed robber. Protection rackets and drugs. Not averse to hanging outside my apartment because he's paranoid about being betrayed. And yet on the verge of tears. Not so strange. Back home in Belfast they had a saying, that even terrorists go Christmas shopping. That it's a job, and when it's done for the day, you become a normal human being, you hire a video, you order a Chinese, you take your kids to school, you shed tears over the natural death of a loved one.

They pull into Sunshine Nursing Home and Hatcher's out of the car before it's properly stopped. Murphy follows close behind; they're met by a nurse, clearly familiar with the funeral director.

'Terry, it was all so sudden, like,' she says, but Hatcher's already past her, moving up the steps and down the corridor.

Murphy sticks with the nurse, allowing Hatcher his time.

'Only happened about an hour ago, one minute he was

right as rain, the next . . .' She's twittering on, making the natural mistake that Murphy actually cares whether Hatcher Snr stays or goes.

Halfway down there's an open door which Hatcher goes through. Murphy lingers in the corridor for a few minutes, not wanting to intrude. No – wanting desperately to intrude, but not wanting to come on like Inch High Private Eye. He leans against the wall, he strains to hear voices, someone says, 'I'm sorry for your troubles,' he gets a shock of static electricity off the carpet and then decides he's been polite enough and ventures into the doorway, fingering his tie awkwardly. His eyes go straight to the bed where the emaciated old man is lying in blue striped pyjamas, his eyes closed, his breathing shallow. A doctor is bending over him, listening to his chest. Hatcher's on one side of the bed already holding his father's yellowed claw of a hand, and on the other side of the bed, just looking up at the new arrivals is . . .

Father McBride.

Bloody hell.

Murphy's jaw has dropped, although not as far as McBride's.

'Marty?' the priest begins. 'What are you—'

'Father McMaster, isn't it?' Murphy cuts in, reclaiming control, keeping his eyes cool and his demeanour warm but respectful.

There's confusion sweeping across McBride's face.

'It was the karaoke, wasn't it?' Murphy continues. 'Nearly didn't recognise you with the uniform.'

'Ah – yes,' is all McBride can manage, but his eyes are darting about like he's stumbled into a dream.

They're saved by the doctor, moving away from the bed and placing a hand on Hatcher's shoulder. 'Perhaps if I could have a quiet word?'

Hatcher looks up, and it takes a moment for him to comprehend, then he nods, yes of course, pats his father's hand gently, then follows the doctor out of the room. The doctor pulls the door closed behind him and Murphy immediately hisses: 'What the fuck are you doing here?'

'Last rites. What the fuck are you doing here?' McBride spits back.

Murphy blows air out of his cheeks. 'Fine language for a priest.'

'Fine language in the presence of a priest.'

Murphy shakes his head. 'I've seen more presence in an alarm clock.'

McBride comes round to Murphy's side of the bed. 'Are you working? Did I give you away?'

'Of course I'm bloody working. And no, I don't think—'

The door opens again and Hatcher comes in, face pale. He sits again and takes his father's hand. He strokes it. There are tears rolling down his cheeks, but his voice doesn't falter. 'Dad,' he says, 'I'm here, I love you, but you can go now.'

33

Father McBride is standing at the top of the stairs when Murphy comes out of the room, leaving Hatcher to his final fond farewells. Murphy hurries down the corridor wondering whether Hatcher will go plastic for his dad. Somehow he doubts it. Plastic is for all the other poor suckers. Hatcher Snr will get the gangster equivalent of a royal funeral. There'll be a horse-drawn hearse, there'll be the old man's name spelled out in flowers, there'll be representatives of other crime families. The Godfather. Or the Grandfather.

McBride starts into, 'Sorry, Marty, I'd no idea.'

Murphy shakes his head and keeps walking down the stairs; McBride glances behind him and sees the nurse coming down the other end of the corridor. He smiles at her.

'How is he, Father?'

'Poor old fella,' McBride says. 'Not too long now.'

She nods and walks on. The sort of inane conversation he engages in every day. When what he really wants to say sometimes is: 'Mind your own beeswax, you cat-faced old hoor.' He doesn't though. He hurries instead down the stairs after Murphy and out into the car park. They stand and chat where they can't be seen from the Hatcher room.

'That was close, wasn't it?' McBride says all big-eyed with excitement.

'Yes it was, 'Murphy says coolly.

'So is it the old guy you're after or Terry?'

'Well, what do you think, Sherlock?'

'That's why you turned up at my church. You were watching Terry Hatcher.'

'Bingo.'

'What's he done?'

'Hazard a guess.'

'Well, he donates to all our charities and sponsors any events we have, so I presumed he was a hood of some description. But I've no idea what.'

'Well, maybe it's better that way.'

'No, come on, you have to tell me. Forewarned is forearmed.'

'That's a lot of shite. What you don't know won't hurt you, if you insist on dipping into the Penguin Book of Clichés.'

McBride sighs. 'Do you think he noticed?'

Murphy shakes his head. 'His dad's dying.'

'Is it insurance fraud?'

'No.'

'Is he selling body parts?'

'No.'

'Give us a clue.'

'No.'

'You're no fun.'

'That's right.'

'OK, OK,' McBride says finally. 'Your business.'

'Yes.'

'Is it tax evasion? VAT?'

'For Jesus' sake, give it a rest, eh?'

McBride gives a resigned grunt and looks back towards the nursing home. Murphy scuffs his shoes on the undulating gypsy tarmac. He needs to change the subject. There's only one direction to take. 'I never got the chance to say the other night. The wife had called to see me. Just before you, you know . . .'

'Oh. Right. Great. That's a good sign.'

'She's moving out of town.'

'That's not so good.'

'With her fella.'

'Oh dear.'

'Won't tell me where.'

'Sorry, Marty.'

Murphy nods to himself. After a while, and seeing as how his old friend isn't saying a bloody word, he says, 'Is that it?'

'Is that it what?'

'Is that the extent of your counselling? I was coming to you for help.'

'We're standing in a car park, I've someone dying on

me and you're on a stakeout, plus I didn't think you were speaking to me because of the tape. I'm really sorry about the tape.'

'Never worry about the tape. I'd been trying to get rid of it for years.'

'Really?'

'Kind of. You did it for me. Fate, or something. And it's not a stakeout.'

'You know what I mean.' He moves closer to Murphy now, manages a reassuring smile. 'Well . . . well . . . if you're really serious about the counselling I . . . well, we could do it properly, lying on a couch, soft lighting, relaxing music.'

'I want you to listen to me, not seduce me.'

McBride sighs. 'Maybe we know each other too well.'

'We haven't seen each other for years.'

'You haven't changed, Marty.'

'And neither have you. Although you've God on your side now.'

'I'm a Catholic, Marty. I always did have.'

Murphy laughs and shakes his head. 'I better . . .' and he nods back at the nursing home.

'Then give me a call and we'll get together. Do a few songs. Talk through the rest.'

Murphy nods and starts to move away.

McBride calls after him: 'You will give us a buzz, won't you?'

'Course I will.'

He's going up the steps when McBride calls: 'You'd need my phone number then.'

'I'm sure you're in the book.'

Murphy's gone. McBride stands watching the door for a moment, then follows him back into the nursing home. He's not entirely sure that he wants to know the inside of Murphy's head. Strangers, that's OK, he can be detached, but your friends, that could be dangerous.

Back in the room, Murphy says, 'Y'all right, boss? Anything I can do?'

'No. No thanks.' He's back holding his father's hand. Murphy stands there, awkwardly. Hatcher glances up. He's been doing some thinking. 'I . . . ah, sorry about what I said the other night. About Annie. It maybe came over like a threat.'

Murphy shrugs. 'Water off a duck's back.'

Hatcher manages a smile. 'She's just so . . . and I'm . . . just protective, you know. And you've done a good job since you arrived, and I shouldn't have . . .'

'Don't worry about it, Mr Hatcher.'

'Well. You know.' He looks down at his father, tears in his eyes. 'I'm going to stay with him until . . . well, the end. You go on, I'll give you a call if I need you.'

'If you're sure.' Hatcher nods. Murphy starts to turn, then stops. He nods down at the old man. 'He . . . well, he seems like a nice old guy.'

'Yeah. He is.'

'Might surprise us yet.'

Hatcher nods appreciatively. 'You never know.'

Murphy walks away down the corridor, fingers crossed that old man Hatcher will linger for a few more hours yet, because there's work to be done.

34

It's like an episode of *Scooby Doo*.

Wind howling outside, lightning crackling through the air, Murphy enters Fond Farewells through a side window. There's an alarm box on the wall, but Murphy clocked long ago that it was there just for show. Who's going to rob a funeral home? And who's going to rob one owned by Terry Hatcher?

He shivers. Different place entirely, in the dark, with just a small flashlight picking out the coffins in the showroom where he's made his entrance. The white one in the corner.

The white one in the corner.

The white one . . .

Walk on, Murphy, walk on, it's only wood.

With a gold cross.

And not real gold at that, not in Hatcher's world.

Nevertheless, he gets out of there as quickly as he can,

then moves up the stairs towards Hatcher's office, his own shadow jumping around him. There are paintings on the wall on the way up, austere old gentlemen staring down, and if he thought for one moment that they really were Terry Hatcher's antecedents he'd be watching closely to see if their eyes were following him, but he knows fine well that Hatcher has picked them up cheap in a junk shop to give Fond Farewells an air of tradition and history. He's actually heard Hatcher tell the newly bereaved that this was his grandfather, and this one was his great-great-grandfather who started the firm, and they believed him, because Hatcher can sell, whether it be faux history, plastic coffins or the idea that your wife is about to have her head ripped off if you don't hand over the diamonds.

Terry Hatcher – Diamond Geezer.

Sharp as one, but maybe not so smart that he remembers to change the security code to his office more than once a week, and with the way Murphy's been lingering close at hand, it's been no problem for him to pick up the sequence. It's not like it's Fort Knox or *Ocean's Eleven*. Five digits and he's in behind Hatcher's desk, switching on the computer. OK, he says, rubbing his hands happily as the screen lights up, let's play follow the money.

Enter Password.

Damn and Fearless Fred falls at the first.

It's not like climbing Everest then discovering you've no film in your camera.

But close enough.

He sighs and then begins to type, plucking wild guesses out of the ether and cursing himself for being technically illiterate. He should be able to hack into it. There must be classes.

Hatch.

Hatcher.

Undertaker.

Stiffs.

Stiffs R Us.

Fond Farewells.

Fond.

Farewells.

Drugs.

Diamonds.

Christ, he thinks, I'm more ET than IT.

And then somewhere in the distance, a door closes.

A draught.

A ghost.

A visitor.

Murphy quickly switches off the computer, kills the torch, then darts across the room to the door and peers out.

Another torch coming up the stairs.

Another burglar?

What are the chances of that?

A night watchman?

No, he would know.

He looks about him, panicking now, there's no way he can get out of the office and not be spotted. He moves back inside. Hatcher has a small private bathroom behind his desk. It's the only choice. He slips back across the floor of the office, aware of every creak now coming through the thin carpet from the tired wooden floor beneath. He's in the bathroom a fraction of a second before the office door opens.

He has the door open just an inch. A torch beam searches the room, then a figure moves across and pulls down a blind. A moment later Hatcher's desktop light goes on and almost immediately, his computer.

Annie.

Of all the funeral homes in all the world, you have to walk into mine.

Murphy's close enough behind her to acknowledge the paleness of her skin, the complete whiteness of her blouse collar, the silky sheen of her blonde hair, and when she moves a fraction he can see the screen and the fact that without a second thought she has typed SIX FEET UNDER into the computer and it's now up and running. In a few moments she's onto the internet and a soft Joanna Lumley voice is saying YOU HAVE MAIL far too loudly. Annie rapidly turns down the volume button, then glances about the room. She blows air out of her cheeks.

'Relax, girl, relax,' she whispers.

She scrolls through mail, and then: 'Bingo.' She smiles to herself. 'Location, location, location.' She reaches into her jacket pocket and removes a mobile phone. She dials and it's answered immediately. 'I have it,' she says, swivelling in the leather chair now, 'it's—'

She doesn't finish what she's saying because she's too

busy screaming at the sight of the insane illuminated face leering at her from the doorway behind her. She shoots back in the chair.

'Jesus Christ Al—'

'Hello, Annie,' Murphy says, the torch held under his chin, lighting his face like the Mad Woman of Shalott.

In the background Murphy can hear a woman's voice on the mobile phone saying: 'Are you OK? Are you all right?' in high-pitched tones.

'Suprise, surprise,' Murphy says, coming fully into the office.

She has a hand on her chest, trying to stop it exploding. 'Yes, yes,' she says to the phone. 'I'll . . . I'll . . . call you back.'

She tries to put the phone away, but with her eyes stuck on Murphy she misses her pocket at the first attempt, then fumbles around for a moment until she locates it. Murphy sits on the edge of the desk.

'Well,' he says, 'I'm pleased to see that the spirit of free enterprise is alive and well in the funeral home.'

'This . . . it's not how it looks.'

'Oh. Right.' He nods sagely. 'Then you weren't breaking into the boss's computer. You weren't studying his emails. You weren't passing on whatever you have to a third party. None of that is true.'

She looks at him coolly, starting to recover herself now. 'Did he send you?'

'What do you think?'

'You can't tell him this.'

He nods. He's in a position of power and he knows it.

'Can't. Won't. Shan't. Might. Could. Will. Either way you won't have much say in it.'

'I was just checking. I've been ripped off before. I have to be sure he's kosher.'

'You have to check that a murdering, drug dealing hold-up artist is kosher? Whatever happened to trust?'

She comes slowly up out of her seat. He has his arms folded and is trying unsuccessfully to keep in his smile.

'OK, Martin. You've made your point. What do you want?'

He shrugs, and she comes a little closer.

'If you try to seduce me,' he says, 'I'm warning you I . . . Oh hell, go for it.'

'I was thinking more of a share of the spoils.'

'Yeah. We could shake on it, then I'd be able to sleep easy. You watch my back, I'll watch yours. This is what you meant by it. Yes indeedy.' He comes off the edge of the desk and lifts the receiver off the phone. 'I think maybe Terry might be inter—'

'Don't,' she says simply.

And he stops because she's removed a gun from her jacket, and she's pointing it at him.

Annie get your gun.

'What're you going to do?' he asks. 'Stay up all night getting bloodstains out of the carpet?'

'No, Murphy, I'm not going to kill you.' With her free hand she lifts her mobile phone to her ear. 'I'm going to arrest you.'

He stares at her.

Keeps staring as she speaks to her phone. 'I need an unmarked car, I need it now.'

And he's winding his jaw back up from his shoes, and the smile has changed from one of superiority to one of stunned incredulity. 'You're the filth? You're a dirty, stinking undercover cop?'

He starts to laugh.

This is so ridiculous.

He's laughing and laughing and laughing, and she looks confused and worried.

'Yeah, it's very funny,' she says, 'very funny, Murphy. Be even funnier when you're inside.'

He's still laughing, he's slapping his knee, he's bent over double. 'You . . . don't understand . . .' he manages.

'I understand more than you think,' she says; and for the merest fraction of a second glances round at the sound of a car passing by outside.

But a fraction is long enough. Murphy suddenly straightens and his hand flashes out and a fist knocks the gun flying out of her hand; she lets out a surprised yelp and starts to move after it, but he's on her; he throws her back over the desk and she rolls off. He goes after her but she flips round and kicks him hard in the stomach. He goes *oooof* and starts to wilt but she makes the mistake of trying the same move twice, and this time when the foot comes flying out he's ready and grabs it and twists it, turning her whole body in the process so that she hits the carpet and he's on top of her, face to face, chest to chest, groin to groin, both breathing hard.

He moves one hand up to her neck, pins her down hard with the other.

His fingers close about her pearl-white throat.

'I could kill you now,' he hisses.

Her mouth opens a fraction, her eyes are panicked, every ounce of her training is telling her to fight for her life, but her heart is telling her to beg for it.

'It would give me the greatest pleasure,' Murphy says, bringing his mouth down right close to hers. 'But if I'm ever going to make inspector, it's probably best not to kill a colleague.'

He moves his hands off her, then rolls off, so that he's lying on the floor of the undertakers, laughing his socks off.

She lies there for several long moments, breathing hard, a million thoughts flashing through her mind at once. Eventually they all converge and come up with what is the only possible response under the circumstances.

'What?'

Murphy manages to kill the laughter for a moment. He shakes his head, then turns onto his side, propping himself up on his elbow as if they're lovers in some post-coital friendly jousting.

'Yup,' he says, 'someone somewhere has made a monumental . . .'

35

'. . . cock up!'

It's not quite so funny now, sitting on the eighth floor of cock-up central, Murdoch, Annie, Carter, Annie's boss Duggan and the big cheese himself Burgess, slugging it out for over an hour now, like Kilroy on a bad day.

'Murphy, keep the lang—' Murdoch is saying.

'No! Why the fuck should I! That's what it is. A fuck-up of monumental fucking . . .' He sighs. He shakes his head. He glares at Annie. Face it, he glares at everyone. 'I put my life on the line every second of every day with these scumbags, I live in their world and it . . . fucking poisons me. And all that time whatever evidence I was collecting was useless because she was compromising—'

'I didn't compromise anything!' Annie's on her feet, yelling back. 'You're the one . . . I've spent three months of my life working towards this.'

'Exactly! A couple of weeks and I've got more than—'

Her boss, Duggan, burly guy in a too-tight suit, rockets in with: 'He isn't even supposed to be working!' He waves a folder in the air. 'He failed his—'

Then Murdoch's up: 'Where did you get that!'

'Why, is it supposed to be a secret that he's—'

'Oh yeah, talk about secrets!' Murdoch shouts. 'Where the fucking hell did she—'

Burgess slams a book hard down onto his desk. 'Enough!' he orders. 'Please,' he adds and everyone falls silent, though the glares they exchange are intense enough to hurt. Burgess sighs. Silver-haired, smooth-talking veteran. He clasps his hands and tries to look encouraging. His teeth are pristine white and his skin smooth. 'This is indeed very unfortunate, a very unfortunate set of circumstances indeed. Not, I hasten to add,' and he looks at Annie first, and then across to Murphy, 'that they are any fault of your own.'

Now he gives Duggan and Murdoch a serious look and they avert their eyes.

'The fact that you are both undercover at the same time, for the same purpose, is nothing more than a catastrophic bureaucratic balls-up, a failure to communicate between departments.' He raises an eyebrow and forces a smile for Annie and Murphy. 'On the plus side, we may be on the verge not only of recovering millions of pounds worth of diamonds, but also of making one of the biggest drug hauls in recent history. The fact that we're so close to this is testament to your sterling good work and your ability to work undercover undetected and unsuspected. The obvious solution, I should think, therefore is to continue as before, independently if you wish, but with the added security of knowing that there's someone else on your side in there.'

They neither nod nor shake.

'Now,' Burgess says, 'when's the drop?'

Murphy gives a slight shake of his head. 'I haven't been able to . . .'

He sighs and picks up what looks like an invitation off Burgess's desk. He examines it as Annie says triumphantly, 'It's tomorrow night. I have location and I have time.'

Duggan is all smiles now.

Murphy fans himself with the invitation.

Burgess reaches across his desk and snaps it off him. He smiles at Annie. 'Excellent. Now then, let's get to work.'

Annie approaches the lift doors, presses a button. As she waits, Murphy comes up beside her. She stares straight ahead.

'So,' Murphy says, 'how about a drink?'

He doesn't mean it at all. It's almost dripping with sarcasm. They both feel foolish.

She looks at him, then rolls her eyes dismissively.

'I'll take the stairs,' she says. 'I could do with the exercise.'

As she turns away and he steps into the lift, he says, 'So I see.'

She hesitates for a moment, ready and able to fire something back, but then walks on. Murphy smirks and descends. As she's pushing through the door to the stairs she glances back up the corridor and sees Inspector Murdoch looking down it at her.

Annoyed by Murphy, she snaps, 'What?' at him.

Murdoch holds up a file. 'Come and have a look at Murphy's file,' he says. 'Everyone else has. You may as well know what you're up against.'

Sometimes you're better not knowing, and she thinks about turning down the invitation.

But only for a moment.

She walks up the corridor towards him. He stands to one side to allow her to enter his office. 'Right balls-up this is,' he says.

36

She stops at the wolf whistle, turns ready to fire dog's abuse at whoever it is, then sees him leaning up against the wall outside, smoking, giving her that look, the one she found so endearing at Fond Farewells but didn't even dare think about. She has hated him for the past six hours, refusing to talk to him because he nearly cocked up the whole operation, but she knows now that a lot of that was her own bad temper, her annoyance at being fooled and duped bubbling out. That and the knowledge that he removed her gun and flattened her with such complete ease. Made her look like a novice.

But he didn't tell them.

Didn't tell them, when he could so easily have, because he lost his temper as much as she did. But he didn't. He gave her that.

Maybe Burgess is right. Maybe nothing has changed except for her having an ally on the inside.

An ally with a flaky personality.

Harsh but true.

She feels desperately sorry for him, but not so much that she wants to put her own life at risk. One slip from Murphy, one flashback, one drunken ramble, it really could be the death of her. She could perform impeccably, but what difference would that make if Murphy suddenly threw a wobbler and plunged them both into the shit?

But she has to admit, he acted the part well. She never suspected for a moment.

They walk towards each other.

He's seen the look before. A hundred times back home, not so often over here.

Sympathy.

It is unlooked for and unappreciated.

Before she can say anything he says, 'Oh, somebody spill the beans, did they?'

Steady. Calm.

'Your boss thought it was a good idea to know what sort of a lunatic I was working with.' She means it good-humouredly, but doesn't earn anything more than a frown. Then she tries to be serious. 'Martin, I—'

But he cuts her off again. 'Been there, done that, let's move on.'

'I just want you to know—'

'That you're there for me if ever I need to talk?'

Deep breath. 'No. I just wanted you to know, that if you mess this up, no matter what Hatcher does, I'll shoot you myself.'

And he smiles finally at that and nods. 'Fair enough.'

'OK. Now you can buy me that drink.'

She leads off, not giving him any further say in the matter.

Except of course that he can walk off in the opposite direction. She turns her head ever so slightly – not so far that he'll think she's looking, but far enough to tell whether he's coming in her wake.

He's standing stock still.

It's a game.

They're in an eighteenth-century pub, built in the past five years. Parchment and quills in wooden frames, and a cigarette machine in the corner. The music in the background is 'The Only Way Is Up'. He knows the song but can't place the singer. Which is no bad thing.

'This feels different,' he says.

'What do you mean?'

'We used to meet up for coffee all the time and chat away. It seemed a lot more relaxed.'

'We were pumping each other for information.'

'It was more than that.'

'What are you saying?'

'That we hit it off.'

'We were acting. At least, I was acting.'

He laughs quietly to himself. He takes a drink. 'So,' he says, 'what's the story, morning glory?'

'My story?'

'Well, you seem to be up to speed on mine. Although I can fill in any grisly details you want.'

'That won't be necessary.' She takes a drink. Her eyes don't quite meet his.

'So what propelled you into the murky world of undercover work? Hollywood movies? An abiding affair with pulp fiction? Lover killed by an East End gang, you join the cops to gain revenge?'

'I just sort of fell into it.'

'Wonderful.'

'I can make something up if you want.'

'OK.'

'OK what?'

'Make something up.'

She looks at him and gives a half laugh, but he continues to look soberly at her. 'Seriously?'

He nods.

She thinks for a moment. 'Well, it's all down to sex, isn't it?'

'Meaning?'

'Well, it's like a constant thrill, but no batteries required. Actors must go around on a high all the time.'

'So you enjoy it?'

'Sex or undercover?'

'Both. Either.'

'Well, both can be pretty hard work right up to the climax, but it's usually worth it in the end.'

He smiles. He takes a drink. She has bought him Carlsberg, and she's drinking white wine. Robbie Williams is now playing on the eighteenth-century jukebox, and it reminds him that he hasn't so much as thought about a song for days and that he must get back to it or he never will be Robbie Williams. Or even Andy.

'So how'd you come by the Japanese?'

'Studied it at university.'

'Why?'

'Different. Interesting. Opportunity to travel.'

'So you must have known about the Fuji connection before you went under.'

'You're insinuating that I'm being used for my Japanese rather than my skills undercover?'

'I'm not insinuating anything. Don't be so touchy. Though I wouldn't have thought Japanese-speaking undercover cops are thick on the ground at Scotland Yard. Or indeed anywhere outside of Tokyo.'

'I can show you my CV if you want. If you don't think I'm up to it.'

'I've seen your CV.'

'What?'

'Murdoch believes in a level playing field.'

She nods thoughtfully, takes a drink. 'So why all the questions if you knew?'

'Just wanted to see if you'd deviate from it. But you were pretty straight. We all exaggerate our CVs. Tell you the truth, I didn't really arrest the Yorkshire Ripper.'

She shouldn't ask, but she can't help herself. 'So, go on then, what did you think of it. The old CV? Though I hasten to add I'm not looking for approval.'

He shrugs. 'Pretty good.'

'I have a better arrest record than you.'

'Let's not score points. Although I have more convictions.'

'I'd say mine were more difficult assignments.'

'Well, that's a matter of opinion.'

'You had no idea, did you?'

'Well, I thought you were far too attractive to be an undertaker. And I mean that in a strictly professional sense. They're usually all old bats, aren't they?'

He glances towards the bar, and she sees that he has blushed ever so slightly. And the sight of it makes her blush ever so slightly.

'It's harder for you,' Murphy says.

'What do you mean?'

'Because you're a woman.'

'Because—'

'I don't mean it like that. I mean, a nutter like Hatcher's pretty full of himself, thinks he can have any woman he wants. I mean, he's not going to come on to me; you got off lightly, getting a black eye. It could have been a hell of a lot worse. And it still could be.'

Annie shrugs. 'It goes with the territory, doesn't it?'

He nods vaguely.

'Why do you do this, Murphy? After what you've been through, wouldn't you be better off doing something else? You know, singing for one thing.'

'I'm not a singer. I mess about.'

'I thought you were pretty good. But I'm serious. Why put yourself through all this shit?'

'Because I want to make a difference, bring peace to the world – oh yes, and be crowned Miss Wyoming.' He shrugs. 'I don't enjoy it exactly. But it keeps me out of trouble.'

She smiles. 'Yeah, there's that.'

Murphy's mobile phone rings. He checks the number, raises an eyebrow. 'It's Hatcher,' he says. Before he answers he says: 'We can make this work.'

She nods. 'All for one, and one for all.'

He answers the phone. 'Murphy.'

Hatcher's voice is broken, full of tears and despair. 'He's gone.'

'I . . . I'm very sorry, Mr Hatcher. What can I—'

'We're bringing him back to the office now, doing it right, but there are arrangements to be made . . .' He sniffs up. 'Relatives to be . . . picked up.'

'I'll be right there, Mr Hatcher.'

'Thanks, Martin.'

Hatcher cuts the line. It's the first time he's called him Martin.

Murphy looks across at Annie. Her own mobile is now ringing. She checks the number, then nods across at him.

Before she answers he says quickly: 'One thing I have to know.'

She waits a moment, then her eyes grow cool. 'Don't you dare.'

'I need to know.'

'No I didn't fucking sleep with him, and I hate you for asking.' She answers the phone. 'Terry,' she purrs.

37

All the way over to Fond Farewells he's thinking about the surveillance photos Murdoch gave him of Hatcher in bed with his girlfriend. He hadn't doubted for one moment that it was Annie in the picture, even though her face was obscured. Even when he caught Noreen and Hatcher at the hotel he had presumed the boss was playing one off against the other. And at Hatcher's party, when he'd been trapped in his private office while Hatcher had it off on the bed, he hadn't doubted for a moment that it was Annie.

He's thinking about what he would do in the same situation. If he ever fell into a relationship with a beautiful woman he was trying to trap. Would he take the sex because it was on offer, then deny it afterwards? Would he fall for her and be tempted to switch sides? Most of all, would he ever reveal who he was and risk the consequences? He's thinking all of this, but he's also thinking about Annie without her clothes on, as he has done several times over the past few weeks. And how relieved he will be if it turns out she has never screwed Hatcher. And disappointed, in a way, if it turns out he's been having private fantasies about Noreen, who, though without doubt a beautiful woman in her own right, with a wonderful figure, does about as much for him as a fish in formaldehyde.

Butterfly.

The blonde's butterfly tattoo.

Only way to prove it, one way or the other.

He wonders how he will get to examine Annie's bum without making it an official request.

As he's approaching Fond Farewells he has another thought, about whether there'll be a sign hanging on the door saying Closed Due To A Death In The Family. He can hardly stop smiling, thinking about it.

In the car park he takes several long moments to compose himself, and then when he reaches the door and sees that there is a sign to that effect, he creases himself again. It's like having a restaurant closed for lunch.

The decomposing composer.

He re-composes himself.

He kicks his foot against the top step and hurts his toe. That does the trick.

Although the sign says closed, the door is open.

There is funeral music playing over the sound system, slightly louder than usual. A funeral home is supposed to feel empty, but Fond Farewells never does. It's far too commercial and busy for that, but today, for once, it does.

There's nobody about. The receptionist's desk is unoccupied. Murphy peers into the showroom, but it's empty as well. He walks on down the corridor towards what they call the 'private room' where relatives are allowed quiet time with their loved one. There is a small black curtain draped along one wall which is never disturbed but behind which the bereaved presume is a small window, but there isn't. It's a dartboard. Murphy knows this because he has played darts with Mitchell and Johnny, sometimes with a coffin in the room, once with an open coffin lying between them and the dartboard, and Mitchell pissing himself laughing as one of his darts rebounded off the board and landed in the neck of the late Mr William James.

But today the curtain is in place, and Hatcher is standing over a coffin. The lid is on, but not screwed down. Johnny stands beside him. They're both dressed in their funeral gear.

It's a busman's holiday, Murphy thinks, but decides not to raise the subject. Instead he stands in the doorway and when they don't notice he clears his throat and says, 'Sorry, Mr Hatcher . . . the traffic. I'm very sorry.' He comes into the room.

'So am I,' Hatcher says, without turning.

There's movement behind Murphy, and he glances back to see that Mitchell has appeared in the doorway.

Murphy says, 'Did he . . .'

'Suffer?' Hatcher nods to himself for several moments. 'Oh, he put up a mighty struggle.' He rests a hand on the coffin lid and traces the fine grain of the wood. No plastic for Daddy, Murphy thinks, only the best.

'When you're in this trade,' Hatcher says, 'it doesn't make your own death any easier. Occasionally, Murphy, we're called upon to exhume coffins – sometimes it's the police or the courts or the hospitals, but sometimes we have to dig them up. Do you know what my father found once? Scratch marks on the inside of the lid.'

Murphy isn't quite sure what to say.

'Urban myth, perhaps, but he swore to it.' Hatcher turns finally. 'Would you like to take a final look, Murphy, before we close it up?'

'No, no thanks.'

'You're not squeamish, are you?'

'No, just I . . .'

He's thinking of his son.

Of course he's thinking of his son.

He saw his son in his coffin, except it looked nothing like his son.

And now he doesn't want to look at an emaciated old man with the life sucked out of him and the innards drained and his holes stitched and cotton wool stuffed in his cheeks.

'Come on, Martin, you're an undertaker.'

'No, I'm a driver. Really.'

'No such thing,' Mitchell says, right up behind him now, and putting a gentle hand on his shoulder.

'Go on, Martin, take a gander,' Mitchell says, and suddenly Murphy knows, because one hood calling him Martin is worrying, but two is a conspiracy.

Murphy steps forward. 'I'm sure you've done a marvellous job,' he says.

Hatcher nods modestly, and Johnny slips back the lid of the coffin.

Murphy steels himself for a hundred things, but not for this.

Before he can look inside, Hatcher reaches into the open coffin, grabs the corpse and wrenches it up into a sitting position.

Except it's not old man Hatcher.

It's bloody and beaten and moving.

There's tape across its mouth.

It's his friend, Father McBride.

His eyes wide and terrified.

'Jesus!'

Murphy is totally thrown. He takes an involuntary step backwards, but is struck hard around the neck by Mitchell and sinks to his knees.

'I always knew you were fucking trouble, Paddy,' Mitchell rasps.

Murphy wants to curl up in a ball, to protect himself and to sleep. The back of his head aches while the front feels numb.

He has a final glimpse of McBride's urgent, pleading eyes, before Hatcher thrusts the priest back down into the coffin, then nods at Johnny, who replaces the lid and begins to screw it into place.

Everything is swimming.

'Like I said before,' Hatcher is saying, but his voice sounds like it's way down at the end of a corridor, 'my father's been to the brink more times than I can remember.'

Hatcher is looking beyond him, and Murphy turns his head a fraction. Old man Hatcher is sitting in a wheelchair, a plastic mask clamped to his face, sucking oxygen, but smiling down at Murphy.

'Y'all right, Dad?' Hatcher asks. His father raises a hand. 'Always had great hearing, my dad, all that time listening out for death's doorbell, and what does he hear but a traitor in the ranks.'

The old people's home, a moment of recognition between Murphy and the priest, but enough to end both their lives.

Murphy forces himself back into the picture.

He will not plead.

He will not deny.

'I hate to say something as clichéd as you won't get away with this, but you won't get away with this.'

There are laughs all round, even as Hatcher removes a gun from his jacket.

'The thing is, Martin,' Hatcher says, calmly raising the gun, 'you won't ever know.'

38

A hair's breadth from death, and then, 'No!'

Annie rushing through the door, alarm etched on her face like a graveyard inscription.

Saved by the belle.

Hatcher hesitates.

'Keep out of it, Annie. He's a cop.'

She looks staggered by this. Her face in Murphy's. 'Are you?'

'Well, that's a matter of opinion.'

Mitchell hits him hard in the stomach for his trouble and cheek, and when he gets back to his knees, still coughing his guts up, Annie smashes him hard across the face. No lady slap from her. He spits blood.

'You know, violence isn't always the—'

She punches him in the stomach. Her face is flushed, her eyes wide. She spits on him. 'Sorry I interrupted,' she says.

No, don't say that, Murphy thinks. Save me. Save me.

His last thoughts are charging through.

He wants them to be about his son, about the wonderful times they had, his wife, the happiness, but instead all he can manage is an angry realisation that Annie has gone over to the other side, that she's been fucking Hatcher, that she's letting him die so that she can make a million and disappear abroad or pull off the arrest and get promoted to . . .

Glory.

That's what they say when people die.

It's what Hatcher says when he's ripping people off with plastic coffins.

Promoted to glory.

Is this your glory, Murphy?

Is this it?

Murdered in an undertakers.

And taking your old friend with you.

He sees Hatcher raise the gun again.

Mitchell's evil smirk.

Annie's smile of triumph.

Hatcher's finger squeezing the trigger.

The Bontempi organ in the background. The Lord Is My Shepherd.

I Shall Not Want.

Old man Hatcher's rasping struggle for breath, six feet from a death rattle.

Death rattle and roll.

Write a song about this, you bastard.

The trigger moves.

It's goodbye from him, and it's goodbye from—

'Wait!'

It's Annie.

'For fuck's sake,' Mitchell moans, 'make up your fucking mind.'

Hatcher hesitates again. 'Annie?'

'If he's a cop, we can make this work for us.'

'Like fucking how?' Mitchell growls.

'Just shoot the bastard and let's get moving,' Johnny adds helpfully.

Hatcher blows air out of his cheeks. He glares at Annie. 'Let's just do it, Annie.'

'I know, I know, but if he's inside us and we get rid of him, then they're going to be all over us. Fuji will be scared off. I know this. He's nervous enough as it is. But if we keep him alive for a while, then we can control them, control the cops. Send them off on a wild-goose chase until the deal is done. Then we kill him.'

'Just shoot the fucker,' Johnny says.

Hatcher looks to Mitchell. 'Shoot him,' Mitchell says. 'He knows too much. We have the diamonds. We can do the drugs another time.'

'There won't be another time!' Annie shouts. 'Fuji needs reliability and security. We cancel, he's got neither and we look like bloody amateurs and the word will be out. We have to go with him now or never.'

'There'll be other deals,' Mitchell says, 'there always will be.'

'No there won't, not on this scale, not in this league. Terry, you've been waiting for this one for a long time, don't piss it away now by taking the easy option. If we've a dead cop on our hands, they'll be all over us. If we use him as misinformation then we can still do the deal, and get away with it.'

Hatcher shakes his head at Annie. 'Mitchell—'

'Mitchell just likes shooting people.'

Hatcher smiles and stops Mitchell with a raised palm. 'Can't argue with that, Mitch.' Then he looks down at Murphy, rubbing at his neck, avoiding eye contact, wondering if he should make a dive for Hatcher and hope for the best.

'I got it,' Johnny says, surprising everyone.

'You got what?' Hatcher says, not turning, not expecting anything as profound as:

'The priest. We bury the priest.'

Inspired, that's what Hatcher says it is. Johnny's all smiles, Mitchell's weighing it up, and Annie thinks it's convoluted and overly dramatic, but has to admit it has its attractions.

Hatcher asks Johnny to go over his idea again, mostly to see if he's capable of outlining the same battle plan twice without getting it back to front.

'We bury the fucking priest alive, right, we had a cancellation down Kilburn this morning, so we stick this fucker in the hole. There's about five or six hours' worth of air in one of those boxes.'

'How do you know there's five or six hours, Johnny?' Annie asks.

Johnny looks a little bashful. 'Well, there's bound to be. You screw the lid down, air gets trapped inside.'

Annie rolls her eyes, but Hatcher's nodding. 'He's right you know.'

Mitchell's nodding as well now, getting over his huff, getting excited. 'Remember we used to do experiments as kids. Rabbits, kittens, if it moved we buried it, see how long they'd last screwed down. Had a hamster lasted three days, though the little fuckers probably don't need as much as a fucking windbag priest.'

Hatcher drums his fingers on the coffin lid. 'So we bury him, then . . .'

'Then Murphy will do whatever we want until the deal's done. If he behaves hisself we tell him where the priest's buried.'

'And what about Murphy himself?'

'Oh, well, that's obvious, we shoot him for being a lying cunt. But this way he gets to save his friend.'

Hatcher nods to himself, then puts his arm round Johnny and gives him a good squeeze. 'Johnny, give a monkey long enough and he'll write himself *Hamlet*. You're a fucking star.'

Johnny's all smiles.

39

The priest knows death almost as well as the undertaker.

Increasingly, it's all he's required for. He's not an old man by any stretch of the imagination, but sometimes he feels like it. He had a calling and went into the Church, he had a vision on the road to Damascus, or more accurately stuck in traffic with a hangover outside Larne, Co. Antrim when he was only twenty-one. Murphy blamed it on a bad pint, but McBride knew better. He'd always been drawn to the Church, just couldn't admit it to his mates. But then he came out with it, and he lost his friends pretty soon after that.

Murphy was the only one who stayed with him, but then he was forced to dump Murphy because you couldn't be a priest and work in the kind of territories he was expected to work in and have a friend in the peelers.

It wasn't exactly church policy, but if you wanted to

have any sway at all with the community, you didn't have peelers for mates.

Just wouldn't have trusted you.

He didn't boot him out, exactly, just never had time to see him; get-togethers that were set up, he broke, or re-arranged, or forgot, until Murphy got the hint.

Must have been about the time Murphy was into Special Branch and he couldn't really hang about with civilians any more, too dangerous for him, too dangerous for the civilians. The cops had a kind of camaraderie of desperation, only trusting each other. A priest? Agents of the IRA, as far as they were concerned.

And then a couple of years had passed and he heard on the grapevine that Murphy was getting married, and the last thing he expected was an invitation. But in through the door it came one morning and he didn't quite know what to do about it. He sent back an acceptance, but thought he mightn't show up on the day, say he was sick or something.

Then out of the blue, the week before, Murphy phoned and said: 'I knew McBride when he used to rock 'n' roll.'

'Murphy?'

'The one and only. What're you doing tomorrow night?'

'I—'

'Good. You're organising my stag night.'

'I'm—'

'Meet you in Lavery's about six.'

'But.'

'Don't wear the priest outfit or you'll get lynched.'

'But—'

'Do you have a problem?'

'No . . . no . . . but we haven't spoken for—'

'So? Are you not my mate?'

'Yes. Of course. But—'

'See you at six.'

'Murphy, Murphy, I would love to . . . but won't there be . . .'

'A whole gang of my peeler mates ready to tear Belfast and a priest apart?'

'Something like that.'

'They're my colleagues, not my mates. You're my mate. Just you and me, kid. See you at six.'

And he was there the next night, dead on six, wearing jeans and a leather jacket, feeling like he was a teenager again, and Murphy was sitting at the bar already well-oiled. They had a great night. They talked about the music and the women and all the old gang and what had happened to them and they got on like a house on fire.

Then breaking with tradition – 'Stupid fucking tradition,' Murphy said – Murphy took him home to Lianne's house, three in the morning, the both of them blind drunk, because he said it was only right that the best man saw the bride before the wedding.

'Best man?'

'Course you're fucking best man, who the fuck else?'

This was turning into an embarrassment of riches, because McBride didn't really have any other close friends – and Lianne came downstairs furious, her hair in curlers and wearing a dressing gown buttoned up nearly to her ears and told them both to fuck off and they laughed themselves silly all the way back to Murphy's place.

Then the wedding, and there was only about half a dozen people there. Murphy's parents were gone, it was only relatives from Lianne's side. And it was great, it being small, so intimate and full of love, and everything went off without a hitch.

Murphy and Lianne were going off to Cyprus for their honeymoon and before they left he called round to see the happy couple. Lianne was fixing her face and he was laughing with Murphy about the stag night, and then he said something about, sure, give us a call as soon as you get back, and Murphy just looked at him and kind of nodded vaguely, but there was something else, like a mask had suddenly come down.

And now, lying in this coffin, waiting for death, he finally understands the meaning of the mask: it was the love of a good friend, it was a good friend saying, no, after this we won't see each other, because what I'm getting into it will be too dangerous for you to be seen with me. Belfast is too small a city for that. This is the end. This has been my way of saying, you were the best, I'm sorry we drifted apart, but let's remember the last few days as cracker fun, and go our separate ways.

A variation of we'll always have Paris.

It's so cold.

He's shivering all over, but he feels it in his feet and hands most. He wants to massage his feet, but they don't build coffins for movement. If they'd buried him in Ancient Egypt he would have had slaves to massage his feet, his coffin would have been as big as a football field.

This isn't Ancient Egypt.

But think positive.

Think of the sunlight.

Think of the air.

Ease your breathing, slow that racing heart.

Think good things, think of the greatness of God and why you entered the Church and what keeps you in it.

He loves christenings, but who bothers these days?

He loves weddings, but they all want to be married in castles by pop stars these days or with sand between their toes in Barbados.

He loves the Sunday service, but there's hardly any interest: he blames digital television, the Internet, gigantic Sunday newspapers and Homebase being open.

But when it comes to death, he's the most popular man in town.

He prays for their poor souls and really means it, just as he now prays for his own.

He has betrayed his friend, and now he will be punished for it.

They came for him in the middle of the night, banging on the front door of the parish house. He stumbled down the stairs, already buttoning himself into his priest's uniform because people don't call at that time of night to discuss the catechism. He opened the door and saw Hatcher's two guys and he prayed hard that it was the old man again, and sure enough that's what they said it was and he felt blessed relief but when he said he'd take his own car, they insisted on him going in theirs, and that's when he knew it wasn't the old man, but Murphy.

They took him to Fond Farewells and they beat him.

You don't beat a priest.

How can you beat a priest? An instrument of God.

He has never been good with pain, but for a long time he told them nothing, even though they had correctly guessed most of it.

But it got to the point where he couldn't take any more, and he gave up his friend.

And now they would both die.

If he hadn't heard their plan it would have been so much easier. There would have been a sensation of movement, darkness, panic of course, but he probably would not have guessed that they were about to bury him alive. Because people don't do that. Yes, he was in a coffin, but it was surely nothing more than a convenient hiding place. A means to transport him from one location to another until all the fuss and excitement was over.

But he had heard, and now he can feel himself being lowered into the ground and knows he will never again breathe God's fresh air.

He's inside a wooden box, so it's already dark, but it's getting darker. He can hear the soil landing on the coffin lid, a pitter-patter at first, then great torrents. Even worse, he can feel the soil vibrating through the wood, like a deaf man hears an orchestra and this one is playing the funeral march. The vibrations grow weaker then lighter and lighter as the layers of soil build up, numbing the sensation.

He has been praying nonstop, praying in his head because the filthy hanky taped across his mouth won't allow him to cry out loud for God's salvation.

Pitch black.

He screams, but no sound comes out.

It's cold.

The soil around him is full of rotting corpses.

Worms.

Please God, please God, please God.

Forgive me.

40

'What the fuck are you talking about?' Murdoch bellows down the phone.

'Don't shoot me, I'm only the piano teacher,' Murphy answers.

The boss is fuming. 'I'm sitting here with sixty-three men. We're ready to go.'

'Well, still be ready to go. Just go somewhere else.'

'You're absolutely certain?'

'No, I'm just taking a wild guess.'

'Murphy, this is—'

'I know what it is. They're nervous. It's a lot of dope. So they've changed the fucking venue. Now deal with it.'

Murphy cuts the line, then hands the phone back to Hatcher. He has just changed the location of the drop by some fifty miles. Hatcher came up with the location, an old quarry which won't have seen such action since it was used as a location for *Dr Who*.

Murdoch's boiling, he has to take the news to Duggan, and together they have to present it to Burgess. Burgess will just look at them benignly and tell them to do whatever they think is best. Because he's on to a winner whatever way it pans out: Duggan and Murdoch have already cocked up the op by keeping their undercover moves a secret, so if it all goes pear-shaped Burgess will blame them, and if it all goes swimmingly he'll claim the credit.

'I don't like it,' Duggan says.

'I don't give a flying fuck what you don't like. I'd trust Murphy with my life.'

'Well, you should think about insurance, because I think he's a halfwit.'

'Like I still give a fuck what you think.'

Duggan sighs and says, 'What're we going to do?'

'What choice do we have? We move three-quarters of our squad to the new location, we keep the other quarter back at the original point just in case.'

'We should call in back-up. Other agencies.'

'You're getting cold feet.'

'Yeah, they go with the fucking shivers I have down my back, because I don't like this one bit.'

'Like I give a . . .'

And it goes on like that for a while, but they're in the shit together and they know it, and they've no choice but to go with Murphy.

'Well done,' Hatcher says. 'Of course I'm not to know if you dropped in any code words or called him by a different name so he'd know something was up. And you might have a bug up your arse. You could be up to anything, but the fact of the matter is your priest friend is underground and you can be fucking certain that's where he's staying until this is done.'

'I understand that,' Murphy says. 'I'm co-operating.'

Mitchell, Johnny, Annie, they're all in Hatcher's office in Fond Farewells, getting their weapons together. It's a done deal, the diamonds and the drugs, but you have to go prepared.

Mitchell, satisfied that his gun is in order, then checks on a blade he keeps up his sleeve, flashing it in and out.

'Very Davy Crockett,' Murphy says. Then when the blade's at his throat he adds, 'That's a compliment.'

'Who the fuck is Davy Crockett?' Mitchell says, glancing back at Hatcher.

Hatcher's laughing. 'You never heard of Davy Crockett? Everyone's heard of Davy Crockett. Even Johnny.'

Johnny gives a thumbs up.

'Who the fuck was he then, smart arse?' Mitchell asks.

'John Wayne at the Alamo,' Johnny says.

'Ah, right.' Mitchell nods appreciatively, and removes the point of the blade from Murphy's throat, leaving only a pinprick of blood. Murphy wipes it away. In a movie he'd be tied up, but he's sitting there like one of the gang, because while his friend is underground, he is one of the gang.

Murphy says, 'Do you know how many ears Davy Crockett had?'

'What the fuck are you talking about?' Mitchell asks.

'How many ears did Davy Crockett have?'

Mitchell shakes his head.

'Two,' Johnny says.

'Three,' Murphy says.

'Whaddya mean three? Nobody has three.'

'Three,' Murphy repeats. 'A left ear, a right ear, and a wild front ear.'

Johnny's looking at him, repeating the answer silently. 'What the fuck are you talking about?'

Hatcher's laughing to himself in the background, Annie's grinning, Mitchell and Johnny are looking at each other, perplexed.

'Are you taking the piss?'

'No,' Murphy says, laughing. 'It's just a joke.'

'You're taking the piss. You think you're so fucking smart.'

'I don't, honest.'

Mitchell now has the knife back up again, same position, pressing it slightly harder. Hatcher looks across now, aware of how fast Mitchell can really lose it.

'Then what's the fucking joke?'

Annie comes up. 'Relax, Mitchell. Davy Crockett used to be known as the King of the Wild Frontier. Front Ear. Geddit?'

She punches Mitchell playfully on the arm, the arm that isn't holding the knife to Murphy's throat.

Mitchell thinks for a moment. 'Very fucking funny.'

'Yeah,' Annie says, 'he's a regular comedian. But then we knew that, we've all heard him sing.'

And that gets a laugh from all of them.

For he's been singing about the whole operation. Told them everything, or a version of everything. No name, rank and serial number for him. Spill the beans, stay alive, work out a way to sort this out.

Mitchell keeps the knife in place for a moment longer. 'You know, Paddy, what I really like about this job is the embalming. It's a real fucking science. But I've never practised on a live subject before.'

Murphy can't nod, or he'll cut his own throat, and he should shut up, but it's not in his nature. 'Yeah,' he says, 'I heard that about your wife.'

The fury springs into Mitchell's eyes, but before he can press home the knife, Hatcher shouts across. 'Mitch! No!'

Mitchell so wants to do it; he glares back at Hatcher, then reluctantly removes the knife. 'It's going to give me so much pleasure to fucking do you, Paddy.'

'It's not Paddy.'

Oh, he's so close to exploding again. Johnny pushes Mitchell away. 'Relax, mate. Here.' He thrusts a bag into his arms. 'Help me load up.'

He gives him another push, and they both walk towards the door of the office. Hatcher shakes his head and laughs to himself.

Murphy shouts after Mitchell: 'How many ears did Captain Kirk have?'

'Fuck off!' comes back from Johnny.

Hatcher lifts his own bag and walks past Murphy on his way to the door. 'You never know when to shut up, do you, Murphy?'

Murphy shrugs.

Hatcher laughs. 'You do what you have to do, just remember where your friend is.' He leaves the room. Annie listens as his footsteps on the stairs fade, then hurries across, the first time she's been able to speak to Murphy alone for over an hour.

'He's fucking dying out there,' Murphy hisses.

'I know, I know.'

'Call them.'

'I can't. It's too—'

'Fucking call them, Annie, this is just diamonds and drugs, but he's dying.'

'We'll all die if we—'

'Call them.'

There are footsteps on the stairs again, moving quickly, and as Johnny comes through looking for something he's forgotten, Annie slaps Murphy hard across the face.

'I fucking hate cops,' Annie says. 'And I especially hate pricks like you. Always a smart answer.' She glares into his face, not minding that she's spitting on him as she speaks. 'Well, I've news for you, Paddy. Comedy is easy. Dying is hard.'

'Actually, I think it's the other way round.'

Annie pulls her hand back to smack him again, but this time it's caught by Hatcher himself.

'Easy there, can't have him too banged up if he's going to drive us, can we?'

He lets go of her hand and she glares at Murphy.

'Prick,' Annie spits at Murphy then turns and tramps out of the office.

Hatcher grins down at him. 'How to win friends and influence people, eh, Murphy? When this is over it won't just be Mitchell wanting to shoot you. They'll be queueing up.' He tosses a set of keys into Murphy's hand. 'Let's go.'

Dear God, dear God, dear God, the priest is saying.

Never such a darkness, never such a need for His light.

It's punishment, isn't it, for almost having it off with the woman.

She was older, and widowed, and he offered a shoulder to cry on, but she wanted more than a shoulder, she wanted his whole jacket, shirt, vest and pants. And he was so tempted. In fact beyond tempted, they got as far as heavy petting, then he made his excuses and left.

No, in fact he made his excuses about suffering an orgasm before he'd even progressed from light petting to whatever else there might be.

Well, he said, there's a first time for everything.

And she started laughing at how pathetic he was and he gathered up his gear and ran for the hills, or sanctuary, swearing to God on his life that he would never break his vows again.

And he kept his promise for a whole week, and then he thought maybe they should try again and this time he would last longer, but when he went round to her house she didn't want to know; and he thought she was just embarrassed and guilty, but she'd get over that, but when he went back the next time she still didn't want to know; and the third time he went she called the cops and told them he was stalking her, and that's how the Bishop got involved and that's how he got transferred across the sea and far away.

An eye for an eye.

He's punishing me.

And He will let me moulder here because of it.

Forgive me, forgive me, forgive me.

Can you hear me?

Are you there?

ARE YOU THERE?

Murphy's in a people carrier in the garage, the doors up ready to go. Mitchell's behind him, Johnny beside Mitchell. Hatcher's in the front seat.

Mitchell peers back out of the vehicle. 'Bloody women,' he says.

Johnny laughs.

'What?' says Mitchell.

'She'll be late for her own funeral,' Johnny says and laughs again. Mitchell laughs as well.

'Whoever said comedy was easy?' Murphy says from behind the wheel.

Hatcher shakes his head, blows air out of his cheeks. He glances at his watch then pulls his door back and hurries across the garage and back into Fond Farewells.

He spots Annie at the end of the corridor, standing with her back to him, a mobile phone to her ear, and immediately he gets a nervous twinge in his stomach.

When he wants to he can move as quietly as a mouse.

He's up close behind her, close enough to smell her perfume, to hear her say: 'Come on, come on, answer the bloody thing.' And then clearly somebody does answer because she breathes a sigh of relief and says, 'Thank God, I thought—'

And in saying it she turns and finds Hatcher in her face. She lets out a frightened shout and cuts the line. 'Christ Almighty!' she shouts and holds a hand to her raging chest. 'Don't sneak up on me like that!'

But there's no smile from Hatcher. His cruel eyes are burning into her. His blood feels like ice. His throat has gone dry. He can feel pins and needles in the ends of his fingers. He's half inclined to just snap her neck now and not bother with excuses. She sees all of this on his grey face, the look of the dead.

'What?' she says quickly, defensively.

'Sounded urgent.'

'What do you mean?' She's blushing.

'Who were you talking to?'

She forces a laugh, at least he thinks it's forced. 'Oh, for God's sake.'

'Who were you talking to?'

'Terry, for God's sake . . .'

'Just tell me.'

'If you must know, I was talking to my mother.' He's not buying it. 'She's not been well. Just making sure she's—'

But before she can finish he's grabbed her hand and yanked the phone out of it.

'Terry!'

'Well, if it was your mother, I just press redial, don't I?'

She tries to grab the phone back, 'Terry, what's got into you?' But he's already spun away and pressed it. She makes another attempt to get it, but he shields it. She tuts and mutters an exasperated, 'Jesus Christ.'

Hatcher listens as the phone rings, then the receiver is lifted, and an elderly woman with a tremulous voice says, 'Annie, is that you, dear? What happ—'

Hatcher kills the line, stares at the phone for a moment, then shakes his head and hands it back to Annie. 'Sorry,' he says.

She glares at him angrily. 'What the hell is wrong with you?'

He shrugs.

'This is the biggest deal of your life, don't fuck it up now by jumping to wild conclusions.'

'You're right. I'm sorry. Murphy.'

She nods, understanding. 'Oh, come here, you,' she says, putting her arms round him. 'Don't turn paranoid on me just because of Murphy. Everything's going to be just fine.'

His head nestles on her shoulder for several moments, then abruptly he twists it up and kisses her properly for the first time. She allows her mouth to drop open and their tongues to meet. She runs her hand through his hair and he puts his hand on her breast and squeezes hard. She lets out a little excited exclamation and giggles. His other hand roams down her back then grips her bum. She moves off his lips and kisses his ear.

'What are you doing, checking for a wire?' she purrs.

He laughs.

She caresses his earlobe with her tongue. 'How come,' she whispers huskily, 'we never got this close before?'

'You wouldn't let me,' he says bluntly.

She laughs again, and this time his hand is up inside her skirt and trying to squeeze in between her legs. She kisses him again, hard, but won't open her legs. She giggles again.

Outside, Mitchell reaches forward across Murphy and blasts the horn.

For a fraction of a second Annie opens her legs.

He feels . . .

And then she sighs deeply and pulls away.

'We have to buy a tonne of drugs,' she says.

'And then we'll make love,' Hatcher says.

'Deal.'

They kiss once more and then hurry back down the corridor to the garage, Annie thanking Christ for good cover stories, back-up and somebody getting the horn.

41

They keep Murphy going with left and right instructions, meandering this way and that until everyone, including Mitchell, is satisfied that they're not being followed. Murphy keeps an eye on the mirror just in case he's misjudged the deeply concerned look he sees on Annie's face and she's somehow managed to alert Murdoch or Duggan or Burgess or whoever the hell is calling the shots. But evidently not. They drive out of the city, towards the coast.

Hatcher sits beside him, a small, unlocked briefcase on his knees, his hands spread palms down on top of it. Inside: millions of pounds worth of diamonds. When he gives directions, there's no fluff, just a tight: 'Left.' 'Hundred yards, left.' When Murphy turns the radio on, Hatcher turns it off. He's nervous. Who wouldn't be?

Murphy tries to concentrate on the road, but in staring into the darkness he keeps seeing McBride's battered face, the bulging, begging eyes.

He's way down deep.

Six hours' worth of air.

It is more than six hours since McBride was screwed down, but presuming air could still get into the casket while it was above ground, and adding Johnny's disappearance for nearly three hours to supervise the burial, Murphy reckons that it's still just possible that his old friend is alive.

He is not a natural optimist, but he has no choice.

He cannot bear to contemplate that his friend might be dead, or that it is his fault.

Six hours.

The natural pessimist inside him reminds him that six is an arbitrary figure, plucked from the air by a hood with an IQ of a woodlouse. There could just as easily have been thirty minutes of air inside the coffin once it was buried, and his priest is already dead.

Or three hours.

Or three hours thirty-six seconds.

Fuck!

'Keep your speed down, Murphy,' Hatcher says.

He eases his foot off and sighs.

He flips on the radio. Hatcher flips it off. He hums, one of his own tunes, until he catches Hatcher giving him the eye and he stops.

He is living the worst kind of country and western song.

Murder and destruction and no trace of a happy ending.

A death's-head ballad; Kenny Rogers could sing it.

They progress from motorway to slip road to dormitory town to a winding country lane. It grows darker still, there are no street lights now, and hardly any other traffic.

Unless Murdoch has recruited spy cows with night vision, they're on their own.

Hatcher seems to relax. He takes gum out of the dash and passes it back. He even gives Murphy a piece.

'Mmmm, Juicy Fruit,' Murphy says, even though it isn't. Then he says, 'Long Night's Journey Into Night. I wish this was fucking over.'

'Don't wish your life away, Murphy.'

Hatcher watches him in the dark for several moments. Then he speaks more quietly. 'I won't ask you any more about your work, Murphy, or what you have on me, I'm not really that interested. If you have it you have it, although your power to testify might be impaired. I'm more interested in the priest.'

'We went to school together.'

'Yes, I know that. I beat it out of him. I'm more interested in how you came to meet him here in London. He says it was chance.'

'It was chance.'

'What do you think the odds of that are?'

'About the same as you getting away with this.'

Hatcher smiles. 'Don't worry about me, Murphy, I'll be fine. It's all worked out.'

'Marbella?' Murphy says.

'I think not.'

'Give us a clue then.'

'No. He says you lost a kid.'

'What's that got to do with the price of fish?'

'It's interesting. Is that why you do this cloak and dagger stuff, to compensate for your loss?'

'No. I do it to catch fuckers like you.'

Hatcher nods appreciatively. 'Not Oscar Wilde exactly, but to the point.'

'Like you know Oscar Wilde.'

'Well, I know Marty Wilde, is that close enough?'

Murphy glances across, sees Hatcher's pale face staring ahead and down at the central road markings. He's talking too much. Adrenaline.

'Do you believe in God, Murphy?'

'No.'

'But your friend does.'

'Up until this afternoon, anyway.'

Hatcher nods, then lapses into his own thoughts again and for a while there is only the steady purr of the engine. The rear of the people carrier is in complete darkness, but for the glow of Johnny's cigarette.

No one speaks for five or six miles. Finally Mitchell says: 'So how many ears does Captain Kirk have?'

Murphy can't help himself. He laughs and slaps the wheel. 'Knew I'd get you.'

'How many?'

'Work it out yourself.'

'How many, Paddy?'

'Take a wild guess.'

'Tell me you fucker.'

'No chance.'

'You're a real fucker, Murphy. I'm going to fucking brain you when this is over.'

'OK,' Hatcher says, 'keep it down.'

'Then tell him to tell me.'

'What are you, three?' Hatcher says without looking back. He sighs. 'Tell him, Murphy.'

'No.'

'Murphy, just tell him.'

'Brush your teeth or Flash Gordon dies.'

'What?' Hatcher says.

'Cartoon I saw once. You don't get anywhere threatening people.'

They all think about that for a moment, and then burst into laughter.

'With certain exceptions,' Murphy adds belatedly.

They drive on for another five minutes, curving road, and then he starts to smell the sea in the air.

In the darkness Murphy says: 'A left ear. A right ear. And space, the final front ear.'

It is greeted with another twenty seconds of silence.

Then Mitchell says: 'Fucker.'

42

Hatcher is standing in front of the vehicle with Annie, staring into the darkness, waiting for a sign. It is 9.50 p.m. and the exchange is scheduled for 10 p.m. He doesn't know any different, but Annie tells him the Japanese are sticklers for detail. If they say ten, it'll be ten, no earlier, no later. His heart's really thumping now, biggest deal of his life, but also because he kissed her and had his hand in her pants.

This is love, he's sure of it.

Not just lust, like with Noreen – they've been going at it so long it's no longer lust even. Habit. A hobby. More fun than building model aeroplanes, but just as time-consuming. Noreen hasn't said a word, but he can read her like a children's book. That's how long he's known her. He thinks she thinks she'll dump Mitchell as soon as the big deal goes through and then they'll head off to the sun and spend the rest of their lives together in the lap of luxury. It'll be hard on Mitchell, but sure he'll have his share, won't he? You gotta be cruel to be kind.

She's dead wrong.

Noreen's beautiful all right, but she hasn't got that . . . thing that Annie has. He knew the first moment he met her. She was the new manager of a bar he was leaning on and when he led the team in to pick up the rent, she refused to hand it over. Normal service would have been to take her outside and give her a working over, but she not only talked him out of it, she talked him into reducing it – of course she didn't explain it like that, but that's how it worked out, index-linked protection money.

What a chancer.

And then when it came time to pick up the next payment, he went himself, and they went out for lunch and he said what's a bright girl like you doing working in a bar, and she said how does a smart guy like you get his kicks burying stiffs? So he said he was more ambitious and she said so was she, and next thing she's working for him, not only organising the business, profits up already by fifteen per cent on the year, but also organising The Business. Nothing he hadn't planned already, of course, he's the mastermind, but she's smoothed out his rough edges, oiled the wheels; what would a guy like him have to say to Johnny Jappo after the niceties were out of the way? But Annie, she chats away like a native and they just love her and trust her.

They're planning big things together.

Of course she doesn't know it yet.

He's planning on her behalf.

Treat her like a lady, like his mum, although of course not like his mum.

Sex with Annie is going to be fantastic.

Electric.

They'll light up North London.

No – they'll light up North America.

He has a place organised in Florida. False names, business cover, extended visa stay. Just need to pop across the border into Mexico once in a while, get the visa renewed. He knows a guy does passports. He knows guys who do most things.

He has sworn to himself there'll be no more drug deals. Too complicated. Too much out of his control. Banks or diamonds, you can just walk in with a double-barrelled and say 'Give me the fucking money!' But all this messing around – no, not now that he's kissed her.

Get this one sewn up first though. Be set up for life.

He glances back at the van and a little shiver runs through him. Murphy. He should have guessed. Everything about him was so convenient. Turning up like that, guitar in hand like he was in an Elvis movie. Wheedling his way in. Always smiling. No wonder he was smiling! But they got him in the end. And now they'll kill him and bury him the way only an undertaker can.

'Cold?' Annie says.

Hatcher shakes his head. 'Excited.'

'I noticed that earlier.'

He smiles. He peers into the mist again. 'Come on,' he says. He shakes his head impatiently. 'Misty night. Four million in diamonds. Ten million in heroin. Four shotguns. Oriental gangsters, a blonde and an undercover cop. Climax or anti-climax.'

'Oh, I much prefer climax.'

He should just grab her now. 'You know,' he says instead, 'if you asked me to drive away with you now – you know, open an . . . antique shop or something in . . . Peckham, I would.'

Annie keeps her eyes on the mist. 'I know,' she says quietly.

'But if I asked you to drive away with me now, open an antique shop in Peckham, you'd tell me to get lost. Wouldn't you?'

'Treat 'em mean, keep 'em keen.'

'I can see living with you is really gonna keep me on my toes.'

'You're putting the cart before the horse, aren't you?'

But she says it in such a way . . . just such a way.

They're going to be magic.

Back in the people carrier, the boys are getting restless. Murphy has had no choice but to put McBride out of his mind. Nothing he can do but stay alive, and look for an opening. It will come, he's sure of it. Their minds are focused on the deal. They're out here in the middle of nowhere, not on home turf now. They're jumpy all right. Jumpy enough for him to wind them up.

He nods ahead at Hatcher and Annie. 'Awww,' he says, 'would you look at them. They're just like Bonnie and Clyde.' Then he holds up an actorly finger. 'Ooops! Bad example.'

Mitchell, his gun out and resting across his lap, smoking

hard, flicking butts out of the half-open people carrier door, already half a dozen of them lying there in the damp grass, merely tuts.

'So, Mitch,' Murphy continues, 'what does the wife say about all these late nights?'

Mitchell isn't in the form for Irish banter. He lifts up the gun and turns it round until the barrel is resting against Murphy's cheek. 'Just remember, Action Man,' he hisses, 'Father Brown is six feet under.'

'It's not Father Brown,' Murphy says, his voice slightly distorted by the cool metal pressing into him. He smells oil and smoke and death.

Johnny glances across, his door open as well, a similar spread of cigarette butts below. 'Relax, Mitch,' he says.

'I'll relax when this fucking thing's over,' Mitchell growls, 'and I'm burying fucking motormouth.' He gives Murphy a prod with the gun, then drops it back down onto his lap.

And then they're coming, out of the mist, but not from the sea like they'd expected, but a minivan and a sleek looking Renault coming down the single road behind them, stopping a hundred yards back and parking sideways, blocking the road and any chance of a getaway on any terms but their own.

Hatcher's armed, but it's beneath him to produce it yet. Instead Johnny comes up behind him, unzipping a bag and producing a machine pistol. Murphy, pushed up beside him by Mitchell, has only really ever seen one like it in movies. Mitchell relies on his trusty double-barrelled shotgun. Probably he has spare ammunition secreted about his body.

Not that he will need it.

Hatcher knows what he's doing.

And Mitchell takes his orders from no one else.

They grew up together.

Lifelong friends.

There are eight young Japanese men coming down the slight incline towards them. Three in front, then Han, then four behind. Only the four at the back are carrying weapons openly.

Annie turns away slightly, feels in her jacket pocket for the gun Hatcher gave her. Safe and sound. Hatcher nods approvingly at her, then returns his attention to the approaching Japanese.

The doors of the second vehicle have opened now, and Fuji begins to walk down towards them, flanked by a bodyguard on either side. A third man gets out, opens the boot and lifts out a leather suitcase. He wheels it down behind Fuji.

Twelve Japanese.

Hatcher doesn't like this balance at all. Everything is agreed, everything is organised, but still he doesn't like the fact that there are twelve of them, and only four on his side. He wants to remove his gun now, give it one last check, let it hang by his side so that they know he means business. But no. He won't. Not yet. Show them he's the boss. He doesn't see Fuji packing one. That's the way to do it. Show leadership.

Annie glances at Murphy. He's saying it with his eyes:

what're you going to do, comrade? The ball's in your court. She looks away. She sees Hatcher's briefcase, filled with the diamonds, at his feet. She should pick it up and run away with it, disappear into the mist.

That's what she would do, if she was twelve.

But now that she's older, she must gamble.

Gamble with McBride's life, with Murphy's, with her own.

Han is approaching now, smiling at her. He stops maybe ten metres away. She steps forward, extending her hand. She speaks in fluent Japanese. 'Han, how are you?'

'Very well, Annie.'

'You came by road. We thought you were coming by sea.'

He smiles again and gives a little shrug. 'I am not a good sailor.'

'What're you saying?' Hatcher hisses from behind.

'Just the formalities,' Annie shoots back, not letting her smile falter for one moment.

Murphy's tensed and ready for he doesn't know what. They're in a narrow car park, accessed by a single road, which is blocked at one end by the drug suppliers' vehicle. Behind him is Hatcher's people carrier, then a sloping manmade grass bank down to a beach and the sea beyond. He can see the first few yards of a jetty thrusting out into the sea, but the rest is lost in the mist; he has no way of telling if there are any boats tied up there. To the left of the car park there is a picnic area with several tables, to the right scrubby bushes leading up the hill to a bank of pine trees, which grow thickly on either side of the road.

Han moves to one side as his father approaches. Annie nods back and Hatcher steps forward with the briefcase. There are now four of them standing in the middle of the car park, the scene illuminated by the lights of the people carrier.

In English Han says to Hatcher: 'May I introduce my father.'

Hatcher extends his hand. They shake. Fuji's hair is grey, cropped short; he does not smile as he grasps Hatcher's hand firmly. He's wearing a heavy beige coat, a red scarf, a white shirt and grey tie. Hatcher doesn't think he looks like a man who normally gets his hands dirty, or perhaps he just likes to give that impression.

If he's so hot, Murphy thinks, watching the little group in the middle of no-man's land, what's he doing dealing with a hood like Hatcher?

Annie says in Japanese: 'You have brought your gifts?'

Fuji turns and nods back at the man with the case. He trundles it forward over the tarmac.

'And the diamonds,' Fuji says, 'you have brought them also?'

'Yes, of course.' Annie turns to Hatcher. 'The diamonds,' she says.

Hatcher nods. 'You sure?'

'I'm sure.'

Hatcher picks up the briefcase from his feet, then hands it to Annie. She lets it drop to her side. She nods at Fuji. He nods back.

It's time.

'May I speak honestly?' she says in Japanese.

'Yes, of course.'

'What are you saying?' Hatcher hisses.

'Shhh. It just a ritual thing.'

'Just get on with it.'

She smiles and nods at Hatcher like it's a compliment, then says to Fuji in his own language, 'Please do not react immediately to what I am going to tell you.'

There is no reaction at all.

'Get the drugs, and let's get out of here,' Hatcher whispers.

'The diamonds are fake.'

Not even a flicker.

'He would rip me off?' Fuji asks.

'I did not know until it was too late. I negotiated in good faith. I would not see you betrayed.'

Fuji nods slowly now.

'What are you saying?' Hatcher demands out of the corner of his mouth.

'Hush!' Annie snaps.

Johnny and Mitchell are worried. They haven't been watching the deal, they've been watching the back-up, and they've seen a shift.

'Hatch,' Johnny hisses forward, 'what's—'

'Shhhhh,' Hatcher snaps back.

'You are very brave, Annie,' Fuji says, 'and I aspire to your high ideals. Unfortunately our heroin is dirty, low-grade stuff we couldn't sell elsewhere. It seems we have attempted to rip each other off.'

'So what do we do?'

'At times like this,' Fuji says, not ruffled at all, 'it is traditional to resort to gunfire.'

Annie nods.

'Please remove yourself,' Fuji says.

Annie nods again, gives the slightest bow. She lets the case of diamonds slip to the ground, then turns abruptly and begins to walk back towards the people carrier.

For a moment Hatcher is too stunned to even try and stop her. 'Annie?' he manages.

'It's a set-up.'

He would love more than anything for time to stand still, to have time to be able to think that one through, the whys and the wherefores and to understand that no, that's not possible, nobody would go to this much trouble – a thousand thoughts but time for only one.

Gun.

In a second everyone knows the game, and it's no game.

They're moving left, right, backwards, forward, guns out, guns blazing.

Hatcher grabs up the diamonds and pulls out his gun in one movement. Fuji is pushed to one side by Han who kicks out at Hatcher even as he goes for his own gun. The foot connects, but as Hatcher goes down he shoots Han in the belly. The young Japanese doesn't make a sound as he collapses down on top of Hatcher.

As Mitchell raises his gun to fire, Murphy drags back an elbow and winds him long enough to turn and dive to his right. Mitchell is hardly fazed, because Murphy's the least of his worries now, bullets are cracking off the tarmac all around him as the Japanese rush forward to protect their boss.

Johnny's got his machine pistol up like a pro.

Fuji lets out a cry and tries to pull his son off Hatcher, but a bullet spins him round. He clutches at his arm, then he's pulled away by members of his gang. Hatcher throws Han off him and scrambles back towards the people carrier as bullets chew up the tarmac all around him.

'Shoot the fuckers!' he screams as he dives behind the vehicle. Annie's already there, her gun out. She starts to raise her head, but Hatcher thrusts it down again. 'No, Annie,' he shouts, then raises his own hand above the bonnet and fires blindly.

They duck down again as a more sustained and concentrated burst of gunfire comes from the Japanese, who are now backing up the hill towards their own vehicles. The people carrier is peppered. Murphy's trying to make it as far as the bushes, but he's pinned down by gunfire from both sides in a slight dip between the road and the stretch of grass.

Annie has her eyes closed tight as holes are punched out of the vehicle above her and the ground around her. Then's there a crack of glass and the lights of the vehicle explode and suddenly everything is plunged into darkness.

Johnny takes advantage of it to stand and spray bullets up the incline towards the Japanese.

They return fire with enthusiasm, and then some.

Mitchell reloads, jumps up, shoots off both barrels, then

tries to drag Johnny back in, but he's having none of it, he's having the time of his—

Johnny drops, clutching his chest.

'Johnny!' Mitchell cries and dives towards him. 'Johnny.'

'Mitch,' Hatcher shouts, 'leave him, concentrate!'

Hatcher stands and shoots into the darkness. Everything has gone pear-shaped, from mover and shaker to arse who got sideswiped, but at least he can stand and shoot at the fuckers. He's out from behind the vehicle now. 'Come on, you bastards!' and Mitch is at his side reloading as he walks.

Engines starting.

The Japanese are scrambling back into their vehicles.

Running under the cover of darkness.

Hatcher reloads. He keeps firing. 'Run, you fuckers!' he screams.

The Japanese are reversing, trying to do three-point turns, obstructing each other on a narrow road with two gunmen bearing down on them. They've crowded back inside, half of them wounded and bleeding and it's too dangerous to raise their own guns now and fire back, they're screaming and shouting at each other as Hatcher and Mitchell draw nearer.

Then the Renault spins its tyres as it straightens and roars away.

A moment later the minivan follows suit.

Even as it goes, its back windows explode and there are more screams from within.

Hatcher and Mitchell keep shooting after it.

They're more or less level with where Murphy is lying.

He sees Han's body just behind them. There's a gun about a metre further back. He keeps his head down, pressed into the grass, his fingers grinding into the chalky soil.

'Terry!' Annie calls.

Hatcher stops, looks back to the people carrier.

'Terry!' Annie calls, more emphatically.

Hatcher turns. Murphy bites the dirt.

Hatcher hurries back behind the people carrier to find Johnny choking on his own blood. Annie's cradling him in her lap; her top, her skirt soaked in blood.

43

Darkness, complete and absolute.

Father McBride has his eyes open, but they might as well be closed.

He has witnessed many deaths in his time, and imagined many more, because when you see it all the time you dream about it, you nightmare about it, but never like this.

Never like this.

This is horror.

He is shivering. And each time the wooden casket gives a little creak, his body gives an involuntary shudder.

He's so scared. He has prayed and prayed but he knows that salvation will not come. God is too busy. There will be better times in the next world, but he wishes God would hurry up and claim him.

The bodies he has seen. Sometimes it's the police or

the social services, they call him in when they've discovered a body, usually some friendless old dear who has lain mouldering in her rancid apartment for six months without anyone noticing.

Stench.

Maggots and flies, maggots and flies.

They're inside him now. Waiting to break out. Just waiting for the signal.

He has no idea how much air is left.

He started out with shallow breaths, trying to conserve it.

Then he thought, no, big deep breaths, let's get this over with.

But now he feels as if he's been underground for days, knocking on death's door but there's nobody in.

He wants to die.

He wants to be promoted to glory.

Dear God in heaven release me.

And then the wood creaks again and he cries out.

It's just the wood.

It's not really the dead all around him, scraping away, trying to get in.

It's not.

It couldn't be.

Dear God in heaven.

44

Johnny's eyes are wide and scared, but even now he won't give in to it. 'Did you . . . get the fuckers?'

'We got them, Johnny,' Hatcher says, going down on his knees beside him.

Murphy scrambles up the bank and across the tarmac towards Han's gun.

He's just reaching down for it, every intention of continuing on and ducking down over the opposite bank, then following it back up to the people carrier and surprising Hatcher when a boot comes down on his hand and he's whacked with something hard round the back of the head.

He is vaguely aware of Mitchell laughing. 'Knew you wouldn't be far, Paddy,' he says, and then drags him to his feet. He marches him back to the vehicle; Murphy can feel blood trickling down the back of his neck. He sees Hatcher looking distraught, Annie stroking Johnny's head.

Mitchell looks down at Johnny. 'Aw, Jesus,' he says.

Johnny manages a bubbly laugh. 'S'only a scratch,' he whispers.

'That's the spirit, Johnny,' Hatcher says. Then to Annie: 'We have to get him out of here.'

She shakes her head. He won't last the trip to the people carrier.

Mitchell doesn't want to look at his best mate dying. He glares at Annie. 'What happened? What did you say to them?'

'I didn't say anything! They were trying to rip us off. I saved you your fucking diamonds.'

'The . . .' Hatcher stands suddenly, panicked because he's lost track of them. 'Where the . . .' and he's looking around him.

'Hatch?' Mitchell begins.

'Shhhh.'

'Have they fucking taken them?'

'No!' Hatcher shouts. 'Of course they fucking haven't! Annie, you—'

'I gave them to you, you must . . . they must be here.' She's looking around her in the darkness, though she can hardly move with Johnny's head in her lap. 'They must be . . .'

And she strains to look under the vehicle.

Hatcher gets down on his knees and peers under. 'Christ,' he says.

He can't remember, he can't fucking remember.

Annie glances across at Murphy, rubbing at the back of his neck. She gives the slightest nod.

'Diamonds, is it?' Murphy says. 'Brown briefcase.'

Hatcher eases back up onto his feet. 'What the fuck are you saying, Murphy?'

'Well, I didn't want them to get damaged, y'know. Thought I was doing you a favour.'

'He's fucking lying—'

'I hid them under a bush.'

Mitchell has his shotgun up, and Murphy can only presume he's reloaded it. 'Where are they, Paddy?'

'Like I say, under a bush.'

'Which fucking bush?'

'They all look the same in the dark.'

He strikes Murphy once across the face with the barrel of the gun and he stumbles back. Mitchell moves with him. 'Hatch?'

Hatcher's shaking his head. 'He couldn't . . . Fuck! Where are they? Annie, didn't you—'

'I was trying to stop Johnny from dying.'

'Am I dying?' Johnny whispers.

'Shhhh, no, you're OK.' She looks despairingly at Hatcher. She has her gun in her jacket, but Johnny's head is restricting her access to it. What was she thinking of, going to help him? The diamonds are only a couple of yards away, she saw Hatcher put them down, but without light they could be blundering around all night looking for them.

'We have to get out of here,' Hatcher is saying.

He looks at his watch. He glances back up the road. The mist is lifting. The moon is breaking through, lightening the dead blackness of the night. Off to the left there are pinpricks of light now – farmhouses. They'll be wondering about the gunfire. The curious will be coming down soon, quickly followed by the police. 'We have to get the fuck out of here,' he says again.

Mitchell hits Murphy with the gun again, and this time he goes down. 'Let me just plug him, Hatch,' he says.

'The fucking diamonds.'

'There'll be other diamonds, and there'll be other deals.'

'There's three million in—'

'We can do it once, we can do it again, Hatch. Stick to fucking diamonds next time, no fucking Japs.'

'Terry,' Annie says, 'make up your mind!' She looks down at Johnny, he's fighting for his breath.

'What's it to be, Terry?' Murphy mimics, rolling onto his back and half sitting up.

Mitchell raises his gun, ready to fire.

Hatcher nods. 'Do him.'

Mitchell smiles, his finger begins to squeeze the trigger.

Murphy's back on his dying thoughts again.

It's getting to be a habit.

But this time it's God.

Yes, God.

Big help, you've been.

McBride in his casket.

At least this will be quick.

A double-barrelled shotgun from close range.

They'll be picking bits of him out of the bushes for weeks.

But again he's cheated in the end, because his last thought is about what he sees.

Mitchell's smile.

Murphy closes his eyes.

He doesn't want his last thought to be Mitchell's smile. But somehow it lingers.

He smells the sea air.

'Any last requests, Paddy?'

'Miss.'

One last breath, and—

'Mitch,' Hatcher says quietly, and in the fraction of a second before he has completely squeezed the trigger, Mitchell hesitates. He eases his finger off the trigger – because accidents can happen – and glances back at his boss. But he keeps the gun trained and he can plug Murphy in an instant.

'What the fuck are you doing?' Mitchell spits.

His surprised reaction is enough for Murphy to open his eyes. He sees Hatcher, standing in the moonlight, and Annie with a gun raised to his head. Hatcher has his own gun in his hand, but held to his side.

'What does it look like?' Annie replies.

Hatcher doesn't turn his head, but his eyes swivel towards her. 'Annie?' he says, and his voice is an odd mix of confusion and anger. 'What are you doing?'

'I'm sorry, Terry – I'm a cop. Now drop the gun.'

Hatcher isn't letting go that easily. He can't anyway. He's frozen solid. If he tried to move his fingers right now they'd snap off.

Murphy pushes himself up onto his elbow. 'To have one undercover cop is unfortunate, to have two is plain—'

'Shut up!' Mitchell jabs the gun at him, then looks

quickly back to the boss. 'Terry, what's she doing, what's she talking about?'

'It's OK, Mitch,' Hatcher says, 'she's not a cop – you're not a cop, are you, Annie? You're a businesswoman, you've hidden the diamonds, haven't you, you fancy them for yourself . . . don't you? Tell me it's the diamonds, Annie . . .'

'No, Terry, it's the thought of getting you, you murdering bastard.'

Her tone is so different. So full of loathing. He can't believe it. Murphy and Annie? Christ, it's like being mugged by Abbott and Costello.

But it's not over, it's far from over.

'Boss?' Mitchell asks.

So far, so Mexican stand-off. Hatcher looks at Murphy, the cheeky grin just poised to slip back onto his face.

'Shoot him,' Hatcher says.

'You touch him,' Annie shouts, 'and I'll shoot, I've no problem with shooting, you fucking hear me?'

'I hear you,' Mitchell says, 'and I don't give a fuck. Let him go or Paddy gets it.'

'It's not Paddy,' Murphy says helpfully.

'You fucker!' Mitchell shouts.

'I swear to God I'll kill him!' Annie screams.

She presses the gun against Hatcher's skull – and he presses back.

'I gave you that gun, Annie,' he says. 'Do you really think I'd let you loose with it after last time if it was loaded.'

She doesn't blink at all.

Of course it's loaded.

She tries desperately to think if she checked.

But it doesn't matter. It's poker.

'Well, if you're so confident,' she says, 'you know what to do.'

He glares at her, then slowly begins to raise the gun in his hand.

'Don't, Terry,' she says.

It's still coming up, ever so slowly.

'You won't kill me, Annie. You love me.'

'Don't do it!'

She's on the verge of blowing his head off when Murphy says to Mitchell: 'Talking of love, this would seem like an opportune moment to tell you Terry's been screwing your wife.'

Hatcher hesitates, just a fraction, but Mitchell doesn't even consider it. 'You won't squirm out of this one, Paddy,' he sneers.

'And neither did she. We have the surveillance photos. They're the talk of the department. In fact they're probably on the Internet.'

'Shut the—'

'Does she have a butterfly on her arse?'

Now Mitchell blinks.

'How else would I know that? Surveillance cameras are brilliant these days.'

'If you have pictures,' Mitchell hisses, 'they're of me and her.'

'Yeah, sure,' Murphy says. 'When's the last time you

had a go at her? She's been working nights, hasn't she? Mostly under Terry.'

'Don't listen to him!' Terry shouts. 'I'd never . . .'

And mid-sentence, with a perfect basketball pivot, he slaps Annie's gun away, brings his foot round behind her and chops her back across it.

The gun goes one way, Annie the other.

The back of her head slaps down onto the ground. She's stunned, but still manages to make one effort to go after it. She gets as far as her knees before Hatcher puts a boot in her arse and sends her spreadeagled across the tarmac.

He steps over her and picks up her gun.

He's laughing now.

Everything they can throw at him, he can throw back, and then some.

So Murphy got inside – didn't he sniff him out?

So the Japs tried to pull a fast one – didn't they run away, crying?

And Annie, Annie whom he would have loved, she spun him a cruel web of deceit without appreciating that he is the biggest fucking spider in the forest.

He stands over her, he raises the gun. She's coughing up her guts.

'We could have been magic,' Hatcher says.

She's not listening, she's in her own place, the defeated, awaiting execution.

Well, here it comes.

But it is a day of false starts, because Mitchell's up behind him now.

'Terry?'

Hatcher turns.

Mitchell pointing a gun at him.

'Mitch, for fuck . . .'

Murphy's keeping his head down. Mitchell's in a different place now.

'Did you, Terry?'

'Did I what?'

'What Paddy says.'

'Jesus, Mitch, come off it. Fucking plug him and let's get out of here.'

'Swear to God.'

'I'll swear to anyone you like, now—'

'How would he know about the butterfly?'

'How would he know about anything? Because he's a sneaky little fucker!'

'You kept going off, we thought you were screwing Annie.'

Annie roars. 'I wouldn't screw him if he was—'

'Shut it!'

'And she was never there nights,' Mitchell says. 'Noreen was always going out.'

'Mitchell, for fuck's sake. You're my best friend.'

'I knew she was doing someone. Just never thought it would be you.'

'Mitch—' but instead of continuing, he snaps his gun up and shoots Mitchell once in the chest.

Mitchell staggers back, his face a hip-hop mix of surprise and pain. He drops to his knees. 'Terry . . .' He pitches forward.

Hatcher shakes his head slowly. 'Mitch, you dumb

fucker. Of course I was screwing her. But didn't we always share everything?' He stands over Mitchell, lying face down now.

'You'd still be tarmacking fucking roads if it wasn't for me. You stupid cunt.' He sighs and then looks at Murphy. 'He was my best friend.'

'There's a vacancy then.'

He almost laughs, but instead he raises his gun and shoots.

Or would have, but it's Annie's gun, and it really is empty.

He laughs and tosses it away. He raises his other gun. He pulls the trigger, and it just clicks.

Shot too many Japanese.

There's a moment when he looks at Murphy, Murphy looks back. He glances back at Annie, who's up on her knees now, ready to pounce.

And there's Johnny's machine pistol lying half a dozen yards away, equidistant between the three of them.

And Mitchell's gun, beneath his bloody chest, but right in front of him.

And then they're off.

Annie dives right towards the machine pistol; Murphy springs up to try and stop Hatcher turning Mitchell, but he hasn't a hope.

Hatcher heaves Mitchell over.

Except he's not dead. He's smiling; his teeth are bloody; but his eyes are open.

Mitchell pulls the trigger of his gun and the bullet explodes into Hatcher's throat and for a moment his arms flail helplessly; blood spurts out as he staggers to his feet and spins around like the garden sprinkler from hell.

Then he's on his knees again, looking around him at Murphy wrestling Mitchell's gun from him, at Annie with the machine pistol trained on him.

It's so much brighter now. He can even see the briefcase of diamonds lying just a few yards away at the side of the road, not hidden at all.

Diamonds.

Diamonds are a girl's best friend.

He always liked girls.

Just never found the right one.

Thought he had.

Right at the end.

The very end.

45

'He was my best friend.'

'You should pick your friends better,' Murphy says, then adds a belated, 'next time.'

Mitchell tries to laugh, but all he manages is a horse kind of groan and a fine bloody mist issues from his crooked, dried-out mouth. 'Yeah, Paddy,' he hisses, 'next time.'

Then they're screaming through the night, leaving the dead to be picked over by their colleagues.

Murphy's at the wheel, Annie on the phone, making sure the bone yard is jumping by the time they get there.

Hatcher's dead. Johnny's dead. Mitchell's dead, but not before he told them where they'd buried Father McBride. One last good thing out of a life devoted to robbing the quick and burying the dead.

'Christ,' Murphy says as they race back to the city.

It's bright now, and although the approaches to London are never empty, it's quiet enough for him to keep his foot to the floor most of the way.

No siren on this machine.

'We'll get there,' Annie says, 'we'll get him.'

'Yeah. Can I have that in writing?'

'Don't snap at me.'

'Sorry.' He glances at her. 'I am.'

'You didn't do anything wrong. He just got in the way.'

'Who will rid me of this turbulent priest.'

'Yeah. Something like that.'

'How do you feel?' he asks.

'What? About the late Terence Hatcher?'

Murphy nods.

She stares ahead. She kissed him yesterday, she let him feel her up, but nobody else needs to know about that, nobody ever will, nobody needs to know how dirty she feels and how happy she is now that he's dead and can't tell anyone. Petty, she thinks, but true.

'I'm fine. I'm wondering how to get it all into a report.'

It was meant to be funny.

They race into Kilburn, find the cemetery.

There are other cars already there. Workers have been dragged from their beds, there's a digger pitching into the fresh soil. The air is crisp, the grass damp.

Murphy and Annie come tearing through the graves. The cold stone crosses and the tombstones with the faded lettering.

We Shall Remember Them, for a while at least.

He hates these places.

He buried his son on a day like this, holding on to his wife, trying to stop her screams while press photographers snapped away. They were on the front pages the next day, their ghostly faces frozen in eternal horror.

Eternal for them, at least. Another day, another murder, another front page.

He doesn't mind the bad guys dying, he doesn't mind killing them, but the good guys, they have to live, they have to keep doing the good things, McBride has to live. Murphy wants to dive into the hole and tear at the muck with his bare hands, but he stands there shivering. Uniformed cops watch, and it's clear that no one has explained to them what's going on. They think they're just pulling up a body so forensics can do a DNA or something relatively run-of-the-mill, but Christ, do you have to do it so fucking early?

Murphy stands shivering on the edge.

Annie looks at him. She squeezes his arm.

Another car arrives and there's Murdoch hurrying towards them, face like thunder.

He comes up beside them and looks into the grave.

'Well?'

'Getting there, sir,' Annie says.

He nods, glances at Murphy. 'That was some fucking wild-goose chase you sent us on.'

'Sorry.'

'He'd no choice,' Annie says.

'I hear they're all dead.'

Annie nods.

'Good riddance to bad milk,' Murdoch says.

Carter has come across the green now, and stands beside Murphy.

'Good work,' he says.

Murphy ignores him.

There's an ambulance pulling through the gates and moving up slowly.

'Optimists,' Carter says.

Murphy scowls at him, but Carter doesn't notice.

Carter rubs his hands together. 'Hey, Murphy,' he says, 'did you hear about the car that crashed into a graveyard in Dublin? So far the cops have recovered three hundred and twenty bodies.'

Murphy nods for a moment, then turns suddenly and grabs Carter round the throat. He walks him backwards, Carter gasping for air, Murphy nearly spitting into his face. 'You open your mouth again, you fucking little—'

'Murphy!' Murdoch shouts.

Murphy throws Carter down onto the damp grass. He points a warning finger at him. 'I swear to God I'll—'

And then he hears it, the scrape of metal on wood.

He hurries back to the graveside. Carter remains on the ground for a moment, massaging his throat, not hurt, exactly, but annoyed because no one has come to his assistance. That was assault. He could have Murphy fired for that.

'Christ,' Murphy says. They've attached a hoist thing to the coffin now and they're winching it up.

'Christ,' Murphy says again.

'It's not your fault,' Annie says.

'Yes it is.'

They lever the coffin across until it rests on the grass, and then they're around it like flies. The cemetery workers have all sort of tools out, but they're not adept at opening coffins, only burying them.

'We're coming for you, Frank!' Murphy shouts. 'We're coming.'

He tears at the coffin himself, Annie tries to pull him back, but he won't go. Then the paramedics crowd in and force him out. He falls back on his arse in the mud. Annie helps him to his feet.

'Christ,' he says.

They're at the screws.

'Frank – Frank is his name?' one of the paramedics says. He bangs on the coffin while the screws are turned painfully slowly.

'Frank, we're coming for you, just hold on, hold on, Frank.'

Murphy's praying now, and he hasn't prayed since he lost his child, and that wasn't a prayer of thanks or forgiveness, it was a prayer of hate.

That's when he walked away from God and all that crap.

But he supposes it's OK to pray now, he's not praying for himself, for his own salvation, he's praying for his friend, little Frankie McBride, the punk rocker, the only punk rocker in Belfast who didn't have his hair spiked, because Mummy wouldn't let him. Frankie who was never a hit with the girls, but they built him up like he was and he basked in it. Frankie who saw God on the way to Larne, and never ever knew that Danny, the drummer in the band, had slipped magic mushrooms into his dinner the night before and he was tripping out of his head. Even Larne looked good, that day. And they stopped the car by the side of the road for Danny to throw up, and the traffic warden came up and said they couldn't stop there and Murphy cursed at him, couldn't he see the poor boy was dangerously ill and where was his compassion, and the traffic warden said if he's gravely ill maybe he shouldn't drink so much beer, because he stinks of it. And Murphy, still pissed, was all for getting out and decking him, except McBride suddenly dropped to his knees and started praying to the traffic warden, convinced he could see the Lord and no one could convince him otherwise, not then, not later, not ever.

Please, God.

How many hours did they give him? Six?

And how many hours has it been?

Eleven, and counting.

It's an inexact science, burying people alive.

Not a lot of scientific papers have been written on it.

Then there's a wrenching sound, and the coffin lid is off.

And now, at the final moment, Murphy cannot look. He drops to his knees and hides his face in his hands.

Christ.

46

Murphy hates hospitals. Big buildings with death certificates. You go in there to get fixed, and you end up underground. It's a fact. Microscopic bugs eat you up and spit you out. Crazy nurses inject poisonous drugs into you for fun. Psychotic surgeons vent their spleen, on your spleen. It's well-known. They give him the shivers. This one is no different. But he puts a brave face on it, because he's being contrite. Although he puts a mask on his brave face, because expressing contriteness is not his forte.

'Well?' he says.

'Well what?'

'What's the capital of Honduras?'

'I've no idea.'

Murphy tuts and shakes his head. 'The brain damage may be worse than they feared.'

McBride closes his eyes. 'What is the capital of Honduras?'

'Caracas.'

McBride nods for a moment, then his eyes blink open again. 'Caracas is the capital of Venezuela.'

'No it isn't.'

'Yes it is. We have missionaries there.'

'Argumentative. Definite sign of personality disorder. The outlook isn't good.'

'Your effin' outlook won't be good if you keep this up.'

'Aw, shucks,' Murphy says, 'sure I brought you a grape.'

McBride shakes his head and sighs. His face is yellowing now, as the bruises mature. His nose broken, jaw fractured, dehydrated all to hell, or nearly. Everything aches, but there is life and light, and he was sure he was dead. When he opened his eyes in the pristine hospital room he was sure he was in heaven, but then he saw Murphy sitting there and was sure he was not.

'Is this Saturday?' McBride asks.

'Sunday.'

'I have a service to take.'

'Sure let's do the show right here.'

'Very funny. But seriously, I'm—'

'You're knackered, take a break. Tell me you forgive me.'

'For what?'

'For getting you into all this.'

'I forgive you. But there's nothing to forgive.'

'I caused you to be buried alive.'

'You caused me to examine my faith.'

'And.'

'Renewed, restored and reinvigorated.'

'I don't follow. He didn't get you out. I did. With a little help.'

McBride speaks a little Zorro. 'The Lord, he Move in Mysterious Way.'

'No, that's Michael Jackson, the Lord don't exist.'

'I think we might agree to differ.'

They look at each other. The room is spartan. It's a private hospital, Murphy's paying for the room because Murdoch wouldn't. Budget. McBride was barely alive when they took him out of the box, he was mostly blue. Another ten minutes and that would have been it.

Murphy hadn't expected this halfway thing: either the priest would be dead, or he'd wink at him as the lid came off and say, 'Had you goin' there for a while, Murphy boy.'

But it was neither, it was paramedics fighting to keep him alive on the way to the hospital, a four-day coma, a predication of brain damage which happily hasn't yet revealed itself.

Murphy hasn't slept since they brought McBride in. He has sustained himself on tea and digestive biscuits.

Annie sits with him part of the time, but the priest isn't really her concern. She's more worried about Murphy. Normal routine for a cop involved in a death is a swift lift to the eighth floor and a psychological assessment, then time off to recover. But she has already made half a dozen excuses for Murphy, because she knows he's not ready to be probed. He was on the edge before, what will this one have done to him?

His friend tortured, nearly killed.

A three-man gang wiped out, not to mention the Japanese.

Ah, the Japanese, disappeared off into the night, never to be seen in these parts again, or at least until they find another mug like Hatcher to peddle their low-grade shit to. The Plastic Triangle.

Murdoch and Duggan have both been up before Burgess.

Arrests were required, the publicity was vital.

What they didn't want was Gunfight at the OK Corral.

And kindly explain why, when this was going down, you and your posse were fifty miles away admiring the view.

While these two gallant officers were fighting for their lives.

Annie smiles at that.

They're going to get medals.

They can wear them out, down to the pub.

Look at us, we're regular heroes.

She showers repeatedly, can't get Hatcher's tongue out of her mouth or mind. And yet feels guilty about not attending his funeral service. They spent so much time together. He pursued her so enthusiastically. He was a cold-blooded killer with a romantic streak. Carter went to the funerals instead. He told her all about them. Noreen in hysterics, old man Hatcher weeping, and dead himself before morning. Three gangster funerals in one day. A big turnout. Heavies at the cemetery gates keeping out the press, the pride of London gangster land coming out to say their fond farewells, and already fighting over the scraps of Hatcher's little empire. Johnny's wife on her knees in the mud. A priest having to be brought in from the other side of the city because all the local ones banded together and refused to participate after what the Hatcher gang did to poor Father McBride.

She has written her report, stayed up all night doing it; Burgess read it, said nothing, but patted her shoulder.

Murphy goes back to work a week later.

Well, not back to work, but a flying visit. Just to say hello. And making sure he avoids the psychiatrist on the eighth.

Half the staff hardly know him, the others pat him on the back and say well done.

They ask him about it, but he doesn't say much.

He goes looking for Murdoch, because he'll be wanting a report. He's going to offer to write it in verse, and then sing it at the Christmas party. Murdoch will see the funny side.

Except Murdoch's at the far end of the corridor, carrying his personal effects in a cardboard box, and somebody whispers to Murphy that the boss has been demoted because of the cock-up over Annie being undercover.

That and the fact so many people ended up dead.

So Murdoch comes down the corridor, stony-faced, saying goodbye to no one. And then he sees Murphy and the stone becomes a scowl.

'Sorry,' Murphy says, 'I didn't think they'd demote you.'

'I haven't been demoted,' Murdoch snaps. 'I've been promoted sideways.'

He turns slightly so that he can continue on past Murphy without having to stop and talk.

'What about my report?' Murphy says after him.

'Give it to the boss.'

Murphy shakes his head. He walks on up the corridor. That's what he hates about this place, they're all here today, gone tomorrow, he might as well report to a dictation machine and a photocopier. They're about the only permanent residents here at New Scotland Yard.

He knocks then enters without waiting for an invite.

Important to get off on the wrong foot.

Annie's unpacking her stuff. She glances round. 'Hello, Murphy.'

She's smiling, clearly pleased to see him. And he feels . . . well, he doesn't know what he feels.

He's not sure whether to run, or buy her a cake.

Epilogue

It's the same apartment. That's how he's different from everyone else. He doesn't create a new identity, a new wallet full of fake IDs, a new apartment, even new friends. He just remains the same and blends in. Ask any of the neighbours and he's just the annoying Irish drunk who makes a racket in the early hours. The one who thinks he can sing. And what friends, exactly?

Oh yes, there's the priest, occasionally we see a priest. Poor man, must be in terrible turmoil for the priest to visit that often.

The same apartment, with the gun taped under the bed, and a suitcase full of children's clothes in a cupboard under the sink.

He's been getting letters from work saying that he has to turn up for his psychiatric evaluation. He wonders if eventually they'll start sending red notices, like electric bills, threatening to cut him off.

But he's been cut off for years.

He makes Leonard Cohen look like Coco the Clown.

He likes that line and will use it in a song, if ever he picks that guitar up again.

Maybe it's time to move on. Buy keyboards and a computer and sampler and other toys and make disco music.

Except, of course, nobody calls it disco music. House. Or Acid. Or Trip Hop. He could do that. Grand Master Murphy.

He could do Gangsta Rap.

He knows enough about gangsters.

And what's rapping but lyrics for people who can't sing.

One day he's just walking down the street and a complete stranger, passing by, says, 'Cheer up – somebody die, mate?'

And it stops him dead in his tracks.

He starts laughing, and for a while can't stop. He goes into a shop and buys a Mars Bar and the girl behind the counter looks at him like he's mental.

'Ever heard of *Candid Camera*?' he asks, and she shakes her head warily. He laughs again and says, 'Doesn't matter.'

The next day he gets a postcard from his ex-wife. The postmark reads Glasgow. She says she hopes he's OK and that she's settling in all right. She had not wanted him to know where she was going, so he can only presume that she's not living in Glasgow at all, but somewhere entirely different. It is designed to say she cares, still, but also to give him a false impression of where she's living so that if he tries to find her he'll fail. Or, alternatively, she would surely know that a super sleuth like him wouldn't be fooled by that trick for one moment, so perhaps she's just doing a double bluff and quietly letting him know where she is in case he really needs her.

Or perhaps Norman is holding her prisoner, beating her daily, and the postcard is a desperate appeal for help. It may say weather fine, city nice, but it actually means please come and rescue me.

Perhaps.

He should hop on the night train and go investigate.

Go deep undercover as an estranged husband trying to recover true love.

He would rescue her all right, and then discover that their love had died, but that luckily he'd met someone on the train on the way up, and after a series of hare-brained adventures, fallen in love with her instead.

He tears up the postcard.

That chapter is over.

And so is this one.

He removes the suitcase of clothes, takes them down the stairs and crosses the road to the public park. He has a lighter, and a small bottle of Sunflower cooking oil.

It is time to say goodbye.

They are only clothes, but they smell of his son. He sits on a bench for a while, with the case closed beside him. He then opens it and runs his hands through the T-shirts and shorts. He lifts a shirt and half covers his face with it, breathing in deep. It's not really his son he's smelling, it's old washing powder and fabric conditioner. But.

There are tears in his eyes.

One of the things his aunt said to him when he lost his son was you're young, you can have another. It was thoughtless and insensitive, like the boy was a pair of shoes, easily replaced, and he nearly tore his aunt's head off.

He shouldn't have been surprised.

When he was fourteen his pet Jack Russell was knocked down by a car. His pet Jack Russell who'd been his from a pup, whom he'd loved so dearly, had been flattened and he was devastated. Four days after they buried him, his aunt arrived round with an almost identical dog and he'd tried to like him, but it wasn't the same. It was like having a schizophrenic round the house, looked the same, walked the same, smelled the same, but a completely different personality. Eventually he couldn't stand it any more and took the dog for a walk and tied him to a tree in the park.

Now here he is, twenty years down the line, feeling like he's tied to a tree in the park.

And the only way to be free involves Sunflower cooking oil and a lighter.

He kisses the clothes for the last time, then pours the oil on them.

He sets the open case on the grass, then kneels beside it and flicks the lighter.

The clothes go up with a woosh! and he stumbles back onto his rear end to stop himself being burned.

'Oi!'

Murphy turns. There's a park warden rushing up, enough epaulettes on his uniform to rule Malawi.

'Oi! You can't do that here!'

Murphy nods vaguely. Memories are rushing past him like he's drowning.

Laughter. Terror. Fear. Guilt.

Thick black noxious smoke is billowing up, it's the synthetics, and people are stopping to watch.

'Do you hear me, you can't do that here! This is a public park!'

He has never really understood before that Lianne was there when they killed the boy. Experienced it first hand, where he only came upon it later, like it was a crime scene. How much worse for her, to see flesh and blood destroyed before her eyes, destroyed for no reason but cruelty and revenge.

'Put that bloody fire out!'

He's rocking back and forth now, watching the flames.

Then there's another voice, one he recognises. 'It's OK – police. I'll look after it.'

'Well, make sure you do . . . bloody disgrace . . . public park, you know.'

And the parky huffs and puffs away and Annie kneels down beside him. 'Hello, Murphy,' she says.

He nods, but his eyes remain on the fire.

He falls forward into her arms, and she hugs him while he cries. She strokes his head and holds him tight as his body is wracked by involuntary spasms. She won't let him go for quite a while.

But eventually he begins to settle, and he touches her hair.

'It's your turn to pay for coffee,' she says quietly in his ear.

'Tea,' he corrects.

If you've enjoyed MURPHY'S LAW, try the first chapter of THE HORSE WITH MY NAME, Colin Bateman's latest novel featuring Dan Starkey, international man of inaction . . .

1

I was shaking hands with the vicar in the rain when the phone rang. I dried off on that week's towel and crossed the bedroom. A voice at the other end said, 'Dubliners are skin-gathering showers of shite.'

I said, 'Excuse me, you might have a wrong number,' and put the phone down. I flipped the answer machine on so that I wouldn't be disturbed again, but by the time I got back to the shower the water had run cold, the vicar had gone and my headache had returned.

I believe you actually have to have the shower in a small, separate room to be able to describe it as en suite; this one sat in the corner beside my bed, the plastic curtain hanging off the railing. You never know quite when the urge to shake hands with the vicar will come on you, so to speak, and this time it had come halfway through shaving in the shower, so I was left with a five-day growth on one side of my face and the other side cut and bleeding from a six-week-old razor which had, according to the packaging on the floor, been cut from the hull of the *Ark Royal*. There remained three inches of water at the base of the shower which was draining away a drop at a time; only with the power off could I hear the weird sucking sound it made as it battled to escape. It had been a while since I'd experienced a weird sucking sound so I decided to investigate. I had two fingers down the drain when the phone rang again, and the machine clicked in. The voice said, 'I'm serious, Dan, they *are*. But give me a call anyway, I might have some work for you.' He left me his number, no code, so I presumed it was Belfast. I recognised the voice, but couldn't quite place it; I was still running possible names through my head when I came up with the remains of a leg of chicken from the drain, the sucking sound ceased and the water started to gurgle appreciatively away. I took a nibble at the leg. It tasted vaguely spicy. I gave some thought to the possibility that I might have stumbled on the Colonel's secret recipe, but not a lot.

I sat on the bed and warmed myself before the three-bar electric fire with the glowing coal-effect façade. In the absence of a television in my little bedsit palace I had taken to watching the façade and been pleasantly surprised at the standard of programming. You couldn't always pick up the Liverpool game but you got a great view of the mountains at sunset. However, I'd managed to put my foot through it a couple of nights before while trying to locate the equally unsweet toilet in the blackness of a heavy session and now it sat dark and cracked like a fellated Krakatoa; from technicolour to black-and-white movies with one drunken footstep. It wasn't my only entertainment, of course. There was a pub round the corner and my laptop, though I used one more than the other. Somehow, the words wouldn't flow, but the beer always would. It had something to do with a little white coffin and the fact that my life was a disaster. I had tried to commit suicide by putting my head in the fridge, which was just about the standard of everything I attempted in life. There was a biography of a fat boxer which had cost me thousands in libel payments, there was a thin novel about a teenage messiah which had been remaindered within six weeks, there was a *making of* book about a hit Hollywood movie which was not, and there were a thousand and one columns taking the pish out of the fighting Northern Irish, except they were now the ones taking the pish out of me. Jobless, hopeless, loveless; generally *less* everything.

I listened to the message again, but still couldn't fit the voice to a name. I finished a can and sat thinking about things for a while, and then remembered why I'd gone to the expense and trouble of showering. I groaned and stood up. I still had my one suit hanging behind the door, but the knees were green from playing football in the park; I couldn't turn up to marriage guidance like that; I would look like a loser. That and the big sign on my head which flashed a neon *LOSER* every time I breathed in. There were tracksuit bottoms and some scuffed trainers under the bed; there was a greyish-white T-shirt with *Harp* written in the corner I'd won in the pub movie quiz; there was my bomber jacket with the lining hanging loose, although you could only tell that if it was unzipped. I'd get there and Patricia would be wearing her wedding dress, just to rub in the fact that she had a date for the divorce hearing.

Fuck it. What was the point? She'd got some big promotion in work and seemed to be rolling in it, but I loved her too much to sue her for alimony. I had a bill in my bottom drawer for a little white coffin, but I wasn't going to bother her with that. What were they going to do, repossess? Over my dead body.

I walked into the centre. It was only about twenty minutes. For once in my life the rain stayed off. There is a Buddy Holly song about *raining in my . . .* but the last word wouldn't come to me. It seemed like it should be *soul,* but I wasn't convinced. Something with *s*: suit, soap, soup. *It's raining in my soup.* I liked that. It wasn't right. But I liked it.

Belfast was buzzing.

That was the slogan they used after the ceasefire. In Stormont they were doing the familiar two steps forward, three steps back, but there was a kind of peace, the kind that involved shootings, kneecappings and riots, about which a lot of reformed terrorists did a lot of tutting and shaking of heads. There was a similar kind of peace about to settle over the headquarters of the Presbyterian Church where the counselling was scheduled to take place. Patricia, in her despair, had found solace in the church, despite our experiences on Wrathlin. Some might argue that I had found solace in a bottle, but I couldn't afford a bottle; solace in a can. The ring-pull mountain sat in one corner of the room; there was no longer any benefit in keeping them; the standard of my beer had dropped with my circumstances and I could no longer delude myself that I was drinking only to attain those air miles, that World Cup football or that outside chance of a Mini Metro. If the men at the ring-pull factory went on strike or some lager version of Auric Goldfinger cornered the market in world ring-pull supplies then I might be in a position to cash in, but in the meantime my ring-pull mountain wasn't enough to convince the bank manager that I was a safe bet on a mortgage, an ATM card or even an account.

I walked through the doomy doors of Church House and told them I was looking for sanctuary. They told me sanctuary was only available on Tuesdays and Thursdays between six and eight p.m., and could I come back. I wasn't sure if they were joking. There were two of them, sisters from the looks of them (although, of course, not *sisters* in the habit and revolver sense), and they wore identical hats and looks of disdain and told me that I'd gotten the wrong day for the AA meeting. I set my can down on the counter and said I was here for marriage guidance, but I could come back for the other one. I suggested to them that they should form a larger organisation called the AAAA, for drinking drivers, but they didn't know what I was talking about.

They pointed me in the right direction, which was any direction which took me away from them, and I heard them fussing and whittering to each other as I headed for the stairs.

There are no elevators in church buildings. It's a fact. Not even for the disabled. I suppose it's something to do with ascending to heaven, or hell in the case of the marriage guidance office three flights up. It wasn't called marriage guidance any more, of course, that was too old-fashioned; there was a proper organisation called Relate, somewhere, but that would have been too straightforward for Patricia. This was my third visit and they should have called it Relate To This You Misanthropic Bastard. Instead they called it Providence. I'm sure there was a reason. It was run by a woman called Mary Boland. When I first met her I told her one of my favourite books in primary school was *The Forest of Boland Light Railway* and she told me to sit down and be quiet or I'd be kept behind. She gave us a lot of guff about love and God and problems and God, all the time Patricia nodding and me staring at Patricia. That was the first time. The second time Patricia slapped me and I pulled her hair and Mrs Boland had to call in a passing curate to separate us. This third time I slouched in and took my seat and smiled at Mary Boland and apologised for last time. She nodded and made a note. Patricia had not yet arrived.

I asked if I could smoke and she said no.

'Drink?'

'No.'

'Drugs?'

'No. Mr Starkey?'

'Call me Clive.'

She looked at her notes. 'Clive?'

'I'm thinking of changing my name. Although I'm more Clive Dunn than Clive of India.'

She blinked and said, 'Dan, Patricia called. She won't be coming.'

'What?'

'She thinks it's pointless. She's decided on the divorce.'

I nodded. 'You could have called me. Let me know.'

'It was only half an hour ago. I tried to leave a message.'

'You have to give at least twenty-four hours for the dentist.'

'I'm not a dentist, Dan.'

'Aren't you?'

I sighed.

She sighed. 'Dan, I know this is all very painful for you . . .'

'Not half as painful as . . .'

'Don't say it, Dan. That was one of her big complaints, that you never take anything seriously.'

'*Au contraire*. Or on the contrary. I take everything seriously. If I happen to be hilariously funny in my responses it's just my way of covering up the hidden pain. It's more of a cry for help than anything. Tears of a clown, as Smokey said.'

We looked at each other for several long moments. Actually she wasn't a bad sort, she was trying to help, she just happened to be blinkered by religion. She had short dark hair and a thin aquiline nose. She wore pale lipstick and a shirt buttoned right up. She closed her file of notes. 'I very rarely say this, Dan; in fact, I'm not meant to. But you know I've been having one-to-one sessions with Patricia, so I happen to know that she loves you. The problem is that you won't talk to her about what happened . . .'

'About dead kid.'

'Dan . . . all you really need to do is go round and talk to her about it. I think you'll find that once you take that first step, things will change. You do have to talk to her, Dan, you know that, don't you?'

I nodded. 'I don't know where she lives any more. The court . . . the police . . . well, you know . . .'

She took a deep breath. 'This could get me sacked.' She opened the file again. She turned it round so that I could see and pointed at Patricia's name and her address on Windsor Avenue. 'On the condition that you won't go round there and throw stones through her windows again.'

I shook my head. 'Nor potatoes.' Her brow crinkled. I shrugged. 'Deal,' I said. She smiled. I stood up. I reached across to shake her hand; she hesitated, suspecting, I suspect, that I would suddenly withdraw it and stick my tongue out like a child, but then she grasped it.

We shook. I held on to her hand.

'I understand your pain, Dan. I had a nephew who—'

I stopped her. 'You don't understand the meaning of the word pain until you've had your pubic hair caught in the rotorblades of the Action Man canoe.' I nodded and let go of her hand. I walked out of the office and down the stairs and out into the street. It was raining.

Raining in my *heart* . . .

I smiled. Buddy. My wife had thrown in the towel, although unlike me she undoubtedly had more than one. Windsor Avenue. It was only a hop, skip and a jump away. People forget how small Belfast is. You can walk almost anywhere worth walking to. I set off. I felt suddenly hungry and stopped off at a Pret A Manger but everything they had left seemed to involve avocados or peaches so I made do with a packet of Tayto Cheese and Onion from the newsagent next door. It wasn't raining so badly that I was in danger of getting soaked. It was vaguely pleasant walking up through the shoppers, the office workers and the tourist.

Fifteen minutes took me to the foot of Windsor Avenue, and then I was standing opposite her house. It was a three-storey terrace on a pleasant leafy street. There was no sign of her car, although she might well have changed it. The likelihood was that she was at work. I contemplated breaking in and shitting in her shoes like a burglar, or just making do with the toilet and forgetting to flush it so that she'd know I'd been there, but I couldn't decide which was more appropriate; not for the first time I was falling between two stools. So I decided what would be would be and rang the doorbell. There was nothing for quite a while. I was just turning away when there came the sound of bolts being drawn back and the door finally opened. I turned back to a tall man with a short beard and fashionably rectangular glasses. He had pale skin and a copy of the *Daily Mail* in his hands, held open with one finger to the page he was reading. He looked me up and down with the blind indifference of a mortician in retirement week.

'Oh, hello,' I said. 'She doesn't take long.'

'Pardon me?'

'I said, would you be interested in a copy of *The Watchtower*?'

'Excuse me?'

'Or double glazing? I find it much more practical to double up. You can look into the window of your soul and be nice and snuggly at the same time.'

'I'm sorry . . . I . . . not today, thank you.'

He closed the door. I rang the bell. 'Only raking,' I said when he opened it a fraction. 'Is Trish in?'

'Patricia?'

'That's the one.'

'No. I'm sorry. She's at work. You . . . ?'

'Oh. Just a friend. Passing by, y'know?'

He nodded. 'Can I give her a message?'

I nodded. 'Tell her that I still love her. That I will always love her. That I have done terrible things to her and we have suffered a terrible loss but that if we just give it a real chance we can work it out, we can go back to what we had, what was beautiful and fun and sexy and just the greatest thing since sliced bread. Tell her she can go ahead and divorce me, that doesn't make any difference, it's only a piece of paper, if she needs time, sure, she can have more time, if she needs me to promise things, I will promise them and this time I will mean it, but just please

God don't throw us away. Tell her I want to talk, I really want to talk, I've seen the light and I want to get it all out in the open. I want to talk. Talk is what I want to do. Talk, and everything will be okay.'

He had closed the door halfway through, but I continued just in case he was still listening.

I turned away. Normally I harbour feelings of violence when Patricia takes a new lover, but there was nothing. I was above it, or beyond it, or beneath it. I started to walk. I was about a hundred yards from home when it finally came back to me whose voice it was on the phone; I knew immediately that I shouldn't call, that it would mean nothing but trouble. And I knew just as immediately that I would.

For Trouble is my middle name.